UNTOUCHABLE

A HOT BILLIONAIRE ROMANCE

ELIZABETH SAFLEUR

This book is a work of fiction. Names, characters, places, and incidents are the product of the author's imagination or are used fictitiously. Any resemblance to actual events, locales, or persons, living or dead, is coincidental.

Copyright ©2015 by Elizabeth SaFleur. All rights reserved, including the right to reproduce, distribute, or transmit in any form or by any means. For information regarding subsidiary rights, please contact the Publisher.

Elizabeth SaFleur LLC
PO Box 6395
Charlottesville, VA 22906
Elizabeth@ElizabethSaFleur.com
www.ElizabethSaFleur.com

Edited by Dana T.
Cover by CosmicLetterz

ISBN: 978-1-7320207-3-3

This book is dedicated to you – my wonderful reader. Thank you for giving up a little slice of your time to read my books. Know that you are appreciated and acknowledged – and always will be.

Hugs to the mental health professionals who every day help people in need -- our men and women in uniform struggling with the aftermath of war or their service, victims of trauma or abuse, and other mentally wounded individuals needing your care. You are heroes to so many. Please take care of yourselves, too.

A huge hug to my BDSM community, which has accepted me with open arms. You are honestly the most generous, well-balanced people I have ever met. We know the difference between abuse and consensual BDSM play; I join you in the effort to ensure everyone else understands the difference, too.

Dear Reader,
This book is a work of fiction, not reality. My characters operate in a compressed time frame. A real-world scenario involves getting to know one another more extensively than my characters do before engaging in BDSM activities. Please learn as much as you can before trying any activity you read about in erotic fiction. Talk to people in your local BDSM group. Nearly every community has one. Get to know people slowly, and always be careful. Share your hopes, dreams and fears with anyone before playing with them,

have a safeword and share it with your Dom or Domme (they can't read your mind), use protection, and have a safe-call or other backup in place. Remember: Safe, Sane and Consensual. Or, no play. May you find that special person to honor and love you the way you wish. You deserve that.

XO ~Elizabeth

1

My future will be made in the next thirty minutes. Okay, perhaps she was being a tad theatrical. But the thought wasn't too far from the truth. London Chantelle took in a sobering, deep breath. Drama wouldn't help her. Carson Drake sat on the other side of that door. She had to focus on business today—and only business.

She smoothed her pencil skirt down for the twentieth time, pulled her shoulders back and marched her Kate Spade pumps into Whitestone International's boardroom.

The men around the table stood as she entered. Carson was conspicuously absent. *Good.* She'd dubbed the company's contentious head of legal and public affairs the "Gladiator." All too often she'd felt like the weaker opponent in the arena of his boardroom.

After the pleasantries of handshakes and good-to-see-yous were over, she launched into her pitch. It took under twenty minutes to explain why she believed Whitestone required a full-scale rebranding.

Isolated at the other end of the vast conference table, CEO Stan Whitestone and his CFO leafed through the thick packet she'd slaved over for two weeks. She sat still and silent in the enormous leather chair, taking the moment to assess his mood. You could tell a lot about someone by watching their face as they read. *So far, so good.*

Mr. Whitestone pushed his copy of her proposal forward on the table. He leaned back in his chair and smiled. *Oh, thank God. He doesn't hate it.*

Her promotion to vice president at Yost and Brennan Communications rode on his acceptance. She desperately wanted that VP title and all that went with it. As vice president, she'd slave over *her* ideas rather than other people's. And the money? For once in her life, she might live in a place with a separate bedroom instead of a studio apartment.

"So, Miss Chantelle, only $500,000?" Mr. Whitestone asked. His CFO stared at him as if gauging his tone. She'd learned over the years that clients didn't often tease, and certainly not the head of a multibillion-dollar contracting firm.

She cleared her throat. "Spending less would be a waste of money. If we can't do it right, then we shouldn't do it at all." *Oh, no.* She led with the punch line. She meant to save that last line until she needed a clincher.

"Well said." A familiar voice filled the room, and the air seemed to shift, along with her luck. The Gladiator had arrived. On cue, her belly flipped at the sound of Carson Drake's confident tone.

"Carson, so glad you could join us," Mr. Whitestone said. "London was just talking about recasting our image."

"So I hear." He strode over to the credenza and poured himself a cup of coffee. The air crackled with the addition of his dominant energy. It was as if he, not Mr. Whitestone, were the CEO.

He took the seat across from her. He fit the oversized chair. Another subtle reminder she was a small player in this

Untouchable

big man's world. His dark eyes raked over her body as if assessing her reaction to his presence. She'd fought so hard to hide the illicit, secret thoughts she'd had about him since they met months ago, but his gaze seemed to penetrate her mind. *Hearing my inappropriate thoughts.*

During their first meeting, she'd had trouble tearing her eyes from his face. She'd spent every meeting since avoiding his dark eyes, as if that would hide her scandalous daydreams. He, on the other hand, watched her every move.

Of course he'd kept a professional tone with her at all times. *Albeit combative.* It was just as well. Her life didn't allow for illusions that Carson elicited with a single, knowing smile. She'd seen how the other women in her office grew all swoon-y over men like him. Men who were accomplished, good looking and oh, so arrogant, and who would turn a woman's focus from herself to him with a wink.

"My apologies, Miss Chantelle. I didn't mean to interrupt." He looked at Mr. Whitestone. "Carter cancelled. I recommend to abort. Effective immediately."

"Agreed."

"Now where were you?" His brown eyes returned to settle on her. A shock of dark hair had fallen over his forehead like he'd finger-combed it all day.

When did the room grow so hot? She casually pulled her blouse a little from her skirt to ease the straining fabric from her clammy chest. *Focus, London.*

She had no time for flirtations. She had responsibilities and a brother who counted on her. Unlike her mother, she would not abandon those dependent on her at the first charming thing out of a man's mouth. Whomever she got involved with—*if* she ever got involved—would not be like any swarthy Casanova her mother had brought home. Good looks always came with a price.

She grasped her portfolio on the table, opened it and

pretended to glance through her notes. *Carson isn't going to affect me. Not today.* She straightened in her chair and squared her shoulders.

"Go on, Miss Chantelle," Carson urged.

"Thank you, Mr. Drake." She pushed a copy of her proposal across the table to him, which he ignored as he casually sipped his coffee. His fingers wrapped around the entire coffee mug. She hadn't noticed how large his hands were before.

She addressed the person who really mattered, Mr. Whitestone. The man who *will* sign an acceptance agreement, she told herself.

"Mr. Whitestone, I understand that discussing your business dealings in the press has been … difficult."

"You could say that," Carson said.

Dammit, she wasn't talking to him.

"Refreshing your image will bring a desirable type of attention to your company. We will sidetrack sensitive information about what you do and how you do it. Instead, we will focus on the expertise of your executive team."

"A new brand based on our executives will invite questions," he said. "Questions we might not want to answer."

"We can deal with them as they come."

"Is that so?" He arched his brow as if he didn't believe her. She noticed his intimidation technique. Well, she wouldn't let Carson frighten her. So what if he'd negotiated six multi-million-dollar acquisitions in the last three years, testified before Congress, and been on every "most successful list" in Washington for the last three years? *So what if I paid that much attention to your credentials.* She knew what she was doing when it came to counseling her clients.

"Mr. Whitestone, we have been working with your firm for over a year. Your competition is getting more ink and more play on social media than you. Media attention requires giving us some news. You need more transparency about your firm." She could feel Carson's regard burn through her blouse, now damp from nerves. Or lust? "I recognize Mr. Drake may not appreciate the process, but—"

"I know all about news generation, Miss Chantelle." His words pierced the air. He was probably annoyed she'd dare challenge him. But she'd also learned over the last four months of handling his company's public relations, he enjoyed verbal jousting on occasion. She had hoped today wasn't one of those days.

He leaned back in his chair. "Tell me something I don't know."

"You have twice the business of any other firm in your field, yet a quarter of its visibility."

"Based on what calculation?"

"Page fifteen of my proposal. Charts and everything." A thin surge of victory filled her at the surprise on his face. But the pursed mouths around the table showed her the snippy tone wasn't appreciated. "We just want to bring Whitestone into the twenty-first century," she added. Okay, probably not the best comeback. But Whitestone International needed a full image makeover, *stat.*

Carson sat motionless. "I fail to see how changing the colors of our corporate logo will be *entering* the new century."

"Rebranding is more than a logo, Mr. Drake. What I meant to say—"

"We know what you meant, Miss Chantelle," Mr. Whitestone said.

"I'm not sure *I* understand." Carson said. "Continue. Enlighten us with your wisdom."

"I apologize if I offended you. I meant we want your audiences to see you for who you really are. Your current branding does not do you justice." *There.* That was a vice presidential thing to say, right?

"I understand you've worked hard on this proposal." He tapped her packet. "But I have serious reservations about spending this money right now. I move we wait a few months."

"Agreed." Of course, the CFO agreed. She'd labeled him the "Miser." He'd rub two nickels together to see if they'd mate before spending either of them.

She gripped her notes tighter. "You have two acquisitions coming up, and launching the news under the new brand would be wise."

In her peripheral vision she caught the other two members of the executive team watching Carson. She'd been in many meetings with this group. As usual, all eyes turned to him when a decision was at hand.

He didn't seem to notice as his unsmiling face focused on hers. A muscle in his jaw twitched. No man should have such perfect cheekbones. Mustering as much fierceness as she could, she matched his gaze. She imagined few people could hold his alpha stare for very long. She wanted to drop her eyes to her lap. She saw him surrounded by a bevy of women dropping before him in supplication. This man had to have women parading through his bedroom every night. Anyone that looked like him would.

Mr. Whitestone's voice cut through her ridiculous musings. "Carson, I agree. But the idea has merit. Miss Chantelle. Tell Mr. Brennan we need more time. You may not get the full budget you've proposed. But we'll consider the effort."

"Thank you." *Thank God.* She really needed $300,000. If she bagged at least that amount, she'd have scored a touchdown for her firm.

She closed her portfolio. "I'll give you a call on Monday to see if you've rethought your position over the weekend. We'd want to get started right away."

"We'll call you." Mr. Whitestone stood.

Carson glared at her. *He looks like he wants to spank me.* She flushed. *Stop it. You are Y&B's next rising star.*

As she gathered her things, she took a deep inhale of the warm scent of tobacco and expensive leather that Carson left in his wake. Her female parts clenched in a very un-executive way. She hoped he couldn't hear the thumping knocks of her heartbeat. Clearly her heart hadn't gotten the I-won't-be-affected memo.

"Mr. Drake," she said before her courage fled. "Did you even read my proposal?"

He turned to her in the doorway. "What do you think?"

She had no idea what to think. The searing smile he gave her held intense dislike. Only Carson Drake could put someone in their place with a grin.

He walked her to the lobby in silence. Her legs rubbed together, the friction heating her thighs. Those foolish, foolish suggestive thoughts returned.

"Miss Chantelle." He held the glass door open for her. His gentlemanly move surprised her. Someone important must be watching.

She skirted around him and outside to join the taxi line before she said something she'd regret.

She checked her watch. It was almost five o'clock. She had two hours until she met Michael—a man who never should have been more than a coworker. He was the last loose end to tie up before approaching Mr. Brennan with the idea of her promotion. And finally advance her life.

As she eased herself into the cab, she noticed that Carson still stood behind the lobby's windows. She turned her back on his curious stare. Perhaps she'd gotten to him. *Nah.* She doubted he gave her a second thought out of the office. She wished she could say the same.

Well, today was a new day. Vice presidents weren't overcome by erotic daydreams. They kicked ass.

~

Carson stared out the window long after London's taxicab disappeared into traffic.

He couldn't tear his eyes away from her today. She kept crossing and recrossing those luscious, tanned legs underneath the glass conference table. Then when she leaned forward to pass him her proposal? The top button of her silk blouse threatened to release. He spent the rest of the meeting anticipating its pop. It didn't.

He wasn't sorry he'd given her such a hard time about her idea to rebrand Whitestone. He'd always had the ability to discern people's true desires and just how far he could push. London needed verbal sparring. Only then would the fatigue and worry in her eyes lift. Her décolletage would flush a beautiful peach color. Her eyes would fire defiantly, and she'd lift that chin in a haughty salute as if he was the biggest jerk on the planet. All her nervousness would vanish.

He stepped into the elevator bank and inhaled London's lingering perfume. The scent matched her personality. *Spicy. And complicated.*

Today, she'd fidgeted on that beautiful ass more than usual, which teased his desire to stroke her defiance even more. *You wanted to stroke more than that.*

She was smart, dynamic and a challenge. *With a great behind.*

While he had no interest in romantic complications, he often imagined the kind of man she would respond to outside the boardroom. It wouldn't be someone who'd break her like a wild horse. Or even relegate her to a corral. No, London Chantelle needed to be haltered, gentled and understood. *All that energy channeled.*

He punched his floor's button and told his cock to stand down. He scrolled through his e-mail on his phone as the elevator lurched upward. London had already sent a follow-up email, ostensibly from her cab. The woman who never quits? *Jesus, what a pistol.* His own pistol remained cocked and ready.

He really needed to get a handle on his reaction to this woman.

He'd learned his lesson long ago. Two years negotiating divorce settlements in his early days cured him of trusting any immediate attraction. He'd seen too many relationships dissolve under the harsh light of day. Men shattered by angry, disillusioned females. He'd encountered a few of those harpies himself, beginning with his first serious girlfriend in college. Now safe, short-term, uncomplicated liaisons suited him fine.

By the time he stepped out of the elevator into his office floor, London's scent had dissipated. But he couldn't shake the image of her slipping those legs into the taxicab. Given it was late on a Friday, he wondered where she was headed. *Not anywhere you are, man.* Jaded or not, he couldn't help thinking what a pity that was.

2

"Control of your submissive goes beyond administering punishments and pleasure," Carson said. Katie shifted once more. He traced a fingertip across the brunette's shoulder tattoo. The ink on her flesh read *Hurt Me*. If only all women came pre-labeled with warning stickers, like this beauty draped over his legs. Perhaps then he'd have understood London's edginess today a little better. *Danger: High Voltage* would have suited her.

For the last two hours he'd tried to stop thinking about those legs. Every technique he used only pushed her deeper into his mind. *And the thought of pushing deep into her.*

Katie wiggled across his thighs and reclaimed his attention. He placed his hand over her lower back. "Be still." He waited. When she finally stopped her attempts to grind into his crotch, he returned his attention to the growing audience for his spanking demo at Club Accendos.

"Settle," he whispered. He willed his usual concentration to rise. After all, he'd agreed to this silly demo.

"Yes, sir." Her words came out garbled. Katie was a screamer, so he'd gagged her. But he couldn't enjoy her usual vocal appreciation of his work, thanks to unshakeable thoughts of a certain PR Princess.

He returned his attention to the ass presented. *Smack! Smack!* Katie's behind grew more heated under his hand. When he palmed her pinkened butt, she pressed into his lack of an erection. It wasn't Katie's fault for his lackluster reaction to her. He'd just been here so many times before.

Katie's flesh jiggled under three more swats. She fell further over his lap, releasing the last of her own tension and settling into the moment. If only he could do the same.

He slipped the gag from Katie's mouth and let it clatter the floor. He eased her up and caught her by the arm as she swayed. Her heavy lids told him at least *she'd* enjoyed their time together.

"Thank you, sweetheart. As you can see, Katie is starting to float. That's when you need to stop. Check in with your sub often and pay attention to the signs. Any questions?" *If there is a God, there'll be no questions.*

No one moved.

"Very good then. No questions." He stood, lifting Katie up into his arms.

He handed Katie to one of the professional aftercare assistants. The crowd dispersed as he shrugged himself back into his suit coat. A drink, that's what he needed.

He headed into the main ballroom, which was now filled to capacity, and picked up his one allowed Scotch from the corner bar. His gaze wandered over the human horde and then rose to the balcony. A tall woman stood on the far end. In a mask of white feathers, a pristine white corset and lace panties, she glowed like a misplaced angel under the soft spotlights shining from the ceiling. Her delicate hands clutched at the mahogany rail. A ponytail of long, caramel-brown hair swished across her upper back. Her skin gleamed like creamed coffee in the subdued light.

He sipped his drink. White was a fascinating color choice. She appeared virginal. *Untouched.*

From all signs, she took great care of her appearance, but he didn't think she was cared *for*. She gripped the bar as if she'd fall over and no one would catch her. No man loved this woman. Well-loved women had a certain confidence, a conquer-the-world countenance.

She shifted her feet and sighed. She looked young. *Hmm, late twenties, I'd guess.* Her posture also struck a familiar pose. The profile she presented teased him with a feeling of déjà vu.

The sound of a sharp slap drew her attention. A man hovered over an exotic beauty tied to a spanking bench. So, his white vision liked spanking. He could accommodate such a desire. *Hmm, mine.*

The alcohol had kicked in, warming his chest and letting his standard emotional control slip for a minute. A familiar loneliness slid into place, a recent regular and *unwanted* guest in his well-ordered life. *Walk it off, man.*

"She's pretty." Alexander Rockingham, his friend and the club's owner, had appeared next to him.

"She's a guest of Accendos. Of course she is."

"Never seen her before. You?"

"I don't know." The white vision taunted him with a feeling of familiarity. He felt he should know her. He really needed to stop cancelling his optometrist appointments.

He turned to the older man. "My paperwork received?"

"Yes. The Tribunal's decision to ban Mr. Landon has been distributed to all the organization's arbiters. They'll distribute the particulars to their members. And the man will never step foot over any club's doorstep again."

"Good." He returned his gaze to the crowd. "His submissive?"

"His *former* submissive is going to be fine. Brond has her in victim assistance."

"That bad?"

"Yes."

He stared into the crowd, unseeing, lost in thought over the woman who'd come to Alexander for help just days earlier. Of course, they'd given her sanctuary. Every Tribunal Council member had pledged themselves to their three laws concerning safety, consent and protection for all who chose their lifestyle.

His gaze rose to the balcony once more.

Alexander slapped him on the back. "She looks like she needs someone like you."

He arched his brow in amusement as Alexander left him watching the woman in white. He couldn't tear his eyes from her. Something about the way she stood...

She pushed off the railing and made her way to the circular staircase on the far side.

He left his drink on a side table and proceeded toward the intriguing figure. Why the hell not? Rarely did he approach someone so early in the evening, but she piqued his interest. Perhaps she sought what he did—pleasure with no complications.

That's why he liked Club Accendos. No hidden agenda. Defined roles. Clear deadlines—usually the end of the night. *No one gets hurt.* He laughed to himself. *Well, not unless they want the pain.*

As soon as the woman's foot hit the second step down, her familiarity clicked into place. *Holy hell. London.*

In his peripheral vision, he watched another man join his progression toward her. He plowed through the crowd to reach the staircase first. He cut off the other Dominant with a flick of his eye. *I'll fight for this one.* The man understood the warning. He walked by, unbothered by the nanosecond exchange.

As soon as London had descended halfway down the stairs, she froze. Her petulant chin lifted as she recognized him. Within seconds, she resumed her descent, her eyes full of her usual bravado.

When London reached the final step, he held out his hand to help her down. "Hello, sugar."

She ignored his offer and tried to scoot by him. He captured her arm, lightly. He didn't want to frighten her, merely get her attention. Her eyes flamed with annoyance and blood rushed to his cock.

She raised her chin. "Excuse me, but we haven't been introduced." Of course her voice contained her signature, throaty impudence.

He raised his eyebrow. *Playing games? Fine.* "I'm Carson Drake. Sit and talk?" He leveled his voice to the business tone she'd recognize, less of a Dominant and more of a diplomat.

Her shoulders relaxed a little but her eyes held debate.

He took her hesitation as a "yes." He circled her waist and led her away from the crowd toward one of the side doors. As a Tribunal Council member, he had a private room—far from any potential interruptions.

London stopped short. "Where are we going?"

"Someplace quieter."

"What if I don't want to?"

"Then you don't have to." He dropped his hold on her waist.

"Just talking?"

"Yes. Witnesses saw us leave. You're safe."

She let him pull her through a gothic arched door. A bodyguard closed it behind them.

He moved them down an expansive hallway lined with closed doors. Only after ushering her inside the last door at the end did he let go of her elbow. She immediately crossed her arms.

"It's okay, sugar. I'm not going to hurt you."

"I'm meeting someone."

"Oh?"

"Yes, so I can't stay long." She worked her bottom lip and shuffled her weight from foot to foot. Her eyes also darted to the bed in the corner. Perhaps she thought he'd take her right away? She knew his identity. She should know he was committed to due diligence. And he had to know why she was here—the last place on earth he'd expect London Chantelle.

He sat in one of two cushioned chairs set before a lit fireplace. He appreciated her luscious curves, beautifully illuminated by the amber glow of the low fire.

"Sit." He beckoned her to join him.

"I like standing."

"Sit." The commanding tones of a Dom brought the expected result. As she lowered herself into the chair, her ponytail licked one shoulder. "Your hair is beautiful in this light," he said. "More golden brown than I noticed before."

She swallowed. "Thank you, um ... I go by Tatiana."

"It doesn't suit you. Why not go with, say ... London?"

Her mouth dropped to an "O" in alarm, and she leapt from her seat.

"Sit. Down." He pointed to the chair.

"Please." Her hazel eyes implored lenience, and her tone of voice surprised him. He liked the beseeching quality. It was quite a departure from her customary unadulterated demand.

"Please what? You thought a simple mask and change of clothing meant I wouldn't recognize you?"

"I hoped ... maybe ... I can't do this."

Before she could complete two steps, he'd risen from his

chair and laid his hand on her shoulder. She stopped. He pressed his torso against her back, sending her firm ass into his crotch. He decided to like her stiletto boots. He was a tall man and they made her the perfect height. He waited to see if she'd object, at which point he'd back off. She didn't move.

He pulled off the elastic holding her hair captive. A curtain of gold-laced chestnut silk cascaded free. He brushed her mane to one side and bared her shoulder. "That's better."

Her breathing sped up. "You said just talking."

"Still, sweetness." He inhaled her scent of Ivory soap and cinnamon Christmas cookies before stepping backward. "We are talking."

She twisted to face him. "Carson, please …"

He liked how her emotions turned in an instant. She'd test his abilities to direct her psychology in a scene. He nearly laughed at himself. *How quickly I have her bound and pleasured in my mind.* "There. Now that's a start. I rather like you begging me."

"I don't beg."

And there goes that chin. "We'll see." He took another step back. His instincts told him she wouldn't bolt.

"Take a seat, London." He returned to his chair. "When you do, hands in your lap. After you listen to me you can decide if you wish to leave. It will be your choice."

She hesitated, then nestled her behind onto the chair opposite him. She placed her hands in her lap. The thumb of one hand worked the palm of the other.

"Take off your mask. Show me your pretty face."

She took a deep breath as her elegant fingers slipped off her disguise, pulling the fastening ribbon through her perfect hair. He wanted to capture her cheeks in his hands. He'd rub off the mask indents and erase the worry imprinted on her forehead.

"How long have you been without a Master?" he asked.

Untouchable

"I-I'm not ..." Her jawline hardened. "It's none of your business."

"That's a shame. I'm good at business." His mouth broke into a smile at the thought of bending her over her desk, papers sticking to her bared breasts, pens falling to the floor. He'd smack her ass with that leather portfolio she carried around like a shield. He wouldn't stop until her engraved initials imprinted her skin.

"Why did you bring me here?" she whispered.

"You're looking for a Dom. I'm a Dom looking for a sub."

She flinched at his final word. "What do you want, Carson?"

What I want. Did it matter? He'd given up what he wanted long ago—a spirited submissive who matched his desires. Someone who might actually stick with him and not drop him the minute a better offer came through. He didn't allow himself to think finding such a woman was possible anymore.

"Time. Willingness. Pleasure." He folded his hands and laid his chin on his knuckles. "Now, I want to know what you want."

"No, you don't."

He raised an eyebrow. "Toying with me will not get you anywhere, sweetness."

"Isn't that what you are doing with me?"

"Hardly." He let silence take over the space.

"Then what?" she whispered after long minutes.

"Patience will be your first lesson tonight. Then I'll consider you."

"*Consider* me?" She gave him a hardened, fuck-off look.

"Yes. Last time. What do you want?"

He let a few seconds tick by. Then he stood. "If you won't tell me why you're here, what you seek, then I can't help."

"I-I didn't mean ... it isn't easy ..."

"You must answer my questions when I ask them. No delay. It's for your safety and mine."

Her lips pursed, her signal she realized she was losing. Her sassiness had its usual alluring appeal—futile, but adorable. She licked her bottom lip, the subtle move urging him forward.

"Stand," he said.

She stood cautiously.

"What is your safeword?" he asked.

"Excuse me? A-a scene. With you? You're a client. If anything ever got back—"

"Then we would both lose. And I don't lose."

"No, you take what you want and damn the consequences."

"London." He walked toward her and she backed around the chair. "What are you afraid of? Afraid you might get what you want? Experience what you've longed for?"

She let out a huff, but continued to retreat as he advanced. He sent her in a backward circle until she closed in on the canopied bed. Yes, most definitely submissive. The urge to discover how deep her desires ran raged through him like a brushfire.

"How would you know what I long for?" Her haughty chin jutted out.

"I want to know, London. Tell me."

"Why?" She'd backed up until she connected with the bedpost.

"Fair question. And one I'll answer. Given you and I dance well together at the boardroom table, why wouldn't we here? Had I known your proclivities, I might have offered. Why didn't you come to me before?" How had he missed her signs?

"B-but you hate me."

Now he *was* puzzled. "No, I don't. You sometimes ... irritate, but I could never hate you. Surely you noticed my tendencies."

"Being a bully in a boardroom does not make you a Dominant I'd be interested in."

"Ouch, London. That hurt." He slapped his chest above his heart but kept his face stony.

"I didn't think you could feel pain."

"Everyone feels pain." Her lips parted when he closed the last inch of distance between them. His thighs touched hers, and he softened his voice. "It pleases me you're here. There's no use in fighting this chemistry." He hooked a thumb on his waistband. "One weekend."

"With you?"

"Yes."

"What will you do with your harem?"

He unbuckled his belt. "Your second lesson. Don't force discipline with a smart mouth."

"I don't have that kind of time." She raised her impertinent jawline—again.

Lesson three: discipline your haughty chin.

"Not enough time to learn discipline or not enough time, in general?" The loud rasp of leather yanked through his belt loops sent her attention to his torso.

"What are you doing?" Her panicked gaze shot to his face.

"I don't have a collar on me."

"I am wholly disinterested in being collared."

"One weekend, London." He grasped one of her hips with his free hand. "If you're disappointed at any time, you can walk. I'll never speak of it again. Our work together will go unaffected. No one—and I mean no one—but us will know."

"Would you put that in writing?" Her eyes filled with mischief.

Priceless. London lured him toward a lightning storm. He could play. Hell, nothing appealed in the moment more than a weekend playing with her. Yes, this is what he wanted. Now he needed to know if she was willing.

"I'll do one better." He snaked the belt around her waist until the leather rested against her hips.

"I'm not a notch on a belt."

"You could never be a notch, London Chantelle. You're the whole belt, sugar."

Her face softened, and the playfulness in her eyes died. He recognized the deliberation behind them, the wonder if she'd be safe, here and at work. She needn't have worried. She might get scared, but mutual satisfaction was the only way his brand of sexual fulfillment worked.

"Say yes or no." He pressed his torso to her corseted body, the last space between her body and his obliterated. "But say yes."

"What will happen if I say yes?"

"What you want. What you've probably always wanted."

Her eyes misted with a surprising vulnerability. "Yes."

3

Yes? Are you out of your mind?

London's first visit to Club Accendos, and she had to run into Carson Drake—the man who hated her. Well, the man who was *irritated* by her. Dallying with Carson—a client!—could jeopardize her promotion at Yost and Brennan. Of course, what if they knew about Michael?

Damn Michael for not showing up. She had a plan. She was going to show him, and herself, that those dark-shadowed desires she'd successfully kept shuttered were best left untouched. But here she was with Carson, a man who tapped into those longings within minutes.

Surrendering herself to a man? *Gah!* Tonight she'd planned to expel those ridiculous desires from her system—those little-girl, save-me, damsel-in-distress dreams she should have outgrown by now. *Not feed them!* She was twenty-nine for heaven's sake and almost a vice president.

Why was she so attracted to this man? She knew why. Why couldn't she finally admit her attraction? *Because of what it says about you, that's why. A needy, vulnerable, gullible...*

Carson's large hands encased her arms and his muscled

thighs pressed into the bare skin above her boots. Holy Jesus, his strength could consume her alive. If she hadn't settled her back against the bedpost, she'd have collapsed in a swoon.

"Your safeword, London." His eyes hunted her face. "I won't continue without one."

My safeword? She couldn't think under such scrutiny. Of course, every meeting, every discussion, every out-of-the-blue telephone call from him forced her to grasp at her composure. She had worked damned hard to hold her own with Carson. But now? Her good sense silently shouted insults at her feminine weakness, that little part of her that said maybe *he* would be different.

Could he be?

Oh, come on.

His eyelids narrowed. "I'm waiting, sugar. Or, I'll have to give you one."

"It's sugar. I've always hated that sweet talk." The old southern endearment reduced her to nothing more than a dessert—unnecessary and an afterthought. Never again would she let herself dissolve like honey on a greedy tongue. That was her mother's domain.

"Fair enough. Sugar." He swatted the side of her behind. A low yelp came from the back of her throat.

Carson backed up two steps. His gaze took liberties with her body. He regarded her ankles and raked his gaze up her legs and torso. His attention stopped briefly at her décolletage. An eternity later, his attention rested on her face.

She took a deep breath and released her clasp on the bedpost. His evaluation—and obvious appreciation—had her nerves on high alert. She'd been under such predacious attention before.

"We need to talk more," she said.

"Of course." He leaned forward but then stopped himself. An almost kiss? He gestured to the fireside chairs.

They sat across from one another, not speaking for a full five minutes. She felt his gaze travel her body.

His voice finally broke the silence. "This might work after all, London."

Her face shot up.

"You've shown more patience than I've experienced from you to date."

Not exactly a resounding compliment, but his words and smile relaxed her a bit ... and warmed her inner thighs. "How is this supposed to work? I mean, this weekend you're talking about."

"That's for us to determine." He ran a finger over his lips. "Would you like to know how I envision our time together?"

She nodded once.

A flash crossed his eyes. "Say yes, sir."

"Yes, sir." If she was going to leap into this likely unwise scene play with Carson, she might as well observe some protocol. *As if I know any.*

"Very good." He stood, peeled off his jacket and draped it over the back of the chair. She regarded the flames peeking around his legs. She wouldn't be caught staring at his broad chest. She'd rather die than let him see how much he affected her. *How he's always affected me these last few months.*

She raised her eyes to his shadowed face. His dark brooding eyes assessed her under a swath of dark hair, his jaw set firm and resolute. "You know the basic rules of a D/s scene?"

"Yes." She swallowed. "Sir."

"Good. Stand. Present yourself to me." He crossed his arms. His warrior stance dethroned any leftover sense of control. Her feminine essence dampened her panties to prove her indiscipline.

She was going to do this.

Yes, she was out of her mind.

Think, London. Monday was two days away. None of her accounts, including Whitestone's, required her attention. Carson would risk just as much as she if they were caught together. She could hear the conversation now. *Mr. Whitestone, Mr. Brennan, Carson and I were at this BDSM club ...*

She almost laughed at the thought. Carson's serious, dark eyes stopped her. *Like he wants me.* A sharp tingle that started low in her belly slithered up her middle.

What if Carson *was* different? Oh, God, here comes the admittance. He'd presented the potential for being exactly the man she'd always longed for elsewhere in her life—a mountain of irrefutable control, capability and ethics. *A protector.*

He hadn't been easy to work with. But his constant cross-examination brought something out in her. She'd done the best work of her career on the Whitestone account, and now she had a chance to advance because he made her prove herself. Repeatedly. Would he be the same outside the boardroom?

Would he make sure his woman was taken care of in all areas of her life? *His.* God, what it must be like to be Carson's. A dampness grew between her legs. She licked her lips, and cool breath ran over them. The sensation jarred slightly. Every nerve in her body had grown more sensitive.

He cleared his throat. "You won't keep me waiting."

Her ribcage clenched under his deep growl. She stood on shaky legs. "Yes. Yes, sir."

"Closer."

She took two steps forward. A mere six inches separated their bodies. A deep inhalation sent her trepidation into overdrive; his masculine scent woke up a ferocious longing.

When he walked around to her back and brushed his fingertips along her collarbone and neck, an explosion of adrenaline made her legs quiver more, not from fear but from a level of desire she'd never felt before.

He swept a lock of her hair so it fell down her back. "Such lovely skin, London. You should never hide beneath business suits."

He tugged on his belt that hung around her hips. She pitched backward and connected with his chest. She shouldn't give in to this. She wasn't being smart. She...

His hand encircled her throat. He pinched her chin and pulled it down.

"You'll control the tilt of this, London. It's a dead giveaway for when you're scared. If you ever want me to stop you'll say 'sugar.' Don't waste my time—or yours—with insolence. This isn't a battle."

She yanked her face free from his clutch. *Uh-oh.* Immediate regret settled in her belly.

He spun her toward the chair and bent her over its arm. The cushion's fabric scratched her cheek as her face brushed the seat. With her ass presented high in the air, he could see, well, everything. Why had she worn such small panties?

A loud crack across her backside ripped a small cry from her throat.

"Impertinent." He chortled. She amused him?

"Carson, don't—"

Smack!

Air shot from her lungs. An unmistakable pang in her sex followed the burning tingle across her ass cheek. He whacked her behind two more times.

She pressed her thighs together, a vain attempt to stem the moisture pooling between her legs. The effect of his hands pissed her off. *He'll see!* His fingertips trailed down her butt seam and pressed between her clenched thighs. She jolted when a finger reached her wet valley.

"Very nice, sweetness." His voice, tainted with approval,

helped ease her embarrassment—a little.

He continued to massage the best spot between her inner lips while his other hand cupped one side of her behind. He made a murmuring, appreciative sound.

Two hours ago Carson nearly tanked her work, his hands pushing away her proposal. His clipped words and rich voice demanded she prove herself. Now that voice made her nether regions jump to attention, and those same fingers touched her in places she ... *Oh, please don't stop.*

She stopped fighting the tornado spinning inside her. She let go. Pricks of light colored her vision. More words drifted in the air. His voice grew muffled. She was upright, and then ... on his lap? His hands tugged on her corset. A strange sizzling sound reached her ears and the pressure on her breasts began to release.

"Breathe, London." His voice cut through her fog.

She took a lungful of air. More zings of fabric filled her ears.

"Again. Deep breaths." He squeezed the steel clips holding her corset together in front. His large hand pressed on the back of her head and her face connected with his skin. A rich, masculine tobacco aroma arose under her nose. She rested against a pulsing vein in his warm, muscled neck. *Masculinity incarnate.*

"One more time," he said.

Her vision cleared. Without thought, she'd been following his orders, taking big gulps of air. She lifted herself from his neck. Oh, no, she'd almost fainted.

His eyes held genuine concern. "Feel better?"

"Yes." She pushed on his chest, but his arms banded her tightly to him.

"Keep taking deep breaths." He pulled the corset free from around her back and threw it to the ground. How did he do that? His belt looked odd and misplaced around her naked hips. Wearing nothing but panties and boots, her skin pinked from the indignity of sitting on Carson's lap, like a wide-eyed child instead of an adult—and practically nude.

When he cupped a freed breast, she startled and pulled back. He tutted in reply. "I've just started my inspection, London. Do you want another spanking?"

Another rush of womanly fluid answered his question.

"Yes, I imagine you do." He tugged on a nipple.

"You're making fun of me."

"Never." He ran his hand down her arm and captured her hand. "I enjoy handling you. I'm glad my touch has a positive effect." He moved to unzip one of her boots while his other arm held her to his chest. "Lift." She lifted her leg closer.

After pulling the boot from her foot and letting it plunk to the ground, she lifted her other foot for similar treatment. He smiled.

An extraordinary wash of calm moved through her whole body as he kneaded one of her feet's arches. The strength of his touch also earned more dampness between her legs. *Please don't let me leave a wet stain on his pants.* Her pride had limits.

"Now, as I continue to examine the beauty in my lap, what other questions do you have?"

"What are you going to do with me?"

He brushed a stray hair from her forehead. "We'll have a short scene here, to test the waters. If you speak your safeword, you'll be free to go. Have the weekend you'd planned."

Did she have plans beyond tonight? Sitting in her own arousal, Carson's erection pressing into the back of her thighs, had blanked her mind. How was she to remember her schedule?

His hands roamed her curves with no hesitation. He lifted a breast and weighed its heft in his hand. She should have minded his assessment. But she didn't.

"If you choose to continue, I'm taking you home with me," he said.

"Why? Why leave the club?"

"It's more private. All rules apply there, as they do here. You won't be harmed. You have my word."

His word? "I don't have any clothes."

"You won't need them."

Oh, God. Another question fought itself forward. "Why did you come here tonight? I mean, if you prefer your house."

He smiled. "To look for you."

~

Carson laughed at her look of disbelief. He'd not known the *name* of the woman he sought tonight. But then London descended those stairs, and landed smack into the middle of his night—and needs. *A beauty with incomparable spirit.*

He dropped his smile. "One last time before we begin, London. Limits."

"Can they be anything?"

"Of course." Why would she ask such a thing?

"Then, no gagging."

He failed to suppress a smile. "Of course. We wouldn't want anything to get in the way of your arguments. No gags."

"I don't like to be cold."

"Are you chilly now?"

She shook her head.

"No ice, then," he said.

She lifted her chin, alarmed.

"Yes, ice is sometimes used. Keep going."

"That's it. It's all I know." She lowered her lashes. "I hate ... not knowing—"

"You aren't expected to know everything, London. I simply require some basic boundaries. At any point you say 'sugar' if things get too uncomfortable. I can't read your mind and I won't tolerate you being harmed." He brushed his lips over her shoulder. "Now, talk to me."

"I-I need some time to think. To process."

A small chuckle escaped his lips. *Processing?* No, she wanted time to talk herself out of their weekend. He was right to make the impulsive decision to take her to his house, something he hadn't done in years. London required privacy. He mentally started a list—London's List—comprised of bits and pieces of her personality. *Feisty. Smart. Nervous. A live wire.*

"This could get messy," she said.

"It'll only get messy if you aren't being true to yourself or honest with me." Another thought dropped into place. "You have more limits. What do you think I'd do that you won't like?"

"You'll go too fast. Can you slow down?"

"Define slow down." He pulled her chin down, swearing a silent oath he'd break her of that habit before the end of the night.

She stared into his eyes. "No sex."

"Define sex."

"No penetration."

"Your pussy by my cock? Your mouth?"

"Your cock. Nowhere inside me. Anywhere."

No sex? *Strange.* If she got inside Club Accendos, she'd presented the necessary medical records to prove herself devoid of any sexual diseases and protected from pregnancy. She had to know what was possible.

"What about this?" He slipped his finger between her legs. Her lip trembled and she let out a long sigh. Her skin fired that beautiful peach color that made his dick protest its captivity.

She grasped his wrist. "Maybe."

"So I may pleasure you in other ways."

London nodded and a new crimson stain spread across her décolletage. Her inexperience should have angered him. He'd encountered too many experimental submissives of late. But he wasn't annoyed with London. Perhaps because he didn't believe her shyness was insincere. She behaved like a woman whose trust had been abused.

Her long lashes fluttered against her cheeks. "Do you always talk this much with your ..."

"Submissives. Anyone you play with should talk, early and often. If they don't, run." She straightened under his harsh tone. But he couldn't stand the idea of another man taking advantage of her innocent exploration. London was smart. But he could tell her ideas of domination filled a pill box. She needed to know what was possible—and what she should never accept, sex or not.

She grew unsettled. Before she wormed her way off his lap, he encircled the back of her neck with his hand. She instantly quieted and leaned into his hand. *Ah.* He added another item to his London List—a desire for control he doubted she knew she had. *But something I've often suspected.*

Carson kept his hold light. "There are many ways for us to be together."

"I'll bet." Her eyes iced over. He'd seen that chilly look from her many times. *Unfortunately.* At least her chin didn't raise at his last words.

She sighed. "So, you will ... or won't—"

"Your boundaries guide everything." He settled both hands onto the chair arms. She could leave if she wanted to. He knew she wouldn't.

London took another deep breath.

"Now are you ready?" he asked.

She nodded.

"Good."

4

Carson scooped her up and set her down on the corner of the bed more gently than she expected. Her legs dangled over the side of the mattress. He smiled down at her as he widened her thighs with his large hands. His dark eyes burned clear through her courage.

He pulled her to the edge so his pelvis connected with her crotch. The ridge of his hard-on ran up her low belly and beyond. *Oh.* The bed had been clearly designed for such a connection. Its height provided an opportunity for many stimulating positions.

He unknotted his tie and pulled it through his collar. He draped it over her neck. "Hang on to this." He ran his fingers down its length, pressing the silk between her breasts.

"Going to tie me up?"

"We'll see." He unbuttoned the top button of his shirt, his silver cufflinks flashing in the firelight. She caught the engraving: CsD. She wanted to know what the "S" in his initials represented. *Probably sex.* Because the man was it —personified.

A smattering of dark hair peeked out from his open shirt.

His biceps strained the shirt sleeve fabric. Even without seeing him nude, she began to understand his strength. Carson Drake may have been an attorney, but nothing underneath his business suit spoke of pushing paper. His body represented a lifetime of breaking granite with bare hands.

"Yes, you may touch me." He placed both hands on her cheeks and lifted her gaze.

Her hands found their way to his abdomen, caressing the hard muscle through his shirt, a betrayal of the desire she wanted to withhold from him—at least until she herself got used to it. She dropped them to her lap. "Sorry."

A low chuckle rumbled from that glorious chest that she wanted to see, to touch, to do so much *more* against—the dangerous more.

He ran his thumb across her cheek. "Yes, patience will be your first lesson. Then I'll address that chin more formally." When his lips touched her forehead in a kiss, every part of her sizzled. He dropped his hold on her face.

As he leaned over her, her teeth seized her bottom lip. She had no option but to lie back as he caged her against the bed. His pecs touched her breasts, her nipples hardening in response.

One hand went between her legs and cupped her sex. His palm connected with her soaked panties. A single push shoved her higher on the bed. She'd never encountered such raw strength in one man.

A whimper escaped her throat when his hand left her crotch. Less than an hour had passed since Carson had pulled her into this room, and already she was a puddle of shameful lust. Her ego screamed its usual insults. *You weakling.* Agreement or not, her body countered. *Please. Take me.*

Carson hadn't expected such naiveté. London's usual hauteur shattered under the most basic display of authority. Yet he caught glimpses of her usual spirit darting behind her eyes. Often prefaced by the tilt of her chin, Diva London threatened to leap out at any moment. But Primal London trumped her.

London's List was going to be long.

Had he known she'd needed handling so badly, he'd have locked the boardroom door one day and had his way with her. Now stripped of a business agenda and paperwork, she wore her need like she sported those ridiculous pastel business suits. *Impossible to ignore. And delicious.*

Her breath quickened through her nostrils. She began to twist underneath him, her conflict evident. *Here we go.* Strong women often had a hard time reconciling their more basic, submissive desires with their need for independence. He'd been here before.

He lifted himself from her body and returned to standing. "Lie back, hands above your head. Grip the headboard."

She obeyed and clasped the bed railing.

"Don't let go. No matter what, London."

She required a certain scene. She needed assurance, a clear understanding he would dominate her and she'd be safe.

As he stood next to the bed, looking down on her, his mind's eye devoured her round plump breasts rising and falling. His imagination feasted on the curve of her hips.

Only when her shoulders relaxed did he touch her. He ran his fingertip from knee to hip bone letting the sensation of her satin skin ignite his nerves. A faint pink line formed where his index finger had laid its trail. She trembled when his finger circled her bellybutton.

His inner negotiator fought with the agreement he had with London. *Two days. That's all to see how much her skin would react to me? Yes*, answered his past experience. Two days was all he could expect from any woman—or all they could expect from him.

He dipped a finger under the elastic of her panties. As he rimmed the flesh under the lace, small moans escaped her lips.

"Look at me." He loved seeing a woman's longing pool in her eyes. Only then could he decipher her strongest desires. London wasn't giving up much, but it was enough for now. Her need to be handled egged him on, a sense of purpose pushing out his earlier cynical mood.

He abandoned the baby soft skin of her belly and began to draw down her panties.

"You said—"

"I meant it." He pulled the slip of silky lace over her knees and her ankles to drop them off the end of the bed. A thin trail of dark hair dusted her seam. *Good.* He'd had enough of grown women shaving themselves clean so they resembled a twelve-year-old.

He circled her calves, his fingertips playing with the tender skin behind her knees. He returned his attention to her face. Scores of questions danced in her eyes.

"You're beautiful," he said. In his thirty-six years, he'd never met a woman who could hear that sentiment enough. Constant assurance was par for the course. It exhausted him —usually.

When her leg muscles grew soft, he ran his hand up her side to cup a breast. She sucked in her breath and arched into his hand.

"How long have you been denying your submissive nature?" he asked.

"I-I'm not sure I am."

"Turn over."

"And let go of the bed?"

"Yes, you have permission," he said, laughing.

∼

Damn attorney. She'd confirmed his assessment of her nature with her question.

At least he gave another favorable murmur when she settled herself on to her stomach and presented her butt to him. She still heated with shyness. Hours ago they were just colleagues. But now?

His hands encircled each ankle and drew her further down until her toes dipped off the end of the mattress. He continued to circle her. A hawk determining which bite to take first? His fingers traced the seam between her ass and leg. The move was assured, graceful, as if he'd done it a hundred times. His hands spoke his intention—incontrovertible possession.

"Spread your legs wider," he said.

But he'd see what she didn't want him to see—pure, wet need.

"Wider, London."

Her toes slipped over the bed edges, her groin stretched, and more damnable fluid gathered in her feminine parts. She flushed anew from head to toe.

"You won't close them, not even an inch. Confirm that command."

"Yes, sir."

He adjusted the belt around her waist so the buckle lay heavy in the small of her back. She tried to focus on the ornately carved, antique headboard instead of the fact she lay spread-eagled on a bed. *Nude. With Carson.*

His jacket fell across her back. Traces of an expensive cologne—his familiar scent—invaded her senses. He pressed another kiss into her hair. "You tell me if you're cold at any time. No sugar required." *A hard-ass and a gentleman.*

Though the room was no more than thirty feet wide, his footfalls grew distant. Strange sounds filled the room. A muffled pop of a wine bottle being opened. The sound of a chair being dragged closer. Her own breathing rasping against the silky bedcover. A small creak from a body lowering to a chair. She tuned in to each sound, assessing the level of threat and what they might entail.

He sipped something? She turned her head to search for him.

"Relax." His voice came from the end of the bed, near her feet, where he could see ... *Oh, no!* Shame burst across her skin. She rose onto one elbow and turned to face him.

"Back down." He leaned forward in his chair, a glass of red wine hanging between two fingers.

"But aren't we going to—"

"Down."

Like a dog sent to its crate, she obeyed. A familiar red thread of anger started low in her belly. She reminded herself she'd agreed to be here, to be like this—spread wide, her most private parts open for his viewing. She wanted it, didn't she? He was going to be different than her past experiences, right?

More time ticked past. She waited. Nothing happened. *This is absurd.* A puff of angry breath blasted from her lungs. "What are you doing?"

"Appreciating."

Another huff of incredulity escaped her lungs.

"Still, London." His hand enclosed her foot, and she choked out a garbled sound. "Easy, girl. Close your eyes. Feel my hand."

"I don't get—"

"I know."

She tuned into his thumb rubbing up and down the arch of her foot. The red light faded behind her eyelids and her breathing slowed, following the rhythm of his massage.

When he let go of her foot, she heard him settle back into the chair.

"This pinot noir goes well with my view. Rich but not too bold. A hint of cinnamon to warm the tongue." Was he reading *Wine Spectator*, too?

"I'd like to take a sip of wine, then put my mouth on you, mix your flavors with it. Would you like that?"

"Maybe." Her sex clenched and a trickle of juice escaped down her pubic bone to wet the sheets underneath her. She swore she could hear him smiling.

More chair creaks filled the space, followed by sipping. "Beautiful."

"What?" she snarled.

"You. London, I want you to think about what I'm seeing. How I might be reacting, looking at you, splayed out for my pleasure." He took a noisy sip.

What he's seeing? Legs quivering from gripping the bed? A wet sheet, damp with her arousal? Or perhaps he could see her ache, an impossibly sharp tingle that wouldn't stop and kept her from relaxing her thighs. When would he start ... something, *anything*?

She adjusted herself on the sheet, unable to stay immobile. She sank her teeth into the pillow, wetting it further. A loud crack from the fireplace sent a spike of adrenaline through her heart—or was that between her legs?—as a log gave way to the flames.

"Feel it, London."

"What, growing stiff?"

His chuckle resonated against his glass. "Growing more aroused."

"I'm not."

"It's nothing to be ashamed of."

Oh, but she and shame had made friends long ago. The slight pulsing between her legs brought her concentration back to her most private place—that special spot that gets so many women in trouble.

His hand clasped the back of her neck and she startled. She hadn't heard him get up. His other hand connected to the small of her back.

"Not yet," he said. "I know you want to come."

Oh, God, she'd been writhing like a cat in heat.

Embarrassed by her craving, she tried to focus her sight on the vine etchings on the headboard, away from him. But when he pulled on her hair a cascade of tingles ran down her spine. Her breathing slowed in time with his playing fingers, now massaging her neck.

When he lifted his hand away, a small whimper escaped her lips at the loss of his touch.

Carson closed her legs till her inner thighs touched. "Now we'll go."

She rose up on her elbows, swiping away the damp hair clinging to her face. She blinked at him in confusion.

He helped her up to sitting. "That was your first lesson. Patience. You also needed to see I'd honor your limits." He eased her forward so she sat on the edge. "Hold on to the bedpost."

As she clung to the post, swaying slightly, she watched Carson stuff her abandoned corset into a bag he retrieved from a chest of drawers in the corner. He also pulled out a robe. After helping her into the short wrap and zipping up her boots, he stood between her opened knees and cupped her chin. "Where is your car?"

For a minute she couldn't recall how she got to Club Accendos. She ran the last two hours through her mind like a tape in reverse. "A cab. I took a cab."

Untouchable

"Good. I'll drive you home."

"Okay." Her lashes fell to her cheeks. Her heart sunk in her chest with them.

"My home," he said.

Her relief at the fact she wasn't being sent away had to show. She knew delayed gratification was part of this dynamic. She just didn't realize how much she wanted him to complete the job now that she'd opened the gates to her desire. *Even though it's going to be temporary.* Not all her good sense had fled.

The plush carpeting muffled their walk down the hallway. Carson pushed a button at the last door before the exit. A young woman opened it and immediately reached out to take her arm.

"I've got her." She pulled London inside a small elevator. She reached out to stop the door from closing.

Carson placed his hand over hers. "I'm not leaving you, London. Carrie is going to help you get your things and bring you back to me."

She nodded and let the door separate them.

Carrie helped her to the dressing room where she retrieved her coat and purse from the locker she'd been assigned. Carrie refused to lace her back into her corset, despite her protest. Instead, the young girl helped her into a simple wrap dress. "Compliments of the house," she said, tying a loose bow around her waist.

On the ride back up in the elevator, Carrie still didn't let go of her arm. Afraid she'd bolt? London's phone buzzed in her hand, signaling unread text messages demanding attention. She didn't have the guts to look. She knew who it was—Michael. A man she hadn't wanted to see in the first place, despite her agreement to meet him here tonight. *To fix things.*

She hoped she wasn't making the greatest mistake of her life, leaving with Carson instead of meeting Michael. What

39

was she thinking getting involved with Michael? He seemed so polished and knowledgeable about things she desperately wanted to know more about. But then when he got rough and refused to back down? His actions were a sharp comparison to the man who waited for her a floor above.

When the elevator doors opened, Carson stood right where they'd left him. Carrie winked at London before releasing her grip on her arm. Something in her wry smile sent a message. She got a sense the woman was proud of her.

Carson helped her into her trench coat. As he pulled her hair free from the collar, he let the long strands run through his fingers. "Beautiful," he said.

She turned to face him. Was that a look of gratitude? He ran his thumb over her bottom lip. She liked it—too much.

"Come." He pulled her toward the door.

"You wouldn't let me, remember?"

"I'd be happy to lift the moratorium on sex."

Curse him. So what if her entire body screamed, "penetrate me?"

He captured her arm and pulled her through the door to his car, which was good. Otherwise, she might have smacked the grin right off his face.

But as he eased her into the front seat of his Aston Martin, she had to admit she liked having an effect on Carson Drake. She inhaled the expensive leather scent of the car's interior as she mulled over her decision to spend the weekend with him. She wasn't impulsive by nature, but he'd treated her honorably in that room. A man of his word, unlike the men she knew before.

She'd too often been pulled into men's laps, pinched and grabbed. Always just for fun, right? What did her stepfather Bert say? *You catch more flies with honey than vinegar, so give me a little sugar?* Well, her days of being the confectionary du jour were over.

Funny, how what Carson *didn't* do made her trust him more.

Yet she couldn't let this weekend get out of hand. On Monday, she'd start with a clean slate. She'd lock in that business, get that promotion, and cleanse herself of needing anything like this again.

She turned to him, now settled in the driver's seat. "Carson, one more thing. I don't believe in happily-ever-afters."

He smirked. "Good. Because neither do I." The car engine rumbled to life.

5

Carson threw his car keys into a brass bowl sitting on a small table at the entranceway. "Have you eaten dinner?" he asked.

She shook her head and forced herself to focus on his face instead of looking around. She didn't want her intimidation at being inside such a palatial home to show.

"Come. I'll show you around later." He headed down a long hallway.

Freed from his attention, she quickly glanced around. From the outside, the Tudor style of the estate home promised wealth inside. The interior didn't disappoint. But the bare wood floors and modern paintings on the wall spoke of a bolder taste than she expected. Several colorful glass sculptures stood on a long, skinny teak table in the hallway.

At the back of the house, the space opened to a large kitchen. Glass balls hung pendant-style over a milky quartz island. Light burst from every direction when Carson flipped a switch.

"I always wondered who lived in these houses." Wow,

she'd somehow lost the ability to keep her thoughts to herself.

"People." He shrugged and opened a refrigerator door larger than most catering kitchens boasted.

"Well, I'm sure it impresses the ladies." She dropped herself into a chair. Her feet were killing her, despite the foot massage given by Carson—twice.

"Does it impress you?" he asked.

"Do you want to impress me?"

"Do you always answer a question with a question?"

"Do you?"

"I never bring anyone here." Carson pulled out a plastic container. "I hope you like lamb."

She swallowed. "I had to. Greek grandmother."

"I recognize the Mediterranean in your skin. But Chantelle is French."

"Stepfather."

Carson returned to the fridge and pulled out two bottles of water. He handed her one. "Here. Hydrate."

She took the cold bottle gratefully, realizing how thirsty she'd grown.

"Do you need to set up a safe call?" he asked.

A what?

"Let someone know where you are," he added. "Then call them periodically to let them know you're okay."

Oh! "No. If you hurt me, you'll have to sign my proposal agreement. For the full $500,000."

He chuckled. "Agreed."

After finishing half of the water, she turned to Carson, who was leaning against the quartz countertop. She wiped water from her bottom lip with a finger. "You're watching me again."

"I enjoy looking at you."

"It makes me uncomfortable. To be observed." *Well, most of the time.*

"A PR person who's afraid of being watched."

"I'm not afraid. But people pay me so they're in the spotlight, not the other way around."

"Come here." He held out his hand.

She set her bottle of water down and stood.

Two steps and they connected, warm palm to warm palm. As he drew closer, her lips parted. *He hasn't kissed me yet. Will he?*

He unbelted her trench and slipped it over her shoulders. The coat fell to the floor.

"Leave it." He gripped her middle and lifted her up to the countertop. She'd never grow accustomed to his strength—never. The snap of the Tupperware container opening broke a vision of Carson brandishing a sword.

"Open," he said and leaned in.

Her knees parted to make room for his hips. He pulled out a small bit of lamb and lifted it to her mouth. *Oh, open my mouth!*

She took the meat and chewed it slowly. She normally had a healthy appetite. She should have been starving, not having eaten since breakfast. She *should* have been. But *normally* she didn't have Carson Drake between her thighs. She jumped when his erection pressed against her mons.

His firm lips curved in response.

"I'm fine." She straightened her back and placed her hands on his rib cage. His stunning presence wouldn't intimidate her anymore. *Focus. Be better.*

His eyes never left her face as he placed another bit of food in her mouth. "Tell me where you're from."

She swallowed. "Nowhere special. Did you grow up here?"

"Does anyone grow up in Washington?" His fingertip lingered on her chin. "So, what about you?"

"Different places. We moved around a lot."

"Military?"

She shook her head.

He lifted more food to her mouth. "I'm from the South. Louisiana."

"Cajun?" She wouldn't be surprised given his dark complexion.

"No, plantation farmers in the far north."

"Ah, that makes sense then." She waved her arm at the ceiling. "From one big house to another."

He laughed and settled his hands on the counter, the dark hair on his arms brushing either side of her thighs. "A gypsy upbringing then. London is an unusual name. Did the gypsies give it to you?"

"Mom always wanted to go to England. Dad didn't. She named me London to torture him."

He arched an eyebrow.

"Always getting to say 'London calling?' whenever I asked a question or called?"

"Don't tell me. You have a sister named Paris." He placed another bite of meat against her lips.

"Un-uh. Only child named after a city."

"Well, London fits."

She flicked her lashes to his face.

"The city is quite ... diverse," he said.

"Mom thought so. We lived there for two years with husband number three."

"I see." He frowned. "My parents are still together."

"Brothers and sisters?"

"One brother. Deceased."

"I'm sorry."

"Me too."

Jesus, this was getting serious. A sudden fatigue set in her bones. She didn't normally talk about her past, and by the looks of Carson's serious face, he might want to get into details. *No way.* She braced to push herself from the counter.

"Don't get down. We're still talking."

"Why, Carson?" She didn't see the point of tripping down memory pain. Wasn't he supposed to be tying her to the bed or something?

He grasped her chin and lifted her head up. His gaze locked with hers and he ... waited. She tried to wrest her face from his grip, but he held her more firmly in response. "You like tilting your chin up. So you'll stay in this position for a while."

Her lips parted.

"Let it go," he said, not unkindly.

She swallowed her planned retort when he circled the back of her neck with his other hand.

His warm fingers cradled her chin. His gaze held her eyes. His hands held her jawline. She recognized his determination in both. Soon she lost touch of everything except the heat coming from his hands and his stare. Her neck muscles relaxed. Her anger withered and she settled more into his gentle cupping of her chin.

When he finally did let go, he stepped backward. The look on his face dared her to look away. When he raised his eyebrows, she lowered her chin. He held out his hand, a clear signal she could ease off the countertop.

"Another lesson." He grinned. "Though I'd say we have a ways to go with that one."

∼

Carson stood in thrall of London, who sat in his old hardback chair, a holdover from his father's study. He doubted good old Dad would have understood his methods. But perhaps he'd have appreciated the nude and blindfolded London, whose bare ass now graced its seat. She wore only his belt around her waistline.

As directed, her ankles circled the chair legs, which deliciously spread open her knees. She presented a portrait of perfect submission. *If she'd stop fidgeting.*

She cocked her head, listening, as he undressed. Now wearing nothing but a pair of well-worn fatigues, he was ready to do battle with her cheekiness—both literally and figuratively.

When he ran his hand from the crown of her head down to the side of her face, she leaned into his touch. He'd secured her hair into a tall, messy ponytail with an elastic, a leftover from a long-ago liaison with someone whose face he couldn't have reconstructed if he'd tried. With London, so seductively perched on his desk chair, all past play faded like century-old wallpaper.

"London, what is the first rule of a Dominant-submissive scene?"

"Listen to you."

"No. The first rule is to stay safe. If I restrained you, would you feel safe or in danger?"

"Protected." Her answer collided with his question. Her chest pinked as if embarrassed by her quick admission.

He understood a woman's deep-seated need to be special, cherished and chosen. But London's answer was unexpected. *From her.*

One weekend wouldn't be enough to solve the mystery of London Chantelle. Yet his desire to take down at least a few of her walls made his cock swell, a signal at least one part of him was up for the challenge. After all, he'd spent countless weekends teasing a sub's trust to the forefront, and its ensuing courage. This weekend wouldn't be any different.

More intense, considering the effect she had on him, but still just a weekend.

"What now?" she asked.

"Right now, all I will allow is that you sit there. Wait. And listen."

He turned toward the massage table he'd set up. As he prepared the wide surface, he didn't hide the sounds he made. Plastic rustled as he encased the table. He snapped a sheet over the top and smoothed it over the sides. He positioned a long neck pillow at one end to help ensure her hair spilled over the edge. Each step invigorated him.

Every candle in his room was lit, over two dozen pillars similar to the ones he'd used in a demonstration he'd given at Accendos months ago. The young girls giggled and screamed as their partners dripped hot wax on their bellies and breasts. No one got burned or hurt. The sensation play simply brought out their innate melodrama. He'd been bored to tears. Right now, nothing interested him more.

After laying London down on the table, he took a moment to admire the wisps of caramel and chocolate strands by her cheeks, her ponytail dripping over the edge of the table.

"Are you cold?" he asked.

"No." She shifted and the plastic crinkled underneath the sheet. "I'm fine."

He freed his belt from her waist. A loud clank when it hit the floor made her startle.

He picked up a bottle of oil and snapped open the top. After filling his palm with the lubricant, he spread it over London's stomach. He moved to her breasts, kneading and then pinching her raspberry nipples. Her back arched into his hands, and her hands grew white from fisting the sheets by her side.

After attending to her arms and hands, he poured more

oil over her pussy. He made sure every hair was coated in the emollient. He wasn't in the business of giving bikini waxes. Soon her thighs, calves and feet wore an oily sheen illuminated by the candles. She glowed like a marble sculpture—if it wasn't for her constant wiggling.

"Relax." He massaged her feet, pulling on each toe and massaging her arch. Finally, her hands unclenched their hold on the sheet and splayed open.

He tipped a few teaspoons of melted wax from one of the candles into his hand. "Tell me if this burns." He spread the warmth over her greased belly.

She inhaled sharply and her hands darted up and then settled back down.

"London?"

"Not burning ..." He could tell she squeezed her eyes tighter under the blindfold.

The wax grew tacky under his palm. More gasps came from her throat as he dribbled a large drop from the candle onto her arm. Her hands jumped from the sheet only to float back down.

"Shh, feel it." He grasped her wrist and angled it away from her body. "Palms up. Don't move." He picked up two pillar candles, one in each hand. "No matter what, London."

He tipped both candles over her wrist. Her fingers danced as the drippings made contact and she gasped. "Oh!" A wax line formed, the edges pooling on the sheet.

"You are being cuffed to the table with wax. If you break these restraints, I'll find something stronger."

She curled her fingers as if she tested the bond.

"Confirm."

"I-I won't break them."

He streamed more wax until she wore a thin manacle on her wrist. The bond barely covered her skin. If she was the submissive he believed, she'd feel it like an iron chain.

"You're mine tonight," he said.

She sent her other arm out, away from her body as if ready for the same treatment. Her acceptance of his handling made his groin tighten in anticipation. Primal London had returned.

He secured the other wrist with a waxy shackle. But her legs would require more than candle drippings. In addition to the soy candles, he'd warmed his largest block of paraffin in a crock pot. If his mother knew what he did with her Christmas gift, she'd lose her final hope of him ever being domesticated.

He dipped a ladle into the wax bath and continued until her ankles wore similar restraints to her wrists. Now cuffed by wax chains, spread wide, he stepped back to admire London's captivity. A small smile played on her lips, finally relaxed. *Finally giving in to the inevitable.*

He picked up a small paintbrush and dipped it in to the pot. He painted a thin layer of wax over one nipple. She arched and sighed under the sensation. He then took one of the larger candles, and holding it high, let a long stream flow over her breast. She cried out and flinched. One hand broke through its cuff.

Her forehead furrowed. "I-I'm sorry. I wasn't expecting it."

"Of course not." He chuckled. "That's the point."

She returned his laughter, but quickly swallowed it back. "Carson? I won't do it again."

He touched her arm. "Of course you won't."

After he re-secured her wrist with more wax, her fingers quivered. Tension in her belly returned, perhaps fighting to lift herself toward him? Her pussy glistened, and not from oil, but from growing arousal. She enjoyed being handled, he thought. He mentally added the sentiment to London's List.

She balled her fists. The thin shackles didn't crack. He

spilled more melted candle on to her waiting body. A seal formed over her breast from drizzling wax, spiral-fashion. *My mark.* "This is the only white you should wear."

He turned to the paraffin wax bath and scooped out a full dipper of the mix. With one long stream, he drew small circles around her other breast. A coiled cap formed over her flesh. She squirmed under the liquid heat, soft moans escaping her lips. More candle drippings formed waxy rivers and tributaries over her belly and her hips. Her skin reddened around the waxy parts from the stimulation and heat.

He traded candles. He'd empty one of its liquid while allowing the others to burn down more, creating their own small pools of melted warmth. Large sections cooled to semi-hardness. Unable to stay motionless any longer, her back arched with each new stream that met her skin. Wax separated and cracked, except for the thin shackles securing her wrists. She balled her fists, as if willing them to stay intact.

By the time he'd moved to her legs, she took in big gulps of air. He ran one long line of warm melted candlewax down one thigh to her knee. A light sheen had formed over her upper lip and forehead. When he crossed her low belly with a large spill of wax, she squealed. Her hands threatened to dart upward. Her manacles barely held. But she stopped herself from completely freeing her wrists and ankles.

His belly clenched. London, the woman who fought his every move in meetings, argued every word from his mouth, now fought to honor his control. The shields she'd erected to deny her desires had begun to fall away.

Now we begin.

"Won't break," she whispered. Her hands relaxed open.

"No, baby, you won't break." *But you'll break through.* He'd pledged himself to her this weekend, and her armor would be no match for his resolution. She'd claimed she wasn't looking for a Master. *Liar*. In a few hours, the pieces had begun to fall away to reveal the real woman.

He'd broken through many subs' walls. He would start out gentle and slow, let them grow comfortable with his hands, his voice and his touch. Their facades would slip. The needs they'd hidden would unfold. And then—and only then —they'd beg for him to scratch an itch they couldn't name.

Jesus, what he could do with London Chantelle. His mental clock ticked loudly inside and saved him from imagining impossibilities. *Like having more time*. Minutes and seconds would dissolve. His forty-eight hours would be up with London soon enough. And then he'd be back where he started—a new countdown, a different sub, another weekend.

~

London's world became heat, her breath, and little jolts from Carson's body connecting to the table. More candlewax poured over her legs. Sometimes zigzag patterns coursed over her skin. Other times, a steady stream poured over knees, hip bones, and her breasts. She grew dizzy from panting.

As a little girl she'd spend hours at the beach squeezing rough, sandy liquid through her fists over her legs until tall, drip sandcastles rose on each thigh. She must resemble such a structure, tall turrets rising from her body. No inch of her body could be exposed. She had to be mummified, encased by wax—and his unerring desire to keep her.

She wasn't truly chained. One flick of her wrist or her ankles and she could roll off the table in seconds. But reacting to him, to his commands and touches, sent crackles of excitement and pleasure up her spine.

"Beautiful." Carson's voice was edged in emotion and approval.

Her pride, so willing to scream at her for her weaknesses, shifted. In this moment she wanted to belong to him. She wanted ... whatever he wanted. *Anchored to his will.*

Under the gummy wax and oil, her body seemed to whirl in a flat spin above the table.

Carson's hand entwined in her hair and pulled, baring her throat. She crashed back to the surface. His teeth nipped her neck and a low growl rumbled through his lips. His fingers touched her pussy. He separated her labia and touched her inner lips, but didn't enter. She wanted to lift her hips, making him dip in further and penetrate her.

The table jarred from a shudder that ran through her, and more wax cracked and separated from her oiled skin. The blindfold dragged over her forehead and through her hair. In the flickering light she had trouble focusing on Carson's body leaning over her.

He spoke no words, but cupped the back of her head and lifted, as if he wanted her to see his work. Thin strips of white covered her body, far less than she believed when her sight had been unavailable. Her breasts were topped with small mounds of wax in uneven ringlets. Long, thin Xs lay on her belly, and reedy wax lines encased each ankle. They'd felt so much heavier when she couldn't see.

She gazed into his face. "I didn't break them."

"No." He laid her head back down and smoothed her hair.

A long scrape of something sharp released some of the hardened shell encasing her forearm. Carson lifted a piece that dangled from the tip of a forked blade. "Time to uncover your lovely skin."

She shuddered at the sight of the knife. The two points curved, like a snake's tongue split down the middle.

He brought an edge down to her stomach and scraped from her belly button to her hip. "Close your eyes."

Her lashes fell. Nothing but tiny flickers of low candle-light made their way through her eyelids.

Scrape. "When you entered Accendos, so many eyes were on you."

"I didn't notice."

Scratch. "Why don't you like being watched? Admired?" Another long graze of the knife down her thigh released more wax crumbles that tickled the sides of her legs as they fell to the sheet.

"Please, don't—"

"Don't what?

"Talk about ... others." She hadn't meant to voice the intruding memories. Her stepfathers eyeing her up and down with salacious grins, like they saw a woman instead of a daughter. And then Michael and his desires?

"I won't let anyone near you," he said. Her eyes fluttered open and found Carson's handsome face. The memories retreated. A long scratch of the blade up the inside of her thigh made her tremble in some unnamed anticipation.

"Are your nipples hard, London?" The two tips of the knife lifted a large piece of wax over her breast. A desire for him to thrust the blade underneath, score the sides of her nipple, washed over her. He wiped his finger across her sensitive peak.

"Ah, God." She couldn't stay flat against the table as he swirled his finger over her nipple. Gummy flakes rolled under her back as she lifted into his touch.

He returned to scratching off more wax bits with his knife. Long scrapes released her legs until only her ankles and wrists remained encased. The handcuffs had fractured and threatened to drop off. But she'd kept her hands and heels glued to the surface.

Carson laid the knife on the small stand next to the table. He placed his hand between her breasts as if checking her heartbeat and gazed into her eyes. "Breathe into my hand."

She let her ribcage fully expand.

He moved to her ankles and crumbled the wax bonds. Flutters of panic and urgency crossed her whole body at feeling his strength. After giving the same treatment to her wrist cuffs, he looked down at her. His hawk-like gaze burned with intention.

Her imagination took over. She ripped her gaze from his face to look at his pelvis. His cock pushed against his OD green fatigues. She wanted him to grasp her hair and drag her closer. He'd unzip his pants, present his cock to her. He'd hold out the thick cockhead for her to wet with her tongue, slicking him so he'd glide in easier. Inch by inch, she'd take him down over her tongue to the back of her throat. He'd grasp the back of her neck, force her to take more, always more. The image was so strong juices trickled down her inner thighs.

He ran his hand down her belly to her mons and without hesitation, slipped a finger deep inside her soaked pussy.

"Oh. Carson!"

"Sir." He swirled his fingers inside her.

"Oh, yes ... sir." She squirmed as his thumb played her clit.

"Do you want to come?"

And more. Make me ... "Yes. Please!"

"Please what, sweetness?"

"More, may I ... ah ..."

He circled her back with his free arm and pulled her closer so she curled into his chest. Even when she began to release her essence over his hand and down her legs, he didn't stop his machinations on her pussy. He drove his fingers deep and hard, milking every last spasm from her body.

When he eased her to her back, she reached up to his neck and pulled a bit of wax hanging from his hair. What would he look like with longer hair? *Like a Roman warrior.* Gold flecks from candlelight danced in his dark brown eyes.

Carson lifted her from the table, her body warm and slick from perspiration and oil. He carried her through the door, down a long hallway and into a bedroom. His room? Then into a Roman bath. *No, wait. The master bathroom.* Her eyesight wandered, an attempt to get her bearings. The pearl white and gray tiles showcased yet more taste than she believed someone like Carson could possess. But why did she think she knew this man *at all* before?

He set her on her feet inside a large glass box. *A shower?* Why wasn't her mind working?

Without letting go of her back, he stripped off his fatigues, one-handed and more gracefully than she thought possible given his large hands. He stepped inside and a stream of warm water turned on immediately—soaking them both. He eased her closer to the wall until her hands touched cold tile.

"Present that sweet ass to me," he said.

She arched her lower back and caught the tip of his cock in her crack. She wanted to turn around, drop to her knees and suckle him until she choked. Instead, as if reading her mind, he settled his hand on her back to keep her in position.

She dropped her head back and pressed backward, tried to capture more of him between her legs. A low sound from Carson echoed in the shower. A signal of amusement? "None of that," he said.

His hands massaged her shoulders, her back and arms. Soapy rivers sluiced down her thighs, rushing between her feminine lips. She closed her eyes. More fingers touched her *there*. She rested her forehead on her forearms.

Her teeth sank into her flesh, a failed attempt to stop a

whimper. "Carson. Sir." She breathed the last word into her skin.

"Yes, London?"

She pushed off and turned to face him—without permission. His hand left her sex. Would he punish her? Drive her to her knees, force open her mouth and use her? *Yes, please.*

His eyes held an irritating triumph. But she didn't have the strength to deny her feelings any longer. She wanted him. Her yearnings were real. Illogical, but true. She wanted to let go, get lost, and spin out of control. *Even if just for one weekend.*

She groaned as he slipped a finger inside her heat, a slow slick glide that made her shudder.

She grasped his forearm. Feeling his strength tipped her to the point of no return. "No more limit on you ... being with me. I want to ..." She grasped his cock, equally steely and hot as the rest of him.

He tutted and she dropped her hand.

"P-please."

"Do you want my cock here?" He pulled his finger out and then pushed back inside.

She arched her hips to reclaim his intrusion. "Yes." She really, really didn't care what she had said before.

He pressed her back into the shower tiles and pulled her knees up around his hips. His mouth came down on her lips and he sank deep inside her in one glide. He held himself in place as if letting her get used to his invasion. His lips began to move, as if testing her willingness. She opened to him fully, letting him take full possession of her mouth. He grew more insistent, his tongue tangling with hers.

Finally, his hips rocked, pressing her against the tile. His hardness took up every millimeter of space inside her. Her aching turned vicious, her need for him to go deeper, harder ... She snapped awake from her trance.

What the hell was she doing?

"Wait. Stop." She released her grip on his ass. She hadn't realized she'd grasped him to begin with.

He leaned back but didn't slip free from her.

She panted in the steamy heat. "I don't-don't know what I'm doing here. Wasn't thinking."

"You're scared." His hand went to her throat.

Oh, love that. Tears pooled in her eyes. She shook her head. "Our agreement. What I wanted ..."

"Third lesson. Don't force it. Tell me what you really want."

His legs quaked under her, his voice edged with a grit. He'd been holding back his own release. *For me.* He moved his hand to one of her wrists and raised her arm high. He pressed it against the wall behind her, above her head. She read his eyes. He knew what he was doing. He helped her decide. But she had to say the words.

The words that have been on my tongue since first meeting you.

She slid her other hand back around to his back. "Take me."

6
———

Carson glared into the bathroom mirror. Drops of water from his hair dripped into the sink. Each soft plink thundered in his ears. *Think, Carson.*

After their heated lovemaking that lasted far into the night, London had curled into his side like a lion cub. She slept hard, finally not squirming in his arms. He watched her chest rise and fall as he wrestled with his random thoughts—bits of information about London that didn't connect. Nothing raised his ire faster than facts that refused to lock themselves into a pattern. And London's List didn't add up.

London hated her vulnerability, yet she was a sexual submissive. She put herself into his hands last night, quickly. *Too quickly*. Then she fought him, only to fall again into compliance. Her desire to be protected? From what or whom? Then he let her break their negotiated limit of no sex. He knew better than to let her take such control.

A phone buzzed in the bedroom and broke his examination. Through the crack in the bathroom door, he spied London twisting in the tangle of sheets. Who'd dare call this early in the morning? When he got to the bedroom, she sat in the chair in the corner, encased in the bed sheet. She cradled her phone between her ear and shoulder while gathering up her boots.

"Yes, yes, I'm sorry. I forgot."

He was close enough to hear a woman's voice chirping on the other end.

She looked up at him, eyes round, almost pleading. "Thirty minutes? Yes ... okay. Bye."

"Where are you going?"

She punched her cell phone into her bag. "Errand."

"London." He pulled her up to standing. "You're upset."

"I'm fine. I just have to go."

"I'll go with you."

"No!" She wrested free of his hold and tried to head around him.

"Now I'm really going with you." No way would he let her add another layer to the mystery she presented.

She turned to face him. "Look. I'll run home, get some clothes, run this errand and meet you back here."

"Telling me what to do?"

"Of course not. But you have to let me do this."

He brushed her hair over her shoulder. "Do what?"

"Jesus, you're nosy. I didn't realize we'd have to bare each other's secrets—"

"It's a secret?"

"Okay, Mr. Attorney." She pushed his chest and he willingly stepped backward one step. She couldn't have moved him in reality. "Let me put on what little clothes I have. One hour, I promise."

That steely look in her eyes told him she wouldn't return.

"Shower first," he said.

"I don't have time." She began to wrap herself back into the dress Carrie had given her. When he tried to stop her fastening her garment, her anger erupted. *What the hell?* "Stop it! I. Have. To. Go." She tugged her arm free and stomped her foot into her boot.

Within seconds, he'd scooped her up and carried her to an overstuffed chair in the opposite corner. "We talk first."

"What, no spanking?" she spat.

"You'd like that too much. Now why are you so upset?"

Her eyes filled with tears. "Please."

He cradled her head with one hand and pulled her into his neck. "Breathe, London."

"I have t-to go do something."

"Okay, I'll drive. You don't have a car."

She let out a frustrated sigh.

Within five minutes, they'd both dressed and stepped out into the foggy September morning. Dew covered his windshield and the squeak of the wipers was the only sound that joined the crunch of tires as they headed down his driveway. She'd given him her home address and spoke no more words.

He recognized the Cleveland Park apartment building she referenced—home to junior assistants, summer interns and other people launching their careers under outrageously small salaries. Given what his firm paid in a monthly retainer, she should have afforded a better address by now.

London worked the side of her head over the cool window glass as if she attempted to roll out a headache. She shrugged off his attempt to rub her shoulder. It took every ounce of control not to pull over, drag her over his knee and slap her ass, hard. He squeezed her knee, a mark silently promising a punishment later.

"Are you going to tell me who we're meeting?" he asked.

"Who *I'm* meeting. You can just drop me off at home. I'll drive from there."

"No." He held up his hand. "No debate." She was in no shape to be behind the wheel of a car.

She pulled out her phone and started tapping. As if

reading his curiosity, she turned to him. "I just had to tell someone why I didn't meet them last night. Something else I forgot."

"I'm sure she'll understand."

London opened her car door before he'd even pulled up to the front of her shabby building. "I'll be right down." She slipped out of the passenger seat before he could grab his belt around her waist and yank her back down.

"Five minutes, London, or I'll knock on every door until I find you." His words met the loud bang of the ancient apartment door closing behind her.

A horn blared behind him as a car urged him to move forward. He pulled up another car length and parked. *Let the bastard go around.*

He glared at the clock on his dashboard. If she wasn't out soon, he'd hunt her down. He made a mental note to later spank her ass to a bright red shade for topping him—now three times this morning.

He took a deep breath. Growing unsettled himself wouldn't help calm London. He'd save it for whoever had interrupted their morning. He hadn't asked London who had called. Work? *No.* She would have said as much. If anyone understood the demands of a career in Washington, he did.

His car door popped open and a jean-clad London slipped into the front seat. She also wore his belt around an oversized shirt.

"For a minute, I thought you might have slipped out the back."

"The thought occurred." She kept her gaze straight ahead and bunched her purse between her legs.

"Where to?"

"One Washington Circle." Her entire body had grown rigid, worry etched across her face.

Saturday morning traffic down Connecticut Avenue was

typical—an exercise in being stopped every forty feet. He managed to slip through several yellow lights. He also cut off a few limos, which made him feel immeasurably better.

When they arrived at their destination, he pulled into the underground parking garage. The sign at the entrance—Southland Rehab—sent a stab through his heart. The mental health facility was second to none in its field, according to his friend, Jonathan Brond. Over dinner one night Jonathan, the head of public affairs for the American Mental Health Association, had mentioned a friend being admitted. A last resort, he'd said.

Carson was going inside with her, no matter how many protests she mustered. "Now you're going to tell me why we're here."

"My brother," she said to the windshield. "That's all I can tell you. It's personal." She yanked the door open.

When he rounded the back of the car, she turned to him, finally looking him in the eye for the first time since leaving her apartment building. "It's okay if you don't want to finish the weekend."

"Don't even think about it."

"I suppose you're following me upstairs."

"Of course."

She heaved a sigh and headed to the door marked "elevators." They rode up to the lobby area in silence. He decided right then and there, he'd take London's arguments over her quiet any day. He rarely grew unnerved. But they headed into something that worried London, badly. If someone she cared about sat inside these walls, her disquiet wouldn't be misplaced. He'd learned that much from Jonathan.

The receptionist smiled when London walked up to the large circular glass desk. "Miss Chantelle. How nice to see you."

"Hi, Janelle. Um, I have to go see Mrs. Roberts. Is she free? She called."

"I see. I'm sorry dear." The receptionist frowned and dropped her voice to a low whisper. "She hates working on Saturdays, you know."

London threw her a weak smile.

"No need, Janelle. I'm here." An elderly woman with a clipped voice waddled up the hallway to them. He recognized the smirk on her face, a look some in Washington had perfected from years of attempted intimidation over others. "I was just about to leave," she said.

London fiddled in her purse and retrieved an envelope. Before she could hand it over, Mrs. Roberts said, "Let's talk in my office, shall we?" She turned on her heel as if expecting they'd follow.

London turned to him. "I'll be right out."

He pushed her toward the hallway. "Yes, we will."

"This isn't your problem."

"Go, London. Mrs. Roberts doesn't like working on Saturdays." His attempt at humor did not earn the hoped-for smile.

When they reached the woman's small office, she'd already lowered herself into her rickety office chair. She steepled her hands, a gesture he'd learned to hate thanks to twelve years of Catholic School. Mrs. Robert's adoption of the subtle Church symbol, often used by the strict nuns he'd encountered, strengthened his dislike of the woman.

"Dear, are you sure you don't want to talk privately?" *Strike that. Hate this woman and the patronizing horse she rode in on.*

He extended his hand. "Mrs. Roberts, is it?"

She limply returned his handshake. "London and I have some business to discuss about her brother's care, Mr...."

"Drake. Carson Drake."

London touched his arm. "Carson, it's better that I handle this ..." Her voice trailed off when he settled himself into a chair that felt as uncomfortable as it looked. He wasn't leaving. London had a brother in Southland Rehab. That fact alone required backup.

He scratched his unshaven chin. "Now, what seems to be the problem?"

"Well, have it your way, Miss Chantelle."

London finally sank into the chair next to him.

Mrs. Roberts pulled her glasses from their dangling position on her chest and perched them on her thin nose. She opened a file folder on her desk. He could make out a long list of figures in columns.

"It seems we'll need to discuss a better payment system."

"I've been making my payments."

"But often very late."

"But I'm almost caught up."

"Barely and you know we—"

"Wait." He leaned forward. Satisfaction filled his insides when Mrs. Roberts looked up at him. He felt less comfort from London's cold stare in his peripheral vision. "Do I understand you're admonishing Miss Chantelle for falling behind in payments? Am I correct in assuming this a mental health institution?"

"Yes."

"It takes insurance?"

"That's run out, Mr. Drake." She threw London an undeserved, scolding look. "We are a private institution that relies on a myriad of funding. You have experience with mental health organizations?"

"I have experience with the law."

One side of her mouth rose up and she leaned back. "You brought an attorney, Miss Chantelle."

"No, I didn't ... Carson ... he's a ..."

They both stared at London. He couldn't have cared less what the old accounting bag thought of his position with London. However, he cared deeply how London herself would characterize his standing.

She lowered her chin to stare at her lap. *Not good.* Her situation was more serious than he'd thought if London was cowed by a bureaucrat.

"Mrs. Roberts, it doesn't matter who I am. But the law states you cannot harass people by calling them at seven a.m. on a Saturday morning."

"I'm well aware of the law, Mr. Drake."

"Then we're done here. London, hand Mrs. Roberts the check." He withdrew his wallet from inside his jacket and retrieved a business card. "You will call me should more accounting matters need immediate attention." He stood and grasped London's arm, now rigid as steel under his hold. She jerked free and tossed the envelope on Mrs. Roberts's desk.

"You call *me*, Mrs. Roberts. Anytime. Obviously you have my cell." London walked out.

Just outside the door, she turned to face him. "You are *not* coming with me."

When her jawline perked up, a shard of hope arose. She wasn't completely daunted. But then she turned right instead of left, from where they originally came.

He followed. "Don't let that troll get to you," he said to her back.

She turned. Her eyes held a volcanic fire beyond his earlier encounters with her temper. "I was handling it!"

"No, you were enduring it."

She huffed and pushed through a set of double doors. One would have smacked him backward if he hadn't caught it with his hand. On the other side of the doorway she turned and angrily pointed through the glass to a wall sign on his side of the barrier. It read "Family visiting hours" with a long list of times and days of the week. "Not family." Her words were muffled and harsh.

He swung open the door. No way would she dismiss him with the obvious.

He tracked her as she navigated the maze of hallways. She didn't say a word to him when he entered an elevator with her.

When they stepped off on the third floor, a sickening antiseptic smell slapped him in the face. Even with the hallway's fluorescent lights bearing down on them as they walked, he felt a darkness. Agony filled the air, not unlike his own brother's hospital room in Germany right before he succumbed to his military injuries.

Three nurses eyed them up and down as they approached the desk. London picked up a pen to sign a clipboard.

"Miss Chantelle." A nurse with a kind face placed her fingers over London's hand. "Today isn't a good day. We had a little bit of trouble with his medication last night. But we're sorting out—"

"I've got this, Brenda." A male voice behind them cut off the woman.

A puffy man belying the brusque voice stepped up to the counter. "London. We had to restrain him last night—just for a short time. To calm him down."

"Not again." She pushed by the man. His name tag skewed as she pushed past him. *Dr. Morgan.*

As Carson strode after London, Dr. Morgan's final words, "we don't want to upset him again," might as well have fallen on deaf ears. *Medication. Restraints.* He wasn't about to let London enter her brother's room alone. But damn, she was fast. She ran smack into an orderly stepping through a doorway. He nearly launched himself at the man after he grasped London's arms with large hands. His tattoo-laden biceps bulged on contact. "Miss Chantelle. Today's not a good day."

The man's name tag threatened to pop off his pec muscle under his T-shirt. "Not good," the orderly repeated.

Carson refused to be overwhelmed by a wannabe prison guard. "We've got this," he said.

The man looked him over. "And you are?"

"Carson Drake." He held out his hand. "Esquire." By the look on the orderly's face, his title registered.

"James. Patient Care Assistant." He stepped aside, handshake not returned.

James leaned down toward London and whispered, "He's not doing too well today." The man's softer tone surprised him.

Carson took her arm. Naturally, she jerked free.

"Thanks, James. But I'm okay. You know that." She squeezed between them and disappeared into the room.

James straightened to his full height. "I'm not leaving. Doctor's orders."

"That makes two of us." Carson inched himself into the room.

London bent down to a shivering man who rocked back and forth in the corner, with his eyes nearly rolled back into his head. She swept his hair off his forehead and sat down next to him. His rocking instantly slowed on contact with London's hug.

"I'm right here, Benny." She looked up at James with angry eyes. "What did you give him?"

James's face didn't move a muscle. "Just a sedative, Ms. Chantelle."

London turned over Benny's wrists. Thin red marks scored his skin, signs he'd been restrained, and not long ago. He couldn't place Benny's age. Lines of anguish traversed his face, and his hairline had begun to recede.

Dr. Morgan appeared in the doorway, a clipboard in hand. "We had no choice, Miss Chantelle."

"So you say." London drew Benny tighter and launched visual daggers at the good doctor. *Good girl.*

The air changed around him, an indication the doctor stepped up next to him. "Mr. Drake—"

"Mrs. Roberts called, didn't she?" he asked. "Saying we were on our way up?" It was the only way the man could know his name.

"Only family may visit during visiting hours. It's not safe—"

"He's not going to hurt London or me." He didn't know why he knew such a thing, but he did.

"It's not safe for Ben. Strangers unsettle him, Mr. Drake. Especially men. We try to keep a calm environment for our patients." The doctor's eyes didn't blink. He fought the urge to point out that the doctor was a man, and obviously one who could do far more harm than Carson could.

The doctor drew his arms around his clipboard. "Our methods—"

"Drugging someone and tying them down? I'm surprised no straight jacket."

"We don't do that anymore, Mr. Drake." The doctor's weary voice didn't convince him the approaches he'd used were any better.

"Benny, no!" London attempted to free her hair from Ben's clenched fist. Benny laughed, a tinny, mad sound that disclosed the man's unwell mind.

James proved his muscles didn't impact his speed when he rushed to Benny and had his hands around the man's wrists in seconds. He pulled the tormented man's hands into his lap more gently than he believed possible. Benny curled into himself, and London sat back on her heels and sighed.

"It's okay, Benny. You didn't hurt me. I'm sorry I got angry." She reached out to touch his hair and Benny raised his arm in an angry retort. James caught it before the damaged man could connect with her. She didn't fall backward in anticipation of a blow, as if she'd resigned herself to receive whatever Benny would dish out.

Carson couldn't—wouldn't—stand by and observe this anymore. He stepped over to London and lifted her to her feet. "Perhaps we can come back later."

"Yes, good idea," Dr. Morgan said. "Give it a few days."

She wrenched herself free of Carson's hold once more, at least the hundredth time since last night. Last evening seemed a long time ago.

"Not until I see he's settled. Only I can do that."

"James, see Miss Chantelle gets whatever help she needs." Dr. Morgan turned away. He'd likely attempted to thwart London in the past, and lost.

"Carson, meet me downstairs in the lobby." She'd leveled her voice as if talking to one of the nurses.

He sat on the side of the bed. "I don't think that's a good idea."

Benny stared up at him and began to shake.

"Mr. Drake." James stepped toward him.

London looked panicked. "Please. Off the bed, off the bed! He doesn't like it."

"I really don't care what James likes. I care more about—"

"No, Benny. *Please.*" She pushed on his shoulder. "Go stand in the doorway at least."

He retreated to the door and leaned again its frame. James also backed up. The two men stood side by side, banished from the action. *Impotent.*

"Benny, this is a friend of mine. His name is Carson." London helped her brother stand and led him to the bed, where they sat together.

He watched London comb Benny's hair and whisper to him. Eventually, Benny lay down on the bed. She kept her

Untouchable

hand on his shoulder and cast a loving, motherly look down on him as if trying to memorize his face.

After Benny fell asleep, she walked over to the two men. "James, tell Dr. Morgan I need to see him."

"He's on rounds."

"Now."

James reached for his two-way radio and walked out of the room.

London's jaw tightened. He could tell she teetered between rage and torment. He wasn't sure if any helpful words existed. He let his lawyer training kick in and squeezed his lips together. He knew when to shut up.

Dr. Morgan shuffled back into the room. Carson stepped back and let London have full access to the man who gripped his clipboard as vehemently as before.

"No more experimental drugs." Her voice was clear and unwavering.

"Miss Chantelle, we don't experiment—"

"You heard me. You weren't expecting me this weekend. Well, expect me more often. In fact, way more often. Three times a week obviously hasn't been enough."

Three times a week. Her devotion to her brother woke something in his heart. Yet a fierce desire to tear her away from the room, from the entire building, never to return, consumed him.

Dr. Morgan's face hardened. "Like I was about to say before you interrupted me, we don't experiment. We are here to help. If you don't agree, I'm sure I can refer you to another facility."

She crossed her arms. His warrior princess wasn't about to leave the battlefield.

The doctor nodded once and backed away. The move might have saved his face. Carson's sorrow for London had taken a sharp turn by the man's denigrating tone. Refer her to a new facility? He would have liked to refer Dr. Morgan to his fist.

It took him nearly thirty more minutes to convince London to leave the sleeping Benny alone. He assured her they could return anytime she wanted. She didn't speak, instead turned and walked out.

He followed her down the hall, into the elevator. They rode down in silence.

When they pushed through the front doors of the facility, she picked up the pace. She trudged to the corner and searched the street. She raised her hand and waved furiously. He grabbed his belt, still around her waist, and yanked her backwards when a yellow cab pulled up within inches of the curb.

"What do you think you're doing?" he asked.

Fire danced in her eyes. "Going home."

With a swipe of his arm, he waved the cabbie away.

She slapped her hands on his chest and pushed. "Leave me alone!"

"No."

She let out an angry "argh" and trudged down the sidewalk toward a quieter, tree-lined street. He stepped in time with her marches.

"I need time. Go home, Carson."

"I'll take you home."

"You're impossible, you know that?" She shook in frustration.

They walked in silence again, side by side for some minutes. When they'd reached New Hampshire Avenue, she stopped and put her hand on a tree. She dropped her face to study her scuffed tennies, and a choked sob released from her chest.

He drew her to a short concrete retaining wall across the

sidewalk and sat her down. His arms banded around her shook under her heaving. Tears soon soaked the front of his shirt. Her crying stunned him into stillness. He clutched her body close to him as if he could squeeze out all the sorrow she'd unleashed.

Cars passed. A couple walked by, ignoring them. Finally, her breath steadied.

"I understand." He realized his words weren't adequate. But in a way he felt he did understand. London's frustration and tension made more sense now. If his brother hadn't died on the surgeon's table, he'd have devoted his life to him as well.

"I don't know how you could, Carson," she said into his dampened chest.

"I know how hard it is when people you love aren't doing well."

She pushed herself away. "Do you? When I was eight, my father hanged himself."

Okay, he wasn't prepared for *that*. Unspoken, insufficient words filled his mouth.

She sniffed. "The night after the funeral, my mom packed me up and moved us to the closest city. St. Louis. That was the beginning."

"Of your brother's problems?"

"No, he was born later. It was the beginning of my mother's quest." She wiped fingertips under her eyes.

He took out a handkerchief and handed it to her. "For?"

"It doesn't matter."

"Everything that has ever happened to you matters to me. You're under my protection."

"Just words, Carson." She never tore her eyes from the street, seemingly lost in thought.

He decided not to argue with her. *At the moment.* But he'd be damned if she walked away believing their weekend was *just words.* He wouldn't let her dismiss the power it could bring to them both.

"What was your mother's quest?" He couldn't continue this weekend without knowing more about who he was dealing with.

"A husband to take her away. She found Bertrand Chantelle in St. Louis."

Ah. "He adopted you."

"Eventually. My mother made him. She said she wouldn't have any children tied to that loser, my father. Then Benny was born and I liked that we both had the same last name. But Bert wasn't good for us. He had quite a temper." She shrugged. "Let's not talk, okay?"

He ran his hand down the back of her head and through her hair, as if he could smooth out the memory of whatever had happened.

"You're good with Benny," he said.

"I could be better."

"No. You're perfect."

"Ha. That was the problem. We weren't perfect. Mom expected it to be different."

"Don't we all?" He pulled her closer again. "Keep going."

"I don't want to."

"Do it anyway."

She laughed into his wet shirt, and he nuzzled the top of her head.

"Benny was ... difficult." She shook herself from his hold again and lifted his handkerchief to her nose. "So Bert first got angry. Then he started looking elsewhere. Made it really easy for Mom to justify putting Benny away. See if removing the problem child would get her husband to stop cheating. Of course, my mother wasn't very capable. She hadn't realized what she was getting with kids. Not really. And I was glad when Bert left. I don't handle anger well."

He rubbed the back of her neck. "Benny's diagnosis?"

"Bipolar. Depression." She dropped her head and fingered his Irish linen square. She looked pale and brittle.

"When?"

"Thirteen."

"That's early."

"Early for him to start thinking suicide."

Each word she spoke dropped in his gut like a stone.

"Then there was husband number three. Mom and he didn't handle it well, either," she said. "They put him in a horrible institution that set him back. That's when I took over." She stretched her back. "I was twenty-three." She announced her age—and the enormous responsibility that came with it—like she'd delivered a weather report.

"What about your mother?"

London half laughed. "She'd never go against her husband's wishes."

"So you did. And you were banished for it." She didn't need to tell him the details. No one London's age would have sole custody for such a troubled sibling without complete abandonment. He understood the concept well.

When his brother had enlisted in the military, his mother got up from the table and walked out of the room. From that moment forward, she'd refused to believe his choice. Even when he died, she stood at his funeral staring over his casket as if the trees held more interest than her youngest child being lowered into the ground at Arlington Cemetery. He still hadn't forgiven her for her callous attitude that day.

He put his arm around London. "You take care of him."

"Someone has to. I used to protect him from their corrections." Her fingers drew air quotes around the last word.

While one hand cradled her shoulder, the fingertips of his other curled around the edge of the concrete wall. "What did they do?"

"Different things. The usual."

His clutch on the hard wall intensified. From their earlier negotiations he knew London's ideas of "usual" weren't at all ordinary. What had she and her brother endured? No wonder she held a shit-ton of anger inside.

She fingered the initials on the corner of his handkerchief. "I'm the only one he has."

"I'll go with you."

She smirked. "Sure, Carson. Playing dysfunctional family is what you want to do on your weekends."

"Everyone's family is dysfunctional."

She held up his handkerchief. "You may be the last man on earth who still carries hankies. What's the S for?"

"Hmmm, changing the subject. Slade. Family name."

"Family." She nearly spat the word.

"You can't choose your family."

She blinked up at him. "Yes, you can. I chose Benny."

"And they unchose you."

"Something like that."

He took a forced breath in. He had little tolerance for anyone who ran away from challenges. He had no empathy for commitments gone unfulfilled—especially the marital kind. And kids? Don't have them if you aren't going to care for them. Stay unattached, like he did.

She rubbed her neck. "Hey, let's definitely change the subject. My head wants to explode."

"No exploding heads on my watch." He nipped her chin with his fingers. "You're not angry anymore."

"I don't have the energy. But don't you dare take over my life. I know what I'm doing." She straightened her back.

"I can't promise I won't help you, London. It's what a Dom does."

She sighed. "I don't know what a Dom does."

He could see her last words cost her. London wasn't

Untouchable

comfortable with her vulnerability. But his job this weekend was to provide the space and the security for her to lay down her sword and let someone else brandish the steel for a while —even if it was hard. He knew what lay on the other side. *Peace.*

He stood and held out his hand. "Come with me."

7

When Carson pulled through the large iron gates of Club Accendos, London's mind finally stopped arguing with Dr. Morgan. In her imagination, she'd screamed at him over and over. But now, faced with the large stone façade of the club, her thoughts turned to Carson—and why he'd bring her *here*.

She picked at the buckle on Carson's belt. "I thought you liked playing at your home."

"We don't have what we need there."

"Oh." If she hadn't been preoccupied by mentally clocking Dr. Morgan, she might have asked him what "stocking room sixteen" meant when he'd barked the orders into his phone on the way over.

Carson turned off the engine and turned to her. "When you step out of this car, you no longer have to handle anything."

"Easier said than done."

"I know. That's why we're here."

He strode to her side before she had a chance to lift herself from his low-slung seat. As she took his outstretched hand, she let out a sigh of relief at the lack of cars in the driveway. She wanted no observers for Carson's plans. *Whatever they were.*

The large mansion looked older in the harsh light of day. Overgrown ivy and boxwoods obscured many of the windows, probably left unruly for privacy. Regardless, the surroundings still screamed money.

She visually drank in the rich interior of the round entranceway. Last night's nerves had overtaken her awareness and she'd missed the club's grandeur entirely. She couldn't have found her way *anywhere*, and the finer details of her surroundings went unnoticed entirely. She'd been preoccupied with trying to find Michael.

Oh, God, Michael. *Well, screw him.* He was the one who didn't show, and he didn't answer her earlier text. She'd deal with him on Monday. Give him her planned speech then. Plenty of women would like to date an executive in Washington's best communications firm. *Or fulfill those darker desires he'd kept hidden behind those charming hazel eyes.*

Carson pulled her into an old-fashioned elevator, straight out of a 1920s movie. He didn't speak, but kept her tightly banded to his side. When they stopped on the second floor, two men stood waiting.

"Alexander, this is London Chantelle." Carson pressed on her lower back to move her forward.

A tall, elegant man with silver hair shook her hand. "A pleasure to meet you, London. I'm Alexander Rockingham. Owner of Club Accendos. And this is my nephew, Ryan." He signaled to a younger man by his side. Under a shock of dark hair, Ryan's eyes held an appealing, and familiar, intensity. Though at least three decades separated them, Ryan and Alexander's family resemblance was uncanny.

"Ryan and Alexander are here as your witnesses," Carson said.

"Excuse me?" She wasn't about to be *witnessed* doing anything.

Ryan took her hand and smiled. "Don't worry, Miss Chantelle. He meant witnesses to your *consent*."

Alexander chuckled. "My nephew is a stickler for rules, as is Carson. But that's good. Ryan will inherit this club someday, hence his involvement in our protocol. You get two for the price of one today. Ryan?"

"Miss Chantelle's paperwork is in order," the younger man answered.

She blushed in recognition. *Oh yes. Her medical files.* She'd nearly forgotten the records Michael had said he'd courier over before they'd meet—or *didn't* meet. He'd said the club didn't let anyone inside without submitting a personal medical history, even as a guest. At first irritated by his request, now she was glad. Such health scrutiny ensured Carson was safe, too—a little fact she should have questioned last night. She rarely chanced anything, certainly not anything around her safety.

"Carson, do you take full responsibility for Miss Chantelle?" Ryan asked.

"Of course."

Alexander squeezed her arm. "At Club Accendos, if you are not a member, a party unattached to a scene must witness the guests' consent before they engage in any kind of play."

"You always do this?" she asked. Carson hadn't mentioned any formal consent practices to her. But then neither had Michael. *Stop thinking about him.*

Ryan rocked back on his heels and gave Carson a hardened look. "She's a novice."

Carson equally met his stare. "Yes."

"Not exactly," she said. "I just haven't done … in a club

before." She wished she hadn't said anything by the serious looks on the men's faces.

"All rules of the house and the laws of the Tribunal will be adhered to," Carson said.

Alexander leaned down to whisper into her ear. "That means no play without willing, informed consent and limits defined."

She smiled up at the imposing man, grateful he answered with no condescension.

She looked over at Carson. "But last night ..."

"Did you engage in a scene here last night?" Alexander arched his eyebrow at Carson.

"Rather a lesson in patience. We then went home."

"I understand." Alexander turned to her. "Carson doesn't break rules. But should anything make you uncomfortable here, at any time, you come see me." Seriousness ground into every word he spoke. "Now, Miss Chantelle, you are about to enter a scene with Carson Drake, a member of Club Accendos. He is a Dominant. Do you understand?"

"Yes." She hoped her voice didn't shake.

"Do you agree to a scene with Carson?"

She looked up at Carson, whose eyes gave no answer. Something eased inside her, though it only made more room for the butterflies in her stomach to swarm. *He's letting me decide.*

"Yes. I consent."

A deep satisfaction crossed Carson's face over her answer.

"Very good. Consent has been granted by the submissive. Miss Chantelle, Carson will go over limits with you alone. We respect your privacy." Ryan straightened and stood before Carson in a way that snapped her to attention. *Ryan's a Dominant, too.*

She took in a lungful of air thick with testosterone.

Between Alexander, Ryan and Carson, she'd walked into a virtual gladiator ring. She'd never shrink before a Board of Directors table again. Balding CEOs and snippy executive assistants paled in comparison to this hallway encounter.

Ryan bowed formally, and then he and Alexander disappeared down the hall.

"What's the Tribunal?" she asked as Carson pulled her down the passage to stop before a large mahogany door.

"A council to ensure proper behavior. And other things." He grasped the brass handle and opened the door wide.

She'd have questioned what the "other things" he referenced were, but the words died on her tongue at seeing what was hidden behind the door. *So much for the 19th Century French artwork.*

The room was at least fifty feet by fifty feet. The walls were painted a dark grey. The ceiling's bright metallic surface shone overhead. She counted seven St. Andrew's Crosses bolted to the floor and reinforced with steel cables and supports so they stood tilted in various angles.

Carson cradled the back of her head with his hand. "There won't be anyone else in this room with us. I've booked it just for us. Special privileges for a Tribunal member." He tucked a piece of hair behind her ear. "Of course, if anyone knew you were here, they might try to crash our party."

She felt herself blush. Twenty-four hours into their agreement wasn't enough time for him to mean such a statement. She had been witness to what flattery can do. Compliments certainly hadn't helped her mother choose wisely in the man department. And there was always a price to pay for such adulation.

"Sometimes people watch through the two-way glass." He nodded toward a long, mirrored pane at least eight feet long.

Okay, not what she wanted to hear or see. "They'll see me?"

"You won't even know they are there—if anyone is there at all. Now remember, 'sugar' will get you out of anything."

"What are we going to do?"

"Quiet your mind. Did you enjoy last night, London?"

Her nether regions answered with a resounding yes. Fluid gathered at the mere memory of what they'd done. She nodded an acknowledgement.

"Last night you said if you were restrained you'd feel protected. Interesting word choice. Perhaps it means you need an advocate. But you aren't sure if that makes you weak or worthy of someone's attention."

He gave words to something she hadn't been able to articulate her whole life.

"You aren't weak, London Chantelle. But you're tired of fighting. Alone."

"Maybe. Probably."

"Yes." He pulled his belt from her waist. "You can always leave. But going forward, whenever you wear this, you're safe. It's a symbol you are under my protection. And don't you dare say they're just words."

When he doubled it in his hand like a whip, a jolt of fear and arousal met somewhere in the middle of her body.

"Any new limits I should be aware of?"

She shook her head.

"Walk over to the cross. Then take off your clothes."

"What?" Her eyes darted to the darkened mirror.

"Now." His voice broke no tolerance for refusal.

She tiptoed to the cross, as if people behind the glass wouldn't see her if she didn't make any sound.

After toeing off her tennies, she lifted her long shirt and pulled it overhead. When she shucked her jeans, a vision of the plain panties she'd thrown on made her flush anew. She peeled them off quickly. Maybe he wouldn't notice?

Now standing in the middle of the room, nude, she shivered. Under Carson's stare her body heated like she'd overdosed on niacin. At this point her eyelashes must be blushing. Why did she feel so shy with him? Maybe because he looked so intently at her? She wondered if after this weekend she'd ever feel seen again. Carson's attention was just so *thorough.*

He engulfed her in a bear hug. "You're cold."

"I'm naked."

"Mmm, my favorite look of yours." He walked around to her back and lifted her hair. He twisted the strands into a long braid. The pull on her scalp sent welcome, warming tingles down her back.

He returned to her front and cupped her face in his hands. "You're like a phoenix rising from the ashes."

"That's a little overstated."

"I'll show you."

He turned her so she faced the cross. He attached her arm to a cuff, and she gasped as she connected with the cold steel.

He secured her other arm to the cross. "Spread your legs."

She widened her legs until they were in line with the angled metal of the cross. He left them unbound.

"I should've directed you to wear your boots."

"You like them?" She turned her head so she could catch his face in her periphery.

"Love them. Next time you'll wear them. I'll redden that perfect ass until you're stomping those heels on the floor, begging me to stop. But I won't." He grasped the back of her head. "Not until you safeword—or come."

A trickle of arousal wet her inner thigh.

The sound of a door opening made her heart startle. "Carson."

"He's not staying," he whispered into her hair.

Heavy footfalls and a loud thunk behind her set her heart into panicked flutters. Another man? *Oh, no, please.* Carson hands wound in her braid and held her head facing forward, while his other hand gripped her hip.

The strange man's voice whispered, "Beautiful." He must have been four feet from her.

"Thank you, Tony. That's all." She heard a door shut.

"London." He placed a kiss on her neck. "No one but us."

"I-I thought …" Her whole body vibrated as her imagination exploded about what could have occurred.

"Just me." He leaned his body into her and her shaking subsided.

But then another, almost imperceptible sound came from somewhere. She turned her head toward the distant noise. Her heartbeat accelerated.

"Eyes forward, London."

Rustling from where his bag lay sent her head twisting around anyway.

Fabric settled over her eyes and blackness joined her anxiety. "Why do you always blindfold me?"

"To help you relax."

Should she tell him it was doing the opposite? More sounds came from somewhere. "Can you blindfold the observers instead?"

He chuckled. "Who might be watching, London? What could they possibly do to you?"

"I don't know. It doesn't matter. I just-just don't like it!" She tested the restraints. Snaps clanked against the metal frame.

His whole body pressed her forward into the cross once more. "You're here with me. No one else."

∼

Carson pulled out his favorite flogger from his bag. With a thick black braided handle and two dozen long suede tails, the whip gave more of a thud than sting, a perfect beginning to his plans.

"Music. Playlist four." Each room had been individually wired, with various "services" turned on by voice command. Music, water, fans—even safewords—were pre-programmed into Accendos's computer system. Such technology proved helpful when hands were occupied and help was required.

A Killswitch Engage ballad poured from the speakers recessed overhead. The songs on his favorite playlist would grow increasingly harsh and loud as they played.

"I didn't take you for a Metal Head," she said.

He huffed out a half laugh. "Atmosphere is important. Besides, this band is underrated. You may know that feeling."

She dropped her head forward. She's ashamed? Just what he'd begun to suspect. The woman he'd known as London Chantelle—the cool, confident business shark—was merely a persona. He understood why she chose to hide the warm and nurturing side of herself. Her compassion could be exploited too easily. But he also knew the cost of hiding one's true self. *Enough.*

Last night he'd told her what he wanted. Time. Willingness. Pleasure. She gave the willingness she possessed. He gave her pleasure. Now he was going to give her time, or rather the removal of time. He'd send her someplace far away from rehab facilities, bills and press conferences. A place where their lives would narrow and amplify at the same time.

He grasped her braid and pulled her head back. "From this moment forward, you are going to be totally you."

"And you?"

"I've always been me."

"Good," she whispered.

He twisted his wrist and the long ends of the flogger swished through the air.

Connecting with a sub in this space was as close to heaven as he'd likely get in his lifetime. It made the lack of love almost worth it.

∼

Swack! London took in a noisy breath as a sting spread across her backside. *He's going to flog me?* For years she'd slipped into public dungeons during out-of-town business trips and been drawn to the whipping scenes. She'd huddle in the shadows, secretly craving the impact of those tails against her skin. The reality hadn't produced what she sought. The first time she felt the sting of a flogger she hadn't liked it at all. Michael had told her that her enjoyment wasn't the point. It was *his* enjoyment he was concerned with, not hers.

Thwack! A growing warmth, like a slow sunburn, spread across her flesh. Two more strikes came rapid against her back. Harder thumps across her backside pushed out small grunts from her throat. *So different.* Carson's strikes were poles apart from her earlier experience—her one and only experience.

The flogger reconnected with her skin across her upper back. The ends of the smooth tails wrapped around her whole torso. More blows, harder but further apart, landed on her back, her behind and thighs. Carson's breath grew louder behind her. Given the impact, he must have been pulling his arm back fully now. Her bottom lip smarted from her teeth's grasp.

The long tails circled her body, the ends licking the sides of her breasts. God, her nipples ached. She wanted to turn around, have him trail those long suede fingers over her breasts. Then maybe move lower until the tails smacked her labia. Perhaps a few might hit right between her folds.

"Beautiful." Carson's voice sounded thick and raspy. His large hand caressed her shoulder, then moved down her back until he reached her ass. He palmed her flesh. She felt his approval.

She cried out as a new pain lanced her to the core. Something that felt like a long rawhide strap raked across her raw nerve endings. *Too much, too much.* She stomped her bare foot and Carson emitted a low, masculine rumble. Rapid, light blows came fast. Her body reached for him even as her cries of "no, no more, stop" ripped from her throat.

Something significant danced on the edge of her consciousness. *Why aren't you calling sugar?* She couldn't wrap her mind around any answer, as she swam in Carson's attention. He didn't stop, and the relentless strikes loosened something inside her. A strange sensation circled her whole body, awakening every nerve ending. The pain spread in a similar pattern, but she began to lean toward *and* writhe away from the burn.

Something important was happening—or not happening. She wasn't hating it.

She arched her lower back, an invitation for him to continue. *Because Carson's not hitting me. Not exactly.* Thoughts floated in and out of her mind, thin as strands of milkweed, not forming into anything logical.

"Ah!" A sharp stripe of pain spread across her backside. He'd switched her!

Before the first sting had a chance to fade, another strike landed on her right cheek. Screams released from her throat as four more cutting stripes of pain sliced her ass. She focused on his panting behind her, and the way he laid two more strikes on her flesh. His precise movements spoke of intense attention, as if working her over became his whole world.

The fabric of his shirt and pants connected with her backside, now a mass of bruised fire. His hands touched her body, like he checked into her state.

She couldn't think anymore. She hung in her bindings and tuned into his exploring fingers. She rolled her head back onto his chest while his fingers touched between her legs. *Oh, yes.* His hand circled her waist and lifted her so she regained her footing. She'd been nearly hanging?

He pinched a nipple. *More pain.* He circled her clit. *More.* The pleasure and pain mixture made her sway.

She bent her knees so she could rub herself against him. He pitched into her harder, causing her to lurch forward. Metal clips banged against the cross. Knowing fingers roughly ringed her clit. She pushed herself up on tiptoes so the crack of her ass could connect with his crotch, now hardened with his own arousal.

"Please." Her voice was no more than a breath.

"More?"

"Yes, please, sir." Her juices trailed down her leg, and oh, her mouth ached from emptiness.

He left her alone again, and the scrape of something being picked up gave her a moment of delicious alarm. *Swack!*

"Present your ass," he said gruffly.

Many minutes passed while he lashed her with the flogger, now circling the cross, letting the ends flick her breasts and her thighs. The ends almost touched her pussy. Underneath her raw, inflamed, yet nearly numb skin, a hunger grew.

She raised on her tiptoes and arched her back as much as she could. Her arms stretched out long. She didn't care what she looked like or who could see her. *Just don't stop.* She wanted more, so much more…

Her own honey coated her thighs. Why wasn't the crosspiece positioned lower? She could rub herself against it, relieve some of the burning pressure between her legs.

"Gorgeous," he hissed and dropped his whip. He began to use his bare palm, spanking her hard and quick. God, she wanted to come. But his rough handling kept her on edge, unable to pitch over completely.

His hands stopped their work. "No!" Her outcry earned her another full-impact swat on her ass.

He uncuffed her wrists, and she buckled into his arms. He roughly turned her. Her back connected with the apex of the cross. He made quick work of reattaching her wrists, and this time, he connected her ankles. She was spread wide, open. *Yes, please.*

She couldn't see his face. Still, she knew he drank in her body, perspiring, bruised, and quaking in her bonds. She arched her back and pushed her breasts out toward him.

His voice broke into her consciousness. "I would never cross any of your limits, like a gag. But your mouth is begging to be filled. Do you trust me?"

"Yes. I need …"

"Yes, baby. I know." A thick dildo split her lips and filled her mouth. "Push it out if you need to."

She sucked on the thick phallus. She wasn't about to let it go.

His fingers pinched her nipple, which sent another pang through her pussy. She shrieked when a snap and sharp pain took over her breast. He'd attached a clover clamp. Nothing else created that kind of agony. She clamped down on the thick rubber phallus, grateful it muffled some of her scream when the pain of the second clamp hit.

His hand caressed the side of her cheek. Without words, she felt he asked her if she was okay. She murmured and pressed her face into his hand. *What is happening to me?*

Untouchable

A light pat on her pussy caused her to lock her knees. A flat paddle tapped again, slowly building to a crescendo of slaps, one after the other.

With breasts throbbing and her clit on fire, she spun in a tornado, unable to land on one sensation. She moved in and out of her usual consciousness, first pain and then pleasure. She tried to clutch at the cuffs, unable to grasp anything.

She suckled the dildo, imagined Carson's large cock. With that image, she released. Her chest heaved. Saliva escaped down her chin. She lost herself in her orgasm.

Rough beard stubble scraped against her neck, bringing her back to Carson. His groin pressed into her and the hard, naked skin of his cock pressed against her opening. She tried to rise up on her toes to give him better access but the ankle cuffs stopped her. He still slid into her, easily. Her head fell backward as he lunged, hard and deep. He grasped her sore ass and pulled her closer. The cuffs kept her from rising, and soon her ankles chafed as her legs were pulled upward from his thrusts.

Another orgasm, stronger and sending her muscles into greedy spasms, left her limp. When he pulled out, he kept a strong hold on her middle. She was unable to stand on her own anymore, gasping and hanging in her restraints.

"Brace, London." His voice sounded strange against the ringing in her ears. As he released the nipple clamps, another hoarse scream was swallowed by the phallus in her mouth.

The dildo gag slipped free. A cloth wiped across her mouth, tenderly. She pitched forward into his body after he unclipped her ankle cuffs and then her wrists.

His hands, lowering her to the floor, weren't at all the same ones that had brutally switched her until she had to be bleeding. Her mind slowly swam to the surface. *We're in a room. At the club.* When he finally brought his hands up to the blindfold, she grasped his wrists. He stopped his motion. He seemed to realize she wasn't ready to see yet, to be brought back completely. She floated in a cloud, feeling weightless and warm.

Carson held her close, on the floor, silently. His hands explored every inch of her body, limp with acceptance of his handling. Not a single muscle flinched at his touches. When his hand cupped her face, a thought echoed through her mind as if he was telegraphing a message. *I've got you.*

~

Carson rarely conducted his own aftercare, instead letting one of the professional attendants take over. But he shook his head at Carrie, who'd silently entered, sending him a questioning look to see if he required help. She must have been watching through the glass. She backed out, and he drew London closer. He wouldn't be separated from her.

He had engaged in hundreds of BDSM scenes. Some light, some heavy, but all with one common element: everyone brought their own reasons for being there. He hadn't realized London's reason until that moment. It was the same reason he was involved: the utter and complete removal of bullshit. *And the dishonesty that this town applauds.*

He kept her face cradled against his neck. He ran his fingers through her hair, massaged her shoulders and ran through their scene again in his mind.

London's nude body, spread open on the cross, had presented a masterpiece. Her total abandonment of control had been the greatest gift he'd been given to date. He knew what it took for a sub to sink into that level of submission. To have her give herself so fully? He felt as high as London looked.

She needs a collar. His thought stunned him, yet he couldn't deny the truth of his desire. Lucky is the man who earned that right. She shouldn't settle for those thin leather straps he'd seen on most of the subs in the club, or those fetish necklaces laughingly called "day collars." No, London needed a substantial circle of metal, engraved with her Master's name, so she'd feel the weight of it against her throat. *A constant promise.*

She whimpered. She needed to lie down where he could attend to the bruises now starting to emerge.

After wrapping her into a robe Carrie had left, he carried her through the door and into the hallway. The aftercare suites weren't far.

"Carson Drake." A man pushed himself off the wall and stepped up to them. "You found something of mine."

He turned slowly to face a wiry man in a polo shirt and khakis. London swayed in his arms, and he tightened his hold. He sharply raised his chin, an obvious signal the man should back off.

The idiot advanced instead. "You disappointed me, London. I'm not used to being stood up." His familiarity with London burned through his chest.

He sent his beady eyes back Carson's way. "Nice technique. But you didn't do it hard enough. An evil stick makes them more obedient."

He wasn't about to get into a conversation with this Polo Preppy who lacked basic observation skills—and manners. As he turned away, the man grasped London's shoulder.

If he hadn't had his arms full, he would have clocked the guy. "Unhand her or lose every finger. Disappear. Now."

"I don't think so." The man dropped his grasp on London and extended his hand. "Michael Headler. London's owner."

8

Carson eased London down into a chair and placed her hands on one of the armrests. "Hold on," he said.

She gripped the chair arm and gaped down at the carpet.

He kept a hand on London's shoulder and turned to Headler, who was still standing before him. "Owner?"

When Carson said the word, London lifted her head and whispered, "No."

"London doesn't agree," he said.

Michael widened his stance and crossed his arms. He dared to smirk. "She's got you by the balls." Headler held out his hand. "London."

A slash of anger sliced through Carson's insides. "London, don't move." He stepped forward. The man didn't have the intelligence to step back. "One more word from you and you'll find yourself spitting out carpet for days."

Carrie appeared out of nowhere. "Jesus Christ, why don't you each just pee on a leg and be done with it?"

The club's assistant pulled London up into a hug. London blinked. She looked like she didn't recognize the woman who'd cared for her just last night. He would be

Untouchable

damned if anyone was taking London *anywhere*. "Carrie, I've got her."

"No, you don't." Alexander's voice thundered down the hallway. "Carrie, please see Miss Chantelle is taken care of."

Alexander may have been in almost sixty, but his long, confident stride had him between the two of them in seconds. He also didn't register Carson's return glare.

"Stand down. Both of you." He jerked his chin toward the elevator. "Come with me."

"After I see to London." Alexander may have saved Michael from being taken to the floor, but he wouldn't be separated from the woman he'd just sent into subspace.

Alexander put his hand on Carson's back. "Carrie will handle all necessary care. Now, to my office. Mr. Headler?"

Carson reluctantly stepped into the elevator. Alexander was one of the few men on earth who could direct him. He wouldn't dishonor any request the man made, especially around the care of a submissive. Alexander's adherence to submissives' well-being was legendary. London wouldn't be harmed by their temporary separation, he told himself. *I just don't have to like it.*

Alexander wisely kept himself between him and Michael, who lazily leaned against the rickety elevator's side wall. They scowled at one another, Carson matching the man's repugnant gaze.

In Alexander's office, a grandfather clock against the far wall made an annoyingly loud clicking noise, the only other sound to join Alexander's slow descent into his executive chair.

Carson folded himself into one of the large leather chairs before the desk. He stretched out his long legs. Prick Michael mirrored his pose.

"What the hell was that downstairs?" Alexander didn't swear often. But he had no ability to suffer bad manners.

"A minor altercation, one I can clear up immediately," Michael said. "It appears Mr. Drake got the wrong impression about London's availability."

"Hardly."

"Just because she didn't mention her previous commitment does not mean it doesn't exist."

Alexander leaned back into his chair. "Mr. Headler, exactly what commitment are you referring to?"

"Some months ago, London pledged herself to me."

Carson looked the man up and down. "I doubt that."

"Go on," Alexander said.

"I realize I'm a new member here, and Mr. Drake here is more established—"

Carson sneered. "You have no idea."

Alexander raised his hand. "Carson."

So, he was going to be forced to listen to Michael's case. *Pitiful*.

"As I was saying, London and I have a commitment. We work together. A few months ago she offered herself to me."

"What do you mean offered?" Carson knew London well enough; she *offered* very little.

"You are a client of my firm, Mr. Drake. I'm sorry you had to get mixed up in our misunderstanding. Yost and Brennan likely doesn't know anything about either one of our ... extracurricular activities. I wouldn't want anything to get between our work together—"

"I've never seen you in my life."

"I'm not surprised. London and I work on other accounts together. Not Whitestone's. Nevertheless, we are connected. I apologize for the *emotion* displayed earlier. You, of all people, should know Dominants can be quite territorial." His face stretched into a greasy smile. The desire to push the man's face into the carpet grew.

Michael turned to Alexander. "As I was saying, London offered herself to me and I accepted."

"Define offer, please." Alexander's cool headedness also irritated. Couldn't he see the insanity of Headler's words? Carson may have known the punk for fifteen minutes, but he knew from the first inappropriate word out of his mouth this man couldn't "own" a woman, and certainly not London. His speech, his mannerisms, his words were too practiced.

Michael sighed. "London is new to our firm. She didn't seem to have many friends."

"You call declaring ownership of someone befriending them?" Carson asked.

"Yes, Mr. Drake. She's a submissive. She needed a Master."

Jesus, didn't he allude that same sentiment to her just last night? His jaw ached from clenching his teeth. "And she chose you?" he gritted out.

Michael returned his attention to Alexander. "We got together some months ago. I accepted the role she sought. End of story. Last night she was to meet me here. She didn't." Michael eyed Carson from foot to head. "Somehow she must have gotten intercepted. I see no reason to disclose private details of our time together. I expected such discretion from your club, Mr. Rockingham."

Carson picked a brunette strand of hair off his trousers. "This has nothing to do with the club or discretion. You just dislike that London chose not to meet you."

"Oh, she would have," he said.

All the things he could do to this man ran through his head like a torture checklist. Release his firm. Get him fired. Reveal him to the head of his agency. Threaten legal action under some privacy statute yet uncovered.

"Carson's correct. Discretion is not the issue here, Mr. Headler," Alexander said. "I only require an explanation of the altercation downstairs and the true relationships—either established or burgeoning." He looked over at Carson on the last word. "And if any house rules were broken."

"I see three, at least." Carson threw his words at Alexander, who gave him a wry smile.

The club's governing body, the Washington Tribunal Council, operated under three laws, all of which the seven standing members had pledged themselves to uphold. Ensured *safety*. Informed *consent*. Intentional *progress* for all.

Michael Headler would know these laws as all club members must. However, Michael likely did not understand the level under which they were enforced. The Tribunal's power was unknown to most people. Carson would be happy to enlighten him on such matters.

"Perhaps." As always, Alexander's smooth tone showed no emotion. "There still lies missing information we need to get from London."

Michael stood. "I'll collect her. I'll get her to talk to you."

He was on his feet a nanosecond later. "I don't think so."

"I don't think—"

"Stop." Alexander's face was as stone cold as Carson's gut felt. "The truth is, it doesn't matter what either of you think."

Michael raised his chin, a haughty salute to Alexander. "What? But you said—"

"The only thing that matters is what London wants and how she would characterize either one of you. And that, gentleman, is something *I* shall find out." Alexander rose to his full height. "I won't tolerate anyone being bullied."

Michael turned his weak chin toward Carson and smirked. "Nothing for you to do then."

Carson wanted to throttle him. "Something can always be done. Alexander, I call a Tribunal meeting."

~

An hour later, the uncomfortable prickling sensation over Carson's skin had grown closer to a brush fire. He wasn't used to being stopped. But before he could slip into the aftercare area to find London, Alexander had halted him with the only words that could.

"Carson, Carrie reports she's asked for time. Remember the second law. The submissive's wishes are paramount. You pledged yourself to it."

The decree clung to him like lead cuffs around each ankle. They stopped him from bolting down the hallway to retrieve London—the *person*, not the property Michael Headler seemed to believe she was.

Instead, he busied himself by firing off text messages to the other Tribunal Council members—Jonathan Brond, Mark Santos, Derek Damon Wright, Ryan Knightbridge and Sarah Marillioux. They'd know an emergency was at hand. He didn't normally text, and certainly not after Alexander's assistant had already called them. But Michael sat at the bar on the other side of the club, when he really should be on his ass in the street. He had to ensure they knew how important their presence would be. A quorum was necessary for his plans.

While waiting for the others to arrive, he passed the time pacing in front of the stairway that led up to the room where Carrie had taken London. From his vantage point, he could see the door they'd vanished into. It might as well have been made of two-foot-thick steel. Even Alexander had been banned by Carrie, which took some guts on her part. As the founder and Grand Arbiter of the entire Tribunal network, Alexander didn't take orders from anyone, anywhere. The other cities' Arbiters practically genuflected in Alexander's presence given the man's connections, and what those connections could deliver.

Of course, Carrie may have been a submissive herself, but

she also was an ex-cop—from Boston. She'd stood before him unwavering.

Carson scrubbed his growing five o'clock shadow. London said she needed more time before her interview with Alexander? That fact worried him more.

Michael's earlier words bounced around in his mind. *Owner, my ass.* Something had happened between him and London. Even if he had to dangle Headler's body by his ankles from the Memorial Bridge over the Potomac, he would discover the truth.

When Alexander had made his decree about both of them leaving London alone, Michael's eyes had glazed, as if he was deep in thought. Carson recognized a man who was calculating.

Damn him. The man had interrupted the best weekend he'd had in years. He'd taken London farther than he'd anticipated. Her response would go down in his history as legendary. In one afternoon, she arched her beautiful back and presented her gorgeous ass, asking for *more*.

His internal countdown clock boomed in his ears. *Only one more day.* Normally it was a comforting sound, the reminder he'd soon be released. He could then continue to live in the moment, on the hard edge of life, avoiding the sentimentality that plagued so many of his friends. *Free.* The preemptive strike had been the basis of such freedom. But now? He didn't feel very free.

~

"The Grand Arbiter of the Tribunal network and Chairman of the Washington Tribunal Council calls this meeting to order. We have a quorum without seventh pledge Ryan Knightbridge." Alexander sat in his executive chair at the far end of the large, round table. "The Chairman calls for silence."

The five attending Council members nodded at Alexander and took their places. Tony closed the double doors behind him, a loud click echoing off the stone floor and walls. He then stood like a sentinel behind Alexander.

"The Chair yields the floor to Tribunal member Carson S. Drake, second pledge."

The other members around the table eyed him curiously. They'd served for years on the Council, and they knew when he wasn't himself.

He stood. "Gentlemen, madam, I called this meeting to lodge a formal complaint against potential Accendos member, Michael Headler, for violation of all three Tribunal laws."

The expressions on their faces told him exactly what he needed to know. Michael was about to experience the full weight of the Tribunal's power. Breaking one law was enough for anyone to be immobilized and likely exiled. But all three? No one before had ever dared.

For the next few minutes he recounted Michael's untenable claims on London. For another infuriating forty minutes, the Council members debated, made motions and amended motions. But by the time Tony reopened the doors, signaling the meeting's end, he had at least half of what he wanted. Headler under formal investigation, on probation at Club Accendos, and more importantly, banished from contacting London until Tribunal pronouncement.

Derek lazily leaned against the club's main bar and drummed his fingers against his glass. "Jesus, Headler's going to wish he'd memorized Dominance for Dummies. Sarah's going to interview him and perhaps offer him training? God rest his soul."

Jonathan laughed. "You have no idea."

"It's not enough," Carson tightened his grip on his tumbler of water, imagining Headler's neck.

"He's got two options, man. Training or eviction." Derek ran his fingers through his unruly copper-colored hair.

"He could choose Sarah's tutelage to avoid exile."

"I would." Mark's tattooed bicep flexed as he lifted his glass to drain the remaining beer.

"That's something I'd pay money to see. The jock being handled by Sarah." Derek grinned. "Carson, surely the more *colorful* rumors about us reached him at some point."

"The *strategic* details we've leaked, you mean. Clearly the finer points of how far we'll go hasn't breached Headler's thick head," he bit out. "London deserves better from us."

He drained his own glass and ran through his mental list of notable points he'd collected on how to handle London. *Her inability to articulate her needs.* She'd have difficulty explaining her needs to Michael. *Her fear about certain limits.* She'd likely been susceptible to going along with anything Michael had wanted, and having it go badly. *Her need to stay in control.* Trusting Michael had been her mistake.

She couldn't have been safe with a man like Michael Headler, a man who clearly thought protocol was merely a suggestion. Law one swam in his head. *Ensure safety—your own and all persons you come in contact with.*

He shook his head. "He doesn't deserve a Council member's attention, let alone Sarah's. She's too good for him."

Jonathan eyed him up and down. "How come you didn't know Headler before this weekend? His agency works for your firm."

"They don't send the whole agency to meetings. And attorneys aren't invited to every meeting."

"Yet you managed to sit in on quite a few with London?"

Yes, he had. Without realizing it until that moment, he'd actually ensured his presence.

"It's not illegal in the District of Columbia to be involved with a coworker," Jonathan added. As a fellow attorney and former member of Congress, Jonathan was as tuned to human resource law as Carson.

"I know a case of bullying when I see it. Law two. Clear, verbalized consent, given freely and without coercion." It was the Tribunal's most important guideline.

"And law number three. All members shall make positive progress in this lifestyle. If Headler is telling the truth and London is unharmed, then we owe it to him to put him on a better road." Jonathan sipped his drink.

Derek pushed off the bar. "Well, Mark and I will leave you two legal minds to debate the state of the union. I left a perfect ass in my bed to come running."

Mark grinned at him. "Which makes it an ordinary day for you."

Carson ignored their attempt to lighten his mood. He watched Derek and Mark head down the wide stairs to return to their lives. If only he could do the same.

Jonathan must have read his desire to take matters into his own hands, as he continued to assess him. "We're going to do this by the book, Carson. Any technical slip-up will hinder justice."

He should have thanked his long-standing friend, the only other attorney on the Washington Tribunal Council, for reminding him of the proper path. *And not overreacting.* But he refused to lock away his emotions. He found himself resenting the rules and regulations preventing the action he wanted to take. The need for restraint and due process left him edgy.

"This is a case of non-consent. She didn't agree to be involved with him. I know it." *I know it.* He knew his words sounded pathetic. During his brief stint at the DA's office how many times did someone proclaim innocence or guilt with no evidence to back it up?

One thing he knew for certain. Headler didn't deserve Sarah's attention. He deserved banishment—something the Tribunal could do like no other organized BDSM network.

Thanks to Alexander, fifteen major cities had seven-member Tribunal Councils watching their local communities. Members came from some of the greatest wealth in the country. With their considerable fortunes, they could enforce deportation from the scene, nationwide. More importantly, they provided medical and psychological help to those whose trust had been violated.

Violated.

His gut roiled at the thought of Headler's lack of understanding of topping a woman like London. *Or anyone.* Though he didn't know the details of her past family life, he knew she'd had her fill of amateurs. *Users.* No woman should suffer at the hands of people whose damned job it was to protect her.

"Man, you're into this woman." Jonathan's stare sliced through his worked-up emotions.

"Yes." No use hiding the truth. Jonathan could smell a lie as well as he. And they'd been friends for a while, often butting heads but always having each other's backs.

"I haven't seen you this hung up on a woman since our days at law school," Jonathan said.

"Yeah, well, Diana was young. She wasn't ready to settle down—until she met Mr. Moneybags."

Jonathan chuckled at their shared memory of the skinny rich kid who spirited Carson's girlfriend away with promises of unlimited credit cards. They'd dumped three gallons of red paint on his Porsche late one night. God, he'd give anything to go back to simpler days, when a man could take matters into his own hands.

"Yvette says hello." Jonathan swirled the remaining liquid in his glass.

His mention of the submissive they'd both befriended long ago, and often serviced when needed, sent an arrow of guilt through his heart. Their last time together hadn't gone well. He and Jonathan had nearly come to blows over the scenario until the truth came out that Yvette hadn't been honest about her state, mentally or physically. *You should have known better. Just like Headler?*

"How is she?" Carson asked.

"Happy."

"Good." He stood and grabbed his coat from the back of the bar chair. "Seems your little grad is ready to tie herself to your sorry ass." Unlike him, Jonathan had found love. By all accounts, his relationship with Christiana was the real thing.

Jonathan slapped him on the back. "If my stepmother's wedding plans don't scare her away. So, you think you've found the one?"

"Maybe."

"And it's killing you to be apart from her."

"Yes." *Oh, Christ. It's been twenty-four hours.*

Carson turned to his friend. If anyone identified with his frustration, it'd be Jonathan Brond. A question he had never asked burned in his gut. "How did you know Christiana was the one?"

A genuine smile broke across Jonathan's face, unlike the toothy grins he'd given the cameras for so many years. "Every time I look at her, I see my future."

9

London pulled the comforter over her shoulders. The room was warm, but she couldn't stop the chills erupting across her skin. She also had the strength of a boiled noodle.

She turned over and winced as her bruised butt met the sheets. Even with the soothing balm Carrie had put on them, her ass cheeks wore a patchwork of red marks and broken capillaries. She was sure she had open wounds. But no real damage occurred. She felt a strange, rising sense of pride at the fact that she wasn't more hurt. And her orgasm? She grew wet at the memory.

Before leaving, Carrie had asked her a few questions about Michael, casually, as if she didn't care about the answers. London knew the technique. She used it herself at work. The second anyone thought their words mattered, they began to hedge their answers. She couldn't remember how she answered Carrie's questions about Michael. She'd simply let the words come out.

She sat up. She was so tired, but Michael's face kept rising in her mind, refusing to allow her to rest.

This situation was all her fault.

Even being in public relations for eight years, she had never found the words for those dark, dangerous places in her mind—in her body. All she knew was her appetite had grown worse in the last year. Then when Michael caught her in a weak moment ... She'd let Michael talk her into things she never should have entertained, let alone acted out.

But Carson? He seemed to understand. Everything sounded so simple when he suggested a weekend of submission. Now twenty-four hours spent with Carson proved Michael didn't have a clue what to do with her and honestly didn't care. Yes, she had disappointed Michael, continuously. Perhaps she wasn't the problem? While he caused similar pain as Carson had, he'd never done anything to have her honey drip down her legs while calling up that hurt.

She rose and went to the full-length mirror in the corner. She turned and examined the long stripes across her butt. She hoped the marks stayed for a while. Maybe she'd take a picture with her phone. A keepsake of her time with Carson. She'd learned by age eight, all good things faded in time.

She pulled on her coat. A gentle rapping at the door interrupted her dressing.

"Come in."

Alexander Rockingham peeked inside. "Decent?"

"That's a matter of opinion."

He opened the door wide and smiled. "In my club, you're right. How are you feeling?"

"Better. The nap really helped."

"I've always said, a shower and a nap can right any bad day."

Alexander's gentlemanly manners shamed her. "I'm sorry to have caused such a scene downstairs."

He sat in one of the wingback chairs near the window. "You caused nothing. Two male peacocks pulling on each other's tail feathers is nothing new here. In fact, it'd been a rather boring day until then." He gestured for her to take the other chair.

"I-I should have handled things a little better." She flinched when her ass hit the cushion.

"My dear, you shouldn't have had to *handle* anything."

She dropped her gaze to her chipped nail polish. "Still ..."

"London, I have to ask you a few questions. Can you explain to me the nature of your relationship with Michael Headler? In your own words."

"He's, uh, my boss. Michael's the head of our largest account, and is my direct report."

"I understand. And outside of work? You dated?"

"Well, no one really *dates* in Washington anymore, but we got together a few times. Wine and cheese happy hours at work. The harbor bars. The usual thing."

"You went home with him."

"Yes. Martinis' fault." She laughed lightly, as if humor would quell her nervousness. "That's when I found out ..."

"He's a Dominant."

"He didn't really say it. One night we sort of just got into it."

"Into what?"

"Well, we were kissing and he pushed my arms over my head. Then, as time went on, he got rougher." She couldn't look at Alexander anymore. She felt like she was confessing the play-by-play of how she got a hickey to her school-teacher. Besides, Carson was rough, too. *But better.*

"You liked it."

"Sometimes."

"Did you ever have to safeword?"

"Michael didn't believe in safewords."

Alexander's lips tightened into a line. "Were you in a CNC relationship with him?"

"A what?"

"Consent non-consent."

"I'm not sure I know what that means."

"I see. Michael's your owner?"

She laughed. "Well, he used to ask me all the time, *You're mine, right?*"

"And you'd say yes."

"Yes, I'd say, sure ..." Because she'd have said anything to make him less angry. But was the price worth it? Was she that cheap? *Just like Mom.*

Before she could fully grasp the epiphany that she was no better than her mother, Alexander stood up. "London Chantelle, stand."

She shot up. His voice could probably make the President of the United States rise.

"Did Michael Headler ever ask you to be his submissive?"

"N-no."

"His slave?"

She huffed out a laugh. "His what?"

"Slave."

Her insides clenched at the vehemence in his voice. "No." Her voice shook.

"Thank you. That's all I needed to know. Sit."

His face broke into a large smile when she folded herself back into the chair. "You are a submissive, however."

"I guess." Why the hell isn't she arguing with him? *Because he's a Dominant. And a good one.* Even feeling that perhaps she'd sold a piece of herself to a man like her mother, she felt comforted in Alexander's presence. His obvious confidence about himself fueled her own courage.

Dominant wasn't a large enough word for Alexander Rockingham.

"You're a Master," she said. In fact, if she could have found a word greater than "Master," she'd have used it for him.

He dipped his chin in acknowledgement. "And Grand

Arbiter of the Tribunal. Has Carson told you anything about us?"

"Not much."

"The Tribunal was founded to uphold the highest standards for our community. We don't allow abusers in our midst. Not here. Not anywhere." His sky-blue eyes clouded to a steel grey.

"I don't feel abused." *Not exactly.*

"That's what I'm concerned about. You may not know what it looks like." His eyes softened. Instead of feeling scolded by his judgment, she felt oddly consoled.

No wonder people spent months trying to get into Club Accendos. Instead of the dark seedy dungeon she'd expected last night, an over-the-top, private boudoir greeted her. But today with Carson? She felt like she'd stepped onto the surface of the sun—burning, bright, and dangerous.

But now he was so angry ...

Alexander tilted his head. "Carson is a good Master."

The marked difference between Carson and Michael once again hit her in the chest.

"He's downstairs, waiting to take you home."

"Oh." Of course, he'd be done with her. Their agreement had to be null and void. Michael made sure of that fact.

"I wish I could stay here." She hadn't meant to sound so pleading. Michael was probably at her house right now, waiting to fire her. First working girl rule? Never embarrass your boss—especially in Washington where appearances were life and death. *So much for being a vice president.*

"You may. The submissive's wishes are paramount. Here and everywhere else." Alexander rose. "You're not wrong to like control—and you're right to make your Doms earn their right to take control. But hiding here won't change anything."

"No. In these surroundings, it'd be the opposite. Too tempting to ... try things."

Untouchable

He cocked his head. "You're either the most reluctant submissive I've met to date or the strongest."

"Michael used to say I'm stubborn. I'm not that strong."

"Are you sure?" Alexander seemed like he really wanted an answer. But it was one she couldn't give.

∾

Carson paced in the main vestibule, glancing up the wide staircase leading to the upper floors and then back to the elevator. London would have to exit the club using one of them, and he'd intercept her. He'd officially been apart from her for more than two hours. One hundred twenty minutes too long.

Alexander casually leaned against the bannister. His half smile followed him as he walked the perimeter of the round portico. He realized he must look like a caged animal. But the pacing kept him from picking up a chintz-covered chair and throwing it at the wall. "Why do you have so many damned prissy chairs in this place?" he growled.

A loud creak from the stairway sent his attention to Carrie, who descended the steps. She held one of Carson's bags. "I figured you'd want to take this." She handed him his small leather satchel.

"Thank you, Carrie. You read my mind."

"All part of the job." She disappeared back upstairs.

Alexander laughed.

"What?" He was in no mood for Alexander's smug superiority—earned or not.

"It's about time you moved some things—or people—home."

So Alexander had prompted Carrie to bring him one of his toy bags. The gesture heartened him a little. Before London, he hadn't brought a woman to his home in years.

111

But now? When he took London home—which he damn well was going to do—he'd want some basic supplies in case she needed him.

Sarah's voice filled the hallway around the corner. "You'll have to abide by the Tribunal's wishes."

"Like hell." Michael trailed Sarah's entrance into the foyer.

"Mr. Rockingham, a word?"

"I see Sarah has met with you."

"Yes, and I refuse to be treated so poorly. I've done nothing—"

"Like hell, is right." Carson strode up to him.

Sarah sent him a silencing, icy stare. Sarah's Domme status deserved respect. She'd been in the scene longer than he had. At the moment, she proved to be in better control than he.

She turned her attention to Alexander. "Mr. Headler has been interviewed. We have his side of the story. My recommendation is training or émigré." Sarah had always reminded him of a thoroughbred horse—spirited, filled with a regal strength and always chomping at the bit for action. And she wanted action. Sarah had clearly determined he'd done enough wrong that he'd either have to accept her tutelage or be tossed on his ear.

Alexander gestured to the large bodyguard who appeared by his side. "Tony will escort you to your car. Then tomorrow—"

"Not without London."

Alexander eyed Michael carefully. He'd grown still, his spine straightening to his full six-foot-five height. To someone not familiar with Alexander, he might have felt assessed. Carson knew Michael had crossed a final line with the Grand Arbiter. He'd only witnessed one other person to be that stupid, a man he'd never seen since.

"I'm afraid not, Mr. Headler." Alexander widened his stance. "London is off limits to you. Her assessment of your relationship with her is far different from your report. London didn't realize when she said, 'I'm yours' you took it as anything beyond a scene. She never imagined you would take it to imply your ownership of her." Acid nearly dripped from his final words.

Michael raised his weak chin. "Same difference."

"Where the fuck did you come from?" Carson realized he'd bellowed. "Do you know who you are talking to?"

Alexander kept his eyes on Michael. "London is free to come and go as she pleases. Of course, she's always been free to do so. We just needed to know the nature of the relationships at hand. Had she been spoken for, then perhaps there might have been a matter to attend to. But now—"

"London and I can go." Michael moved toward the staircase.

Alexander's hand stopped him. "Not exactly. At Club Accendos, we take our etiquette very seriously."

"So Sarah says."

"Sarah is a member of our governing body. The Tribunal." Alexander articulated the syllables with great care. Did Michael understand? If pushed far enough, the Tribunal could ensure identity reassignment and federal prison sentences. It had no less than sixty individuals under permanent care and more than two hundred abusers under permanent watch. If you were an abuser and a non-U.S. citizen? Swift and permanent deportation from the United States.

"I've heard of it," Michael said.

"Then you know we don't throw terms around lightly. Owner is a significant claim to make on someone. One you clearly don't grasp. Tomorrow Sarah will meet with you to discuss your options. If you do not choose her offer, you will be excluded from here and any other organization, world-wide. Until the Tribunal readmits you, you'll stay away from any organized club. And London is under our protection."

Carson sucked in a deep breath. London's safety was guaranteed. Carson's protection would keep her safe; Alexander's protection would render her untouchable.

Alexander peered over his shoulder. "Sarah?"

"I'll call you." Sarah folded her arms over her chest and stared at Michael.

"I see," Michael said through gritted teeth. "And London?"

"Is going to stay here," Alexander said.

"What?" Carson and Michael nearly said the word together, which returned his anger.

"What do you mean she's staying here?"

"What I said, Carson. The submissive's wishes." Alexander's words ran through him like he'd been shot with a nail gun.

"Actually, I'm not." London stood at the top of the stairs. Carrie had a tight grip on her arm.

Smug, self-satisfaction bloomed across Michael's face. Carson grew tired of wanting to cuff him.

He met her descent. "Are you okay?"

She grasped both his wrists as he captured her face in his hands. "Yes. I'm ready to go." She let him take her arm from Carrie's and lead her down the stairs.

"Mr. Rockingham—"

"Alexander." He gave her a rare, paternal smile.

She returned his grin. "Thank you. For everything. I'm fine now."

Alexander pulled out a card from his inside jacket pocket and gave it to her. "My private cell phone number. Should you ever require help."

London took it and turned to Michael. "We'll need to talk. On Monday. I can explain."

Untouchable

"You don't owe him an explanation." Carson ran his hand through his hair. He was beyond done with the niceties.

"Yes, I do," she said. "I'm sorry for any misunderstanding we might have had."

"We'll talk, London," Michael said. "Believe me, we'll talk." His nostrils flared as he walked away.

Alexander studied Carson until he couldn't stand the man's evaluation anymore. "What?"

"Nothing." Alexander winked at London before turning down the hall.

London's shoulders hunched forward, and her eyes scanned the floor as if studying the Wenge wood parquet. Insecurity seemed an implausible trait for London yesterday. Today the depth of her self-doubt pained him.

"I want to go home. *My* home." She peeked up at him through her lowered lashes. "Will you go with me?"

"Try and stop me."

∼

London felt her chest heat as Carson's eyes flicked over her tiny apartment. A blue chenille blanket lay draped over her old couch. An old bouquet of daisies sat wilting in a vase on her tiny dining alcove table. Why hadn't she straightened up? *Oh, perhaps it was because you weren't planning on returning with Carson Drake?* But when he returned his attention to her, he smiled. "Your place looks like you."

"Worn out?"

He frowned and did that face-cradle thing with his hands, a move she'd grown to love. "Homey. You need to sleep."

She wasn't tired. Instead, her insides felt fractured and jittery. She teetered on the edge of losing her mind. For God's sake, she'd pissed off a senior executive at her firm.

She was probably now unemployed. The bills weren't going to pay themselves, especially not Southland Rehab's invoices.

Carson rubbed his thumbs over her cheeks. Something about the way he held her face made wallowing in pity not an option. His body's energy formed a bubble around her. He *helped. That's what a Dom does*, he'd said.

"I owe you an explanation," she said.

He pulled her down to her couch and onto his lap. She winced at the burn from her welts.

"Still hurts? I have something for it." He braced to rise, but she stopped him.

"Later. I-I kind of like it." She shrugged. "It makes me feel …"

"Alive. I understand."

"So, now I need to talk. There's more to the story."

"Start at the beginning," he said.

"The job at Yost and Brennan was an answered prayer. It meant I'd be able to do so much more."

"Travel, expense accounts, hang with the elite." He smiled.

"No, for Benny." She couldn't have cared less about any of those perks. She'd just wanted to be able to take care of her brother.

He tucked a stray hair behind her ear. "Go on."

"I was put on a large team. Cisco's trade show PR. Michael's largest account. So, he sat in on a lot of meetings. The execs only do that when it's a major customer. He was nice to me. He let me ask stupid questions." She smiled into her lap.

"I've never heard you ask a stupid question."

"Ha! So I *irritated* you with my charming personality?"

"Your questions made our meetings last longer. I liked listening to your voice. How did you end up with Michael?"

Carson always did get right to the heart of the matter. "One week, we had some big wins. The whole firm came out

Untouchable

for the Friday wine and cheese, our reward for working so late all the time. They hold them so we don't bolt early on Fridays." She laughed, trying to keep the conversation light. "I should never drink without food. I'm a lightweight. And, well, it's just so clichéd it's stupid. He followed me when I went to look for cups or something."

Carson's jaw tightened.

"He didn't attack me, Carson. He touched me ... in a way I just knew he had certain proclivities." Her lashes fanned over her cheeks as she lowered her gaze. "I had always wondered what it'd be like."

"He's not a Dominant. He may like to top, throw his weight around. But a Dom? It's something you are or you aren't. No need to prove it, and he certainly shouldn't have coerced you. What did he do exactly?" His face grew too serious.

She shouldn't continue. The way he handled Michael— one of her *bosses*—had to stop. Carson's temper proved unpredictable. He liked the avenging warrior role. But what if he learned about her last time with Michael? *He'll explode.* She nearly shuddered at the memory, herself. Friends of Michael's that he'd invited into a scene. Eyes assessing. Hands on her. *If you won't come for me, you'll do it for them,* Michael had said.

"London," Carson said. "Tell me."

His voice broke her trance. "He liked to restrain me and make me beg. He got rougher, um, over time. It, well, *he* didn't feel right, even though ..."

"Even though your urges didn't abate."

She examined her fingernails harder. When he lifted her chin to look up at him, his eyes held no judgment. "Good girl. Keep yourself safe, first. Remember?"

"Yes, I remember." She'd learned more from Carson in a weekend than she had in years on the sidelines. Too bad that direction was a day late and a million dollars short. "I'm not so safe at work."

"He can't hurt you there. I'll be sure of it."

"You don't know that. You see, when I said I wanted to stop, he began hinting, little things, really." Should she even tell him this? Yes, he needed to know how serious her situation had grown.

"What do you mean?" he asked.

"How disappointed he was in this presentation or how this article I wrote wasn't 'polished' enough. One night, we were both working late and he cornered me. Said I should reconsider his offer, how I needed it, needed *him*. Then when he said he'd go to Jason—"

"Jason Brennan." Carson's face colored.

"President of the agency."

"I know. I cosign Whitestone's checks."

"There's a VP position open. I was hoping to land it. But now? Carson, I can't afford to lose my job." Did he understand what that would mean? If Yost and Brennan fired her, getting *any* other PR job would be difficult. Agencies gossiped worse than sororities. They'd blackball her.

"He threatened to 'out' you to your boss. Why would Brennan listen to him and not you?"

She snickered bitterly. "How long have you been in this town? It's a guy's network. If anyone would be ostracized, it would be me. I couldn't take that chance. But then I thought of something."

He cocked his head.

"I'd show him I wasn't *really* a submissive. Maybe then he'd back off. Go find someone else."

"So you came to the club last night to meet him to…fail?"

"I guess so, when you put it that way."

"Under the law this is blackmail. It *will* stop." The finality of his words terrified her. She shouldn't have told him any of this. But when he held her like this, his large hands on her hips, his cock pressed into her most needy, disobedient place, she found it impossible to suppress the truth.

"No, please, my work will find out, and then they'll find out about you—" Her words stopped when he grasped her cheeks in each of his palms.

"London. The Tribunal is more powerful than you know. He's a potential club member and will be dealt with accordingly."

"That won't stop anyone from firing me."

"You'd be surprised."

Surprised? This Tribunal he talked about would have to produce a miracle. Washington's currency was influence. No one liked admitting they didn't have it, and they'd go to the ends of the earth to maintain whatever corner of the power grid they believed they owned. Michael Headler would crush her career forever because of one fact. He'd failed with her. He wouldn't allow his disaster to stand.

She laid her head on Carson's shoulder. "Carson? Can we not talk?"

He cocked his head as if appraising her state. "You should sleep, London."

"No, please." She pushed her pelvis into Carson's firm crotch. Even angry, the man sported a perpetual half hard-on.

A few beats of silence fell between them, his dark eyes assessing her. *Or making me wait.*

"Please. It will ... help."

"Stand." His voice switched from concerned investigator to stern Master in a second. It was a subtle, but significant, difference. One man wanted to know things, the other knew everything already.

She did what he asked and stood ... and waited.

His eyes burned new trails over her body. She didn't

mind. For the first time in her life, she didn't mind being watched. *So long as it's Carson.*

He unhooked his belt from around her hips and let it fall to the floor. "Now, take off everything but your panties."

"Yes, sir." This is what she wanted. *No talking.*

After stripping down to her panties, now damp with new arousal, he clutched her hips and pulled her closer. His fingers dug into a bruise and she winced. She liked the gentle reminder of their scene.

He trailed kisses down her low belly to her feminine ache. As his tongue reached out to touch her growing heat, she moaned. He grew more aggressive, teething and tonguing her captive opening. Who cares if the psychological experts said never to use sex to fix problems? Those people probably didn't have problems. They certainly didn't have their hands on Carson's hard, broad shoulders like she did right at that moment. If they had ... *Oh, God.* He caught her around the thighs and continued to suck through the fabric until she buckled into his hold. Before she could peak, he stopped and lifted her off her feet with his impossible strength. More pain lanced through her tanned ass as he let her slide down the length of his body and through the loop of his arms. It made her want him—between her legs, hot and hard.

He must have had the same idea, as he carried her into the bathroom. Seconds later she found herself nude under cascading water in her shower, her bare skin to his bare skin. Carson barely fit under her showerhead, but it didn't deter his movements.

"Turn around," he said. Splashing sounds echoed as he lathered up her French milled soap bar—one of the few luxuries she allowed herself. He kneaded her shoulders and soon cinnamon-and-orange-scented streams of water sluiced down her back.

"Such beautiful stripes you have, London." She wiggled

her ass against him in reply and he laughed. "My ass." He pinched one of the welts and she yelped.

He moved his attention to her breasts, hands molding down her belly and into her crotch. As he washed her front with his hands, she sent her hands back to touch his legs brushing against the back of her thighs. *So hard.* He had to do push-ups and squats in his office all day to maintain such muscle tone.

"Hands on the wall," he said.

Her upper body leaned forward and her palms settled on the cool tile. He caressed her butt with slick hands. Her trance at such lavish handling stopped when he roughly separated her cheeks, like someone inspecting merchandise. Her pussy clenched at the thought, and her lower back arched in response. When his finger drew a small circle over her back hole, she pushed into his touch until his fingertip dipped inside a millimeter. She gasped at the intrusion, but was proud she'd captured him.

Her moment of superiority was short-lived.

While he didn't remove his finger, his other hand moved to her front and grasped her throat. Her arousal spiked again at his message. *I'm in control.* He gave a gentle squeeze on her neck, as if he wanted to make sure she understood his complete meaning.

She couldn't help herself. She clamped down on his finger lodged in her backside. She groaned at the understanding that—in this moment—Carson *was* in charge. He claimed ownership of her body. *So, this is what it feels like.* She almost came at the thought.

He suckled her shoulder as his teeth lightly sunk into her skin. His finger pressed into her backside more. Unrecognizable, carnal sounds from her throat bounced off the wall. Her past experience with anal sex was minimal and unpleasant—something degrading to live through to please a man. But when Carson inserted a second, soaped-up finger, her whole sex plunged into an overwhelming neediness.

Just when she thought she couldn't take anymore, he let go of her throat and moved to her clit. She lost herself in pure sensation. She could barely keep her hands on the wall. She wanted to grasp his body somewhere, anywhere. Only his intention kept her hands firmly attached to the tile and away from him.

Something else danced around the edges of her mind. Something *important*. But she couldn't think anymore—because she was coming.

When her orgasm subsided, his fingers slipped free. His arm banded around her waist to keep her upright as he pressed her further into the wall.

Rhythmic lapping sounds filled the shower. Without having to see him, she knew he slicked up his cock. Would he take her right here and now? *Yes, do it.*

He turned her so her front connected with him. His cock slipped between her legs. She squeezed her thighs together to capture his hardness, to rub herself back and forth. Another orgasm built just from her thoughts of him slamming her against the wall to complete his possession.

The damned mind reader chuckled and grasped her ass, which smarted a little from the hot water beating against her bruises and welts. She liked it. Just like at the club, she yearned to lean into the pain. He held her tight, not letting her wiggle and move to rekindle the sensations.

His eyes locked on hers. "Not yet. Back against the wall. Legs spread. Hands overhead." He released his hold and his eyes dared her to disobey. But nothing on God's green earth could cause her to defy Carson in that moment. Her world relied on pleasing him. Pleasing him brought thrilling consequences.

She reconnected with the wall, the cool surface calming

the fiery parts of her ass. She widened her stance and raised her hands, crossing her wrists above her head.

Carson kept his eyes on her face while he washed himself, excruciatingly slowly. He ran his hands down his arms, over his chest and legs. He took hold of his cock and ran his hand up and down its length. Need trickled down her legs. She felt raw, dirty and so turned on by her own stance—and his motions—she couldn't stay still.

She dropped her eyes to the engorged, red mushroom head of his cock. A desire to take him in her mouth, touch the deepest parts of her throat, overtook her senses.

"Kneel." He must have understood her overwhelming hunger to feast on his erection.

She dropped to her knees and reached for his legs, mouth open. He grasped her head and forced her gaze to his face.

"Hands behind your back. Grab your forearms." His voice wasn't angry, irritated or even stern. It held the same conviction that pulled her into this utopia last night. *Say yes,* he'd said. She wasn't sure she could give a different answer to Carson Drake ever again. Yes. Always yes for my...

"Now, London."

She boxed her arms and blinked up at him.

"I'm going to use your mouth. All of it. Confirm," he growled.

She nodded and opened her mouth in reply.

While one hand kept a firm grip on her head, the other guided his cock, now rinsed clean of soap, between her lips. He slowly worked himself into her mouth. The tip of his erection went as far as she'd ever taken a man. When her throat clenched, he eased out a little. She didn't want him to back off, so she suckled the underside with her tongue to urge him forward.

The smile in his eyes was all she needed to suck harder. A moan rumbled in his throat. A heady sense of accomplishment from his obvious approval made her want to grasp his legs and pull him deeper. She wanted to undo him.

His hands held her head and, inch by inch, he thrust deeper. Her throat opened fully. He growled and she almost came from the sheer force of his driving. Digging her fingernails into her forearms to stop herself from reaching out, she concentrated on his use of her mouth. And he did use her, harshly and fully. She couldn't hold herself back. She exploded, her cries muffled by his own release jetting down her throat.

As soon as he pulled himself out, he eased her up and shut off the water. "So good and so bad at the same time. Now, what should I do with you?"

Anything you want.

10

Carson hadn't seen London's masochistic streak at first. But now? How far and deep it ran was unknown. Their run-in with Headler required a course correction. She needed to remember she was safe—again.

After assessing London's marks from their former play, he determined where he needed to be careful and where the bruising might add to her enjoyment. He had to take her slowly tonight. No matter she enjoyed pain. She needed time to recover.

He sat her in an old-fashioned desk chair found under a pile of her clothes. He positioned her legs so one hung over each armrest.

"Keep those pretty thighs spread wide." His words earned a half smile from her lips.

He bound her with scarves found hanging off the back of her closet door. Each leg dangled over a chair arm and allowed him to secure her wrists to her ankles. He stepped back to admire the full view of her spread, sexual treasure.

The small curls around her sex glistened with moisture. If

he'd known London grew instantly wet from bondage and the anticipation it brought, he'd have come in his pants every time she drew out her laptop's power cord in a meeting.

He tuned in to the finer details of her form. The fine curve of her bottom lip quivered in longing, and her skin glowed in the low light. At any time, any man would consider London a beautiful woman. Tonight, she rivaled any female who ever lived, any mythical deity immortalized in songs and poems. How could any man resist?

Another item slipped to the top of London's List. *Goddess.*

Before he lost himself in her pleading eyes, he tied another scarf around her head. When blindfolded, she'd melt faster and farther into all the pleasure he planned to give. He then sat down in a chair across from his beauty.

"London, remember last night when I said I'd like to taste you, mix your flavors with wine?"

"Yes." She smiled, her cheekbones rising. She cocked her head when he pulled the cork from a bottle he'd found in her wine rack. "I've opened your 2006 Scott Paul Audrey Pinot."

"I was saving that for a special occasion."

"Then I chose wisely." He poured the wine into the large goblet he found at the top of her cabinets. She obviously didn't entertain often. The glass had been tucked high above her reach.

He took a sip and swirled the exquisite liquid over his tongue. He released it down his throat. "Excellent."

"Do I get any?" Her lips pulled into a smile.

"Oh, yes, sweetness. You're going to get some, and more."

He dropped to his knees and took another draw of wine. After swallowing, the flavors still on his tongue, he placed his mouth on her opening. She sucked in air and arched her back.

"Ah," she cried as his mouth worked her sex. Her head

lolled backward and her soft keening sounds urged him on. He dragged her hips forward another inch, giving him access to all her pleasure points. By the time his tongue rimmed her back opening, she moaned and writhed on the chair, tugging at the scarf bonds. When he moved back to her clit, she was so wet, loud sucking sounds filled the room from his work.

She lifted her head when he stopped abruptly. "W-what?"

"Patience, sweetness." He rose and set himself back in his chair. After sipping more wine, he leaned into her for a kiss. He released the pinot into her mouth and a small drip of red wine escaped down her chin. He lapped at it like a puppy.

"More?" He pressed his mouth against her lips again. "Or more of this?" He thrust a finger into her willing pussy.

"More of everything." Her mouth held that same determination he'd seen in business meetings. Yes, he'd been blind about London.

He remembered the first time she walked into his boardroom, hand outstretched as if to say, *I'm not afraid of you.* Her strength and resolve had overridden her need to surrender. Conflict was inevitable for most alpha submissives. The need to yield had to cohabitate with their need to control their own destiny. But someone like London—with her past? The stress must have been unbearable.

Now he knew the price she'd paid when she said yes to his proposal last night. It had to have been hard, not knowing if he'd understand, honor her struggle and show her a way through.

He knelt and took custody of her pussy. No one *owned* London Chantelle. But if she required possession—even for a while—he'd oblige.

Carson proved his magic once more. Time stopped. Her life was again measured in orgasms he granted. He brought her up to the edge, pulled back to ease her downward, and then brought her up again. He'd spend a few minutes nipping her neck, her bottom lip and her collarbone. He'd then return south to drive her mad—until her very existence lay between her legs.

Finally, her legs quaked so badly, she pleaded for relief. I don't beg, she'd told him. *But I do.*

He kneaded the underside of her legs, indented from the harsh chair legs. Fabric released from her head. Her eyesight homed in on his erection, now pointed northward with want. She licked her lips. "Carson, please."

"Yes, baby." He gently put her legs down. She noticed he was careful to avoid the angry red marks from his merciless caning.

He laid her on the bed. "On your stomach. Lift."

After scrunching a pillow underneath her ass so it rose high in the air, he forced her knees apart. Carson's back connected with hers and he breathed into her hair. "What do you need?"

More. "Please, let me ... you." She could barely speak. She lifted her ass as words failed to express how much she wanted him to take from her.

He reached into his bag and pulled out some items. A pressure against her anus made her grunt. She relaxed her back channel as his lubed finger dipped inside. A thrill ran down her legs at his returned attention to her backside.

Another bottle snapped open. Carson rubbed something cool on her hurt spots. *He worries about me.* His care made her eyes prick.

Wet, slick sounds soon followed the tear of a condom packet. She pressed her ass back toward him in invitation.

She craved the pleasure and pain this man inflicted. She wanted to be of service to her man. *Mine.*

He took renewed guardianship of her clit—*his* clit. Small circles. Moaning. His slick and hard cock. A harsh pinch to her ass.

"Easy," he said when she tensed as a second finger entered her. She pushed backward to capture him deeper. He twisted his fingers slightly while quickening his other fingers over her clit. The pain and pleasure she craved returned. Could she ever live with one without the other again? Who'd want to?

His cock pressed against her back opening. "Open up for me," he whispered. As he breached her muscle, she cried out at the sharp pain. He returned his fingers to her swollen nerve center. Juices flowed down her legs and she rocked her hips backward. She needed to pitch into the agony, feel it everywhere. He'd called her a phoenix. *So, burn me.*

As she writhed and he worked himself into her more, she moaned at the indescribable feeling of fullness.

He grasped both her hips when she began to undulate harder. But only when he fisted her hair and yanked her head backward did pleasure spike inside, hard and fast.

"Squeeze down on me hard," he bit out. She clasped his cock with muscles she'd never known she had. The clenching ignited her desire further, and his hard use of her ass pushed her into yet another new zone. She wanted his cock to the hilt, as if anything less meant failure. She'd had no idea being impaled in such a carnal way would feel so good—like wild animals mating instinctively.

When his balls finally banged against her backside, she knew she'd come in seconds, violently. Guttural sounds filled her bedroom, from both their throats. She was close, so close.

"You'll come when I say," he rasped. His words delivered a

torture that shoved her violently toward orgasm. She snarled through clenched teeth.

"Hold it." He pulled her back so she sat in his lap, now impaled on his length. She tightened her back channel once more. Little waves of pain around her opening made her gasp for air.

"Now, London. Come *now*." His words set off a detonation. She grasped his wrist and tuned in to his strength as her own wail deafened her. Only the pulsing in her rear told her he'd joined her freedom.

"Easy baby." He pressed her down to the bed so she lay on her stomach. Gasping for air, she felt a sore, slow pull as he left her body. His bag rustled by the side of the bed. Cool wipes touched her bruised behind. His hands were then … gone. *Water running. Carson? Don't leave me.*

Carson's silhouette filled her bathroom doorway. "London?"

He returned to her side and tenderly cleaned her up with a warm washcloth. After dropping the cloth to the floor, he pulled the bedcover down and he eased himself under to scoop her into his arms. Carson pulled her close and she dissolved into his body. She whispered who he was to her into the air—who he *really* was. He leaned up on his elbows and took her face.

"What did you say?"

Her eyes moistened. *"Master."*

~

Carson sat on the edge of the bed. He'd eased away from her body reluctantly. But he had to get word to Alexander. After what he had learned from London tonight, he should have called Alexander immediately. But London had needed him first.

Her beliefs about herself had been taxed in the last day and night. Add an altercation about her brother's care and Michael Headler's nonsense, and anyone would have careened off a cliff. But not his London. *His.*

She slowly turned over, and her hands seemed to search for him in her sleep. He honestly, never in a million years, believed he'd find a woman to put up with his ass for very long. Now he'd been chosen. London had called him Master. He nearly came unglued at her naming him.

He scrubbed his fingers through his hair. No matter she had called *him* Master, her control over him was undeniable.

He studied the dark floor and slowly shook his head. *Truth time.* Real men don't lie, not even to themselves. *But you have—for years.* Man, he hadn't been living for the last few years. He'd measured teaspoons of his attention bound with caveats and rules and timetables and for what? To ensure his own safety. *Untouchable.* Just like London—though for vastly different reasons. Well, no more preemptive strikes.

He dragged himself out to the living room. He picked up his pants from the floor and retrieved his cell phone.

London had battled through life alone for too long, always the white knight for those she loved. Who championed her? Who rescued her? His jaw firmed. Headler couldn't touch London tonight, but *he* would damn well reach out and touch him.

Her cell phone vibrated on the coffee table. Michael's name flashed on the screen and then disappeared. Another noise showed he'd texted her.

He had no time to deliberate. What he was about to do might be considered prying. Well, London was under his protection now. With one swipe of his finger, he pulled up Headler's message. A picture appeared. He turned down the volume and tapped the image. A video. London on all fours.

Blindfolded. Shaking. Headler's voice. One word typed below. *Remember.*

He stopped himself from crushing the phone in his hand.

Headler had just moved into new blackmail territory. Carson would fucking destroy him.

After forwarding the video to himself, he then sent it to Alexander. *Watch this. Tribunal acts or I do.*

He quickly erased the video from London's phone and blocked all calls and texts from Michael. He'd figure out how to address his phone takeover with London later.

He sent his gaze back to the open bedroom door. Her breathing was barely audible, but he knew from this moment forward he could pick it out of a screaming match in Parliament.

His phone shuddered. *Tribunal reconvenes tomorrow. Four p.m.*

Not enough to tamp down the rage he felt, but Alexander's message was a start. He'd make them act. A training session with Sarah? Headler didn't deserve her attention or a second chance. If he had his way, the man wouldn't have a future, not in Washington, not anywhere. Now knowing the extent of the man's transgressions, he would be evicted from London's life and any other future victim's—forever.

A plan spun in his mind. He'd persuade London to visit Benny tomorrow. He would go to the Tribunal meeting, where Headler's future would be determined. Any claims on her would be dissolved.

His phone buzzed with another message from Alexander. *About time you fell in love.*

His insides should have clenched down in annoyance at the man's assumption. Instead, he chuckled at his insight. He rubbed his eyes. "Fuck me."

A slight rustle sent his gaze up. London stood in the

doorway, wearing nothing but a sheet. "You weren't there. When I woke up."

"I'm here." He ushered her back to bed, where he might never leave. London's safety was all that mattered. He would do anything for this woman.

11

London picked up another fried doughnut—her fourth. A house specialty, Carson had said. The homemade confections were so good, they should have been illegal.

Carson buttered another biscuit and set it on her plate. "I can't believe you've lived in Washington for eight years and you've never had brunch at the Tabard Inn. I'm going to identify all the places you *should* have gone to in your first five years of living here. Anything you haven't tried, we'll do."

"We will?"

"It's the least I can do. My PR rep needs to be worldly, to be sophisticated and to understand this town inside and out."

"Oh, yes, I guess you're right." Her heart sunk a little at his attention to her career, even though at the moment her work life required more help than any other part of her life.

"I'll add a few special places, certain attractions not everyone knows about. Or *needs* to know." He squeezed her knee and renewed hope returned.

She licked cinnamon sugar off her lip and nervously glanced about the crowded room. People might see his possession of her leg. Of course his hand had barely left her thigh since they sat down.

When they'd arrived at the Inn, he'd pulled her from his car's front seat into a slight hug. He'd kept his hand on the small of her back up the short steps. He held her hand all the way to the table, seemingly unconcerned about the gazes that followed their every move.

She never used to like being manhandled in public. But she loved Carson's constant touch. Her panties dampened at the mere memory of his treatment.

A table nearby seemed particularly interested in whatever Carson did. One woman with wispy white hair kept leaning back in her chair, as if trying to listen to their conversation.

"You know a lot of people here, don't you?" she asked.

"D.C. likes its traditions. Nearly all the same people come here every weekend." He lifted his chin to a gray-haired man across the room who nodded his recognition to Carson. "You liked your biscuits and gravy?"

"I don't usually eat this much in one sitting." *Or in a month.* She put her hand on her belly, now pressing against the thin fabric of her dress—a pale yellow gauze that had always made her feel feminine, almost delicate. When she stepped out of her bedroom in the dress, Carson's smile showed approval. She liked that her choice pleased him.

He lifted his mimosa. "To doing things differently."

She clinked her glass against his and swallowed the remains. "I also don't drink on Sunday mornings."

"What do you typically do?"

"Go see Benny."

"That's next on the agenda."

She was surprised he'd think of such a thing. "Really?"

"Of course. Whatever you need, London."

She twisted her napkin in her lap. "So, it's Sunday."

"So it is." He finished his drink and set it down. "You're wondering about our weekend. It ending."

"A little."

One side of his mouth lifted. "Well, given we were so rudely interrupted yesterday, I'd say you owe me at least another day."

"I'm sorry about yesterday. I mean, it was a lot to be dumped on you."

He placed his hand over hers. "Nothing that happened is your fault."

A waiter dropped the check in a small black portfolio next to Carson, and he removed his hand. The release of warmth had a greater effect than she liked.

"Um, Carson?"

He signed his name and looked up at her. "Yes? Need something else?"

"No, I mean, maybe." She let her lashes fall to her cheeks. She couldn't look him in the face. She didn't want to have to ask what she wanted to ask. She didn't want to *feel* what she felt. But a well of emotion had lodged itself in her heart and threatened to tear her apart if left to grow anymore. *Why was this so hard?*

So much had happened since Friday, when she and Carson fought over her proposal. Suddenly, work seemed very far away, yet so close. She still cared about her job. Given her life, she couldn't afford *not* to care. But Carson evoked a kind of hope for something different, something other than the path she'd carved.

For two years her sole focus had been climbing up the career ladder. *For Benny's sake.* But now? With Carson's eyes casting concern down on her, she wondered what it might be like to consider something more.

The assumption was dangerous. She'd learned long ago

not to want more than she had. She looked up at the man who was most definitely more than she'd ever dreamed.

Carson's eyes sparkled. "You want more than one day."

"Yes, and I don't know what to do with that. So, you can drop me off at Southland. I know you don't do long term. So, let's just finish things off on a good note. Not pretend and make it any more awkward—"

"No." His hand clutched the edge of her chair, and with a loud groaning scrape across the tile, pulled her closer. Several heads turned to look at them, including Miss Nosey at the next table. Carson didn't notice or seem to care.

Foolish tears pooled in her eyes under his regard. He ran his thumb under one eye and captured a few before they fell. "None of that." He grasped her hands.

"Don't worry. I'm not trying to manipulate you into anything or—"

"I know." He tipped her jaw up. "You haven't done that haughty chin thing in a while. I kind of miss it."

"I doubt that."

He laughed. "London, did you know the weekend was a made-up chunk of time, invented by a New England cotton mill to give certain workers two days off between five-day work weeks? Before the early 1900s, no one knew what a weekend was."

She smiled. "Sounds like something the business world would invent. Things were simpler before our jobs became so important."

"Exactly. We should do the same. No weekend. No weeks. Just time."

"Friday, when we first got together, you said you wanted three things. One was time."

"Yes. Your time."

"And now?"

"I want you all the time."

"All the time?" She had to repeat his words, to let them sink in fully.

"Yes."

Tears welled on her lids. Her resolve to go back to her life—the one she crafted so carefully—withered under the heat of his gaze. She twisted the linen napkin in her lap, back and forth until it nearly ripped in her hands. "I-I'd like that."

He stood up and held out his hand, which she took. "Good. Let's go see your brother."

A strange, floaty feeling took over her legs. For the umpteenth time this weekend, she was unsteady on her feet. Carson's hold around her waist helped her with her balance. She looked up at him as he moved her toward the door. When he smiled down on her, the clouds in her mind parted. *Oh. I'm happy.* She hadn't been happy in so long she almost didn't recognize the feeling.

~

Carson scored one of the three visitors' parking spots in the tiny outdoor lot. An uncomfortable feeling crawled over his skin. Why so few cars? While they avoided the depressing, dank garage underneath the building, he didn't like that it meant no one was visiting the people inside Southland Rehab. They needed visitors.

He vowed London would get to visit Benny as often as she liked. Once he figured out how to get her into a new job, away from Michael Headler, he'd be sure she had anything she desired.

He clutched her hand all the way to the elevator. *Like family.* In a moment of pure bliss, he pulled her closer to his body while they waited for the elevator to arrive. He wasn't sure what being with London "all the time" entailed. He'd never been good at relationships. But if he could negotiate a multimillion-dollar contract, ensuring all possible future scenarios were covered, he could figure out how to be with someone *not* temporarily.

When they stepped off the elevator, the familiar sickening scent washed over him like a foul tide. How long did Benny have to stay at Southland? Why hadn't they found a halfway house or other better establishment? He added correcting Benny's situation to his to-do list for the week. It felt good to have something meaningful to do for a change.

London tore away from him. "Let me go in first, see how he's doing. Join me in five minutes?"

He smiled at her nurturing side. *She'd be good with children.* Jesus, he'd made some leaps in his mind, oh hell, his heart, rather quickly. "Sure, baby. I'll be down in a sec."

She bounced down the hallway. He hoped he was the reason she moved lighter than he'd ever seen her.

A gruff male voice interrupted his appreciation of London. "Sir, only family is allowed on Sundays."

"Throw me out, then." He didn't even turn to look at the latest rent-a-cop guarding people who no one cared to visit in the first place.

"Carson Drake?"

He turned to look at the man who called his name. "George Johnson?"

"I thought I recognized you yesterday. How the hell ya been man?" The large black man pounded his back in a hug.

The last time he had seen George, Carson worked for the DA. George had run into some legal trouble. He recalled the man was more concerned that his girlfriend wouldn't marry him than about going to jail. *I thought he was crazy.* He now understood at a level he didn't know existed before.

"Fine. How are you? What's happening with Tanya?" he asked, hoping he got her name right.

George waved his hand, showing off his wedding ring. "Got a second baby on the way."

"Congratulations. Got the girl and the family." A deep spike of happiness speared his chest.

"I'm blessed, man. Great family. Good job."

He scoffed. "This place is depressing."

"Ah, it's not so bad. They're really trying to help."

"Really? You're not lying to me?"

"No, man, the docs are good."

"Thanks. I needed to hear that today." He looked down the hallway into the vortex that had sucked London away from him.

"Whattaya doing here?" George asked.

"Seeing a new friend. Benny Chantelle."

"Oh, the architect. Yeah, Benny."

"The what?"

"Benny likes to build things. He'd always wanted to be an architect, before, you know, things took a turn for the worse. Good man. A little mixed up in the head, that's all. Hey, you ever settle down? Benny's got a hot sister." George winked at him.

"Yes, I know."

"Oh, no, you tapping that thing?" He must have sent George a deadly look as the man stepped back a little. "Hey, joking. Man, you got it bad."

"I don't know what I've got."

"Oh, you do. Takes one to know one. You're in love." George cocked his head. "Come on, the nurses won't bother you if I escort you down there. They like me here."

Carson knew he wasn't bragging. The man's affability was palatable. Why hadn't he noticed it before?

When they reached Benny's room, George took him by the arm. "Approach slowly. You tend to charge forward like a bull. Good lawyer skill, but—"

Untouchable

"Not so good with people."

"Well, you got the hot sister to go out with you. You musta done something right. She never looks at anyone." George laughed and turned his gaze to a nurse trying to get his attention.

He looked into Benny's room. Where was London?

Benny sat hunched over a table. He pressed the pencil so hard to the piece of paper before him, the tip broke. "Dammit." He didn't seem to notice anyone was about to breach his personal space—full of clothes and magazines strewn around his bed.

He could see Benny had drawn a series of buildings, one to each piece of paper, now scattered around his chair. Each one contained a series of transparent boxes floating in space.

He cleared his throat. "That's a good city you've built."

Benny looked up and scraped his chair back. "London?"

"Not sure. Do you know where she is?" He nearly backed out of the doorway to go look for her, when Benny beckoned him closer. "I'm building a house."

"Like Philip Johnson?"

"You know him?"

"Yes, the glass house." He glanced over Benny's house plans. Long lines. Meticulous. "I've always wanted to build. To get the right proportions, the right space."

"People don't understand proportion anymore. They all want to build a house to match overstuffed furniture." Benny scrubbed his scalp.

"Like Pottery Barn."

"I hate that place."

"Yeah, no subtlety." As if he was the king of refinement. "But the Washington Design Center..."

"Yeah."

He was talking furniture with a bipolar suicide case?

141

London's brother. A sense of responsibility for Benny's well-being took him by surprise.

"So, this house you're designing. For you and London?" He sat down next to Benny.

"Someday. I started at SCI-Arc. Then ..."

"You've got talent."

Benny didn't say anything, but instead bent back over his paper. "She likes you," Benny said. The sudden turn in conversation almost didn't compute.

"You think?" *She does?* His heart moved inside his chest at the thought that London *liked* him. *What are you, in seventh grade?* Perhaps he was pitched back into junior high. His emotions certainly hadn't been as messy since those days. *Until now.*

"She never introduced me to anyone before." Benny fiddled with his pencil.

Carson didn't know why, but he felt like he'd just been knighted.

"She likes you more," he said.

Benny smiled and turned back to his drawing. Several minutes passed before he realized London was still missing.

"Benny, I'm going to go get your sister."

He walked the hallways. He found the ladies' room tucked into a corner, locked. He asked an exiting nurse about London. She simply shrugged.

He was about to retrace his steps when London's voice echoed down the hall. *Distressed. Arguing.*

He ran down the corridor and found a small lounge—stained chair cushions, a sagging couch and magazines haphazardly strewn across a cheap wooden coffee table. London stood in the middle of the room, arms crossed. She sent a seething look to Michael Headler.

When Michael reached for her arm, Carson had his hands around the man's neck in seconds. He pushed him into a row of chairs lining the far wall. "How the hell did you get in here?"

"Hey, let-let go," Michael managed to gasp.

London's hands were on his back. "Carson. We were just talking!"

A pair of brawny arms wrenched Carson's neck hold loose from the man. George had pulled him backward. Michael sputtered and dropped into the chair under him.

"Mr. Drake, sir, calm down," George said.

"Get out of my way, George. Or so help me God—"

"Or, what? You gonna defend yourself in criminal court?"

He took one step backward and assessed George's calm face. He wasn't used to losing his temper quite so baldly, or so often like he had this weekend. He certainly wasn't used to having the obvious pointed out to him.

"Now everyone back down for a minute. You okay, Miss Chantelle?" George peeked around him.

"I'm fine, George. Thanks."

"Well, I'm not. Thanks for checking in." Michael coughed a few times.

"Who are you?" George asked him.

"A friend of London's."

Carson stepped forward. His chest connected with George's hand.

"More like her blackmailer," he spat. "I know what you've done."

Michael huffed out a laugh and shook his head. "If that's what she's told you, London has a greater imagination than I thought. Though I'm beginning to see her skills have been overrated." He stood up and arched his back like the peacock he was.

Carson caught the veiled threat. "Don't even think about it, Headler. Her job is not in question. Your ability to avoid jail, however—"

"Carson, stop." London's angry voice was the solitary thing that could have stopped him from setting Michael back down on his ass.

"Let's take this outside." Carson glanced at George. "It's a ... private matter."

Michael rubbed his chin. "London, you didn't get my text?"

"No. My purse must still be in the car." London sighed. "Michael, I'm sorry—"

"Don't you apologize to him." He knew he'd given London a harder look than she deserved. But when she raised her chin, he recognized he'd gone too far. He tried to soften his voice. "London, this man cannot threaten your job or your ability to advance because you don't want to date him." He'd used the PG phrasing for George's sake. "And he certainly shouldn't have shown up here."

"She wasn't at home, so I knew she'd be here. Wanted to get a jump start on our conversation before Monday."

He stared daggers at Michael. He knew this game. "More like you didn't want anyone at the office to hear your threats or inappropriate actions. If you ever go to her house again, I swear to God—"

"Threatening me?"

"Good. We understand each other."

"Stand down, men." George crossed his arms and looked over at London. "Miss Chantelle, you're a nice lady. But we're going to have to take this outside. We don't want to be upsetting the patients."

"Of course, George, thank you." She jerked her head at Carson and Michael.

"I'll be accompanying you all." George held out his hand. They followed him down the hallway until they reached Benny's room.

London paused. "George, will you see they get out okay? I'm going to Benny."

"I'm staying with you," Carson said. "Headler can go with George."

"No, Carson. I need you both to leave." Each word was wrapped in tension.

Benny stood up, but didn't advance. That same distrust he'd seen yesterday colored his eyes. "So many." He backed up.

"It's okay, Benny. They're not staying," London said.

"Hi, Benny. I'm Michael." Headler moved into the room before anyone could stop him and snaked toward London's brother.

Benny screeched and backed up against the wall. "Not taking me, not going, not going!"

George was behind Michael in seconds. "Man, what the hell you doin'?" He half-dragged Michael back and out of the room.

Benny screamed. Carson's heart nearly stopped from hearing the sound of pure terror emitting from Benny's mouth. London rushed forward, but Benny had slumped to the floor

"It's okay. I'm here, Benny. Listen to me. It's me. I'm here." London tried to hug her brother. But the petrified man punched and kicked, trying to move further back, only to be stopped by the wall.

Carson had no choice. He yanked London away before she'd be pummeled by her own brother. "Wait, get back."

"No, let me go!" London's strength was no match for him, but she fought so hard he finally had to let her go or risk her getting hurt. She dropped to her knees and pulled Benny into a hug. He stopped his yelling and rocked back and forth.

Carson didn't know what to do. So he stood there, like a

third wheel, witnessing London wrestle with her brother's demons. Helpless. Ineffectual. *Again.*

Shoe squeaks in the hallway grew nearer. Two orderlies stood behind him in seconds. They ran around him like he was nothing more than a piece of furniture in the way.

London raised her hand. "Back off. I refuse care. Thank you." The two men straightened. Renewed respect for London's deft handling of the orderlies surged through his whole body. *Add it to London's List.*

"We'll be just outside," the taller one said. The other crashed into Carson's shoulder on his way out. They barely moved him. But the warning was clear. He better not create any trouble. They were in charge.

But they weren't. London held the floor.

"Carson." George had stepped up behind him.

"Does he get like this a lot?" he asked, never taking his eyesight off the brother and sister on the floor.

"No. But strangers, especially men, scare him. Miss Chantelle, need me to get the doc?"

"No, George. Benny will be okay. Give us a bit? Make sure Thing One and Thing Two stay outside." Carson would have laughed at her viewpoint of the two orderlies but her eyes held so much sadness, his eyes pricked.

"Carson. Wait for me in the parking lot. I'll be down as soon as I know Benny's settled." She smoothed hair off the man's damp forehead. Benny's eyes had glazed and his breathing labored. But at least he wasn't screeching like he'd just descended into hell. Something told Carson he'd landed there long ago.

12

George leaned so heavily on the car hood of Carson's Aston Martin, he'd likely leave a dent. Carson couldn't have cared less. George pulled out a pack of cigarettes and offered one to him. He shook his head, though if he'd ever had the inclination to smoke, today would've been a perfect day to start.

"Miss Chantelle's got a lot on her plate."

"Yes." He knew George meant well. But he wasn't about to get into London's life with him, no matter the guard's intentions. Once he started, he'd wind up into such a ball of rage he might punch the first person he saw, including George.

He thought he'd tamed his temper long ago thanks to daily strenuous workouts and the help of good friends like Alexander and Jonathan. Yet this weekend, the usual control he'd fought so hard to build had slipped—repeatedly. He hadn't let anyone get under his skin like Michael Headler in years.

"Don't you need to go back to work, George?"

"Nah, shift's ended. Besides, got strict instructions from Miss Chantelle. Gotta keep you out here."

He huffed. "George, I need you to do something for me."

"Don't worry about that dandy, if that's what you're wondering. He won't be back. I've seen to it. This place is pretty guarded."

He should have laughed at George's assessment of Michael. *Dandy.* The term fit perfectly. *A man who believed his own press.*

"Counting on you, George. I need you to do something else, too. Go in and ask her to come out?" He rarely asked for help. People came to him. He hated having to ask. But his options had run out.

"Worried she won't?"

"Just a feeling."

George crushed his cigarette under his boot. "If I was you, I'd let her have tonight. Women need their alone time."

"Would you have done that with Tanya?"

He laughed. "Hell, no. But maybe I would've been married to her sooner if I had."

George pushed off the car and lumbered inside.

He checked his watch. One hour until the Tribunal meeting. He tapped out a text to Mark Santos, who had as much access to the private security industry heavy hitters as he did. London's apartment needed to be monitored even though London wasn't going back to that dump. She deserved better. But he'd hoped Headler was the idiot he knew him to be. If he showed up, his presence would add to the harassment charges he'd file first thing tomorrow morning.

He tapped his jacket pocket, where he'd nestled London's phone. He planned to turn it over to Mark. One phone call and his IT specialist contacts would wipe the video from the phone and the cloud.

Damn Headler.

Carson paced like a panther in his cage. *Where was London?*

∼

London took a deep breath before pushing open the door. George had said Carson would spend the night in his car if she didn't at least come down and say something. She didn't want to deal with him right now. But she knew Carson well enough to know he rivaled a pit bull in stubbornness—the same trait Michael had accused her of having.

Why couldn't Carson just give her some time to think? She'd broken so many promises to herself already. The minute she took her eye off the ball—her future—things deteriorated. *Good going, London.* Make it right, she told herself. She had to get Carson to back off so she could make it up to Michael and secure her job. Maybe then she could finagle some way to still be considered for that promotion. She knew what to say to Michael to repair his ego. Her mother had taught her at least that much. *You could do better.*

She blinked into the flat September sunlight and stared at Carson's back. He gazed over the traffic on Washington circle, both hands in his pockets. His black pants drew tightly over his butt. His hair was so dark, in the sunlight it sparkled midnight blue. God, he was gorgeous.

Focus, London. "Carson."

His head snapped around and he strode over to her quickly. He engulfed her in his arms and pressed kisses into the crown of her head. When he circled his hand to the back of her neck, her inner thighs melted.

"How's Benny?"

She pulled back and looked up at his face. "Napping. It's what he does after an episode."

"How are you?"

"Fine."

"No, you're not."

"Fine, then I'm not." She wrenched free. She tried the car

door, but it remained locked. "Carson? Open it please? I need my phone to see Michael's text."

"It's not there. I erased it." He pulled her phone from his jacket pocket.

"What? Give me that."

He placed her phone into her hand. She angrily swiped her finger over the screen. He didn't need to look to know she wouldn't find any messages dated past Friday.

"You didn't need to see the video he sent. Of you. Of your last ... encounter."

Her breath left her body. "He-he ..."

"Taped you. Blindfolded. Bound." Carson caught her around the middle before she had a chance to fold.

"I told you. He's blackmailing you. But don't worry. Alexander has it and—"

"What? You sent it to other people?"

"The Tribunal, which will deal with Michael." He grasped her face in his hands.

No, she had a better plan. She shook her head free. "I need to go see him. I know what Michael wants. He wants to know he's won and—"

"No—"

"Carson—"

"I forbid it," he gritted through his teeth. "You will not go crawling on your hands and knees to the Headler boy."

Forbid? "Excuse me?"

"You aren't going to see Michael and you're not going home. He's probably waiting for you there."

"No, he's probably at the office preparing my termination letter. Forget ever being promoted. Thanks for that by the way."

He grasped her arm. "He can't fire you. I'm meeting with the Tribunal and it will be over. You'll come home with me."

"Still treating me like your sub?"

"You're wearing my belt."

She'd grown so used to wearing his belt, she didn't notice it anymore. She reached for the buckle when his hand stopped her.

"Don't." His eyes narrowed.

She released her hold on the buckle and leveled her gaze on him. Two could play this game. "Submissive's wishes," she said.

"What?"

"Alexander said you had to abide by the submissive's wishes."

"Yes." He circled his hand around her neck and pulled her closer. "What do you need, London?" He ran his fingers across the little dip at the base of her skull. Her pussy tightened and she swallowed. *Not so fast, Carson Drake.* She was capable of making this situation right, with or without a man. Couldn't he see that?

"Stop it!" She pushed against his chest. "Sugar."

He dropped his hands. For the first time she saw pain in his eyes.

She froze in place, not sure what to say next. Oh, God, she didn't mean it. Could she take it back? She only wanted him to stop, to listen to her. But she'd run out of words.

She needed to do this on her own. Why couldn't he see? "C-Carson?" Okay, she managed that much.

"The submissive has spoken, and I'm late for a meeting." He then turned and got into his car. He never looked back.

Her heart, already full of cracks and fissures, broke apart and fell to the pavement.

∼

Carson yanked the door and it banged into the wall. Tony threw him a stern look.

"You ever go home, Tony?" The man seemed to live at his post at Accendos.

"They're waiting for you, sir. Mr. Rockingham and Mr. Wright ..."

Tony's words faded as he marched down the hallway to the Tribunal meeting room. So, London pulled her safeword and bullshit rules on him? He had more up his own sleeve. After texting Mark with a request for surveillance, starting immediately, he felt a little better about leaving her, even temporarily.

He pushed open the door to the Tribunal room a tad gentler than the front door. This time when it connected to the wall, the handle didn't leave a dent.

"I call this Tribunal meeting," he said before even sitting down.

"In a hurry, are we?" Derek asked.

"Well, it is Sunday," Alexander leaned back in his chair and presented his irritatingly calm demeanor. Sarah, Jonathan, Mark and Derek mirrored his stance around the Tribunal table, which raised his ire even more.

Alexander continued. "Given we met twenty-four hours ago, I'll forgo the formalities to go right to our discussion. We're here to discuss the formal charges brought by Tribunal member, Carson S. Drake. He has lodged a complaint against new member, Michael Headler. Our investigation has shown Michael's claim of ownership is—"

"Bullshit," he said.

"False." Alexander threw him a not-unkind look. "Sarah ascertained that Mr. Headler does not understand basic terminology, protocol or any of the basics of such a relationship."

He stood. "This man has gone beyond a simple protocol breach. He has threatened someone under my protection— our protection, Alexander."

"You know what my protection means, Carson."

He nodded. He may have been one of the few people on earth who understood the depth of Alexander's words.

"He shows no sign of stopping. He took a video of her and surely has blackmail plans. He went to her apartment this morning, and when he didn't find her, he showed up at Southland Rehab."

"Southland?" Jonathan asked.

"Her brother is being treated there for suicide attempts." No use sugarcoating what he'd learned.

Genuine concern flooded Jonathan's face. In an odd turn, Carson realized the blessing of his life. He had friends. They sat around this table. London and Benny had only each other. His emotional volcano threatened to erupt at the thought.

"Headler created a scene at Southland. He's been banned. But I don't trust this man to stay away from London."

"They work together?"

"Which is going to be an ongoing problem," Alexander said. "It is *her* work, Carson."

"Headler is blackmailing her. The video, remember?"

"Back up. Video?" Derek looked uncharacteristically stricken. As the owner of twelve nightclubs up and down the East Coast, Derek knew the power of visuals.

Alexander tapped his phone and London's distressed whimper filled the room. Each Tribunal member leaned forward to catch the brief snippet of London, nude and defenseless.

Jonathan leaned back. "What does he want?"

"London back. If she doesn't give in, he's threatened to go to the president of her agency."

"And do what?"

"What do you think, Derek? Sit down with a cup of tea and compare notes on flogger materials." He ran his hands through his hair. "Are you people listening to me? The man is resolute in his ignorance. He doesn't want to learn. He wants—"

"To be right. I'm familiar with that particular brand of ego." A slight twitch in Alexander's face broke the man's cool.

"Has she been harmed? Any residual issues we can help with?" Jonathan sat forward in his chair. Carson knew why he asked. The Tribunal's network of psychological care, medical facilities and physical rehabilitation—all friendly to the BDSM community—rivaled the Mayo Clinic. If London had been injured in any way, she'd receive real help.

"I've got that covered. No victim assistance required. She's going to be fine. But she needs more than words of our protection."

Jonathan slowly nodded. "What do you need?"

"Headler gone. I'll help London with her brother. As for his blackmail? I'll sue his ass from here to eternity if he threatens to reveal this or anything about her, this club or her foray into this lifestyle. She'll get another job. Washington's practically recession proof around employment. But I need to know the Tribunal is taking this seriously. I want Headler neutralized. And assurances he won't talk."

"Sarah?" Alexander nodded to the petite brunette.

Sarah slipped sheets of paper from her leather portfolio and handed everyone a copy.

Carson scanned the paper. "A gag order? Seriously? Then he gets trained by you? Over my dead body."

"Or his." Derek lifted his eyes from the agreement. "Sarah, you're really going to do it? Man, he's in for it." He laughed.

Carson threw the paper, and it floated to rest in the middle of the table. "Unacceptable. You can't train an asshole to be anything but a well-behaved asshole. He'll still talk. Not enough."

"It's what we start with. The three laws, Carson," Sarah said gently.

He shook his head, emotion getting the better of him. "She can't handle this on her own, Alexander."

"Has she asked for your help?"

"If one more person tells me she has to go through anything alone—"

"She asked for you to back off, didn't she?" Derek asked.

"We had an argument, that's all. She said she needed time."

"Then she has spoken." Alexander leaned back in his chair.

"Don't pull that submissive's wishes crap on me. I've heard it enough."

The man smiled. "She learns quickly. Carson, we will handle Headler. In the meantime, you'll honor London's wishes. Mark tells me you requested surveillance. Agreed. But let London have some breathing space."

"Do you realize what you're suggesting, Alexander?" Jonathan turned to the others. "Would any of you be warned off the women you loved?"

"Or man," Sarah said. "No, probably not."

For once Carson didn't mind the two being in cahoots.

"Let her come to you, Carson," Alexander said. "Trust me."

Let her come to me? "No."

Mark finally looked up from his phone. "Surveillance is in place at her apartment and her work. My man followed her home. If Headler shows any signs of getting rough, he will intervene. You have the phone?"

"Not anymore."

"Not needed." Mark said. "I'll get my people on it. Cell phone networks are easily cracked. We'll handle wiping the video from the cloud." God bless Mark. Carson hadn't even had to ask for that help.

"You people scare me," Derek said.

Sarah graced him with a rare smile. "You forget you're one of us."

"Hey, I just come for the group therapy."

"Enough," Carson said. "I'm not sitting around twiddling my thumbs."

Derek raised his chin. "We're not the mafia, man."

"Don't make me go to the mafia."

"Carson." Alexander's voice stiffened everyone in the room.

Alexander rarely pulled rank. But his voice often was enough to remind anyone within earshot who held the greater power. "Sarah will execute this plan. If Headler slips up, even once, you know what that means."

"Siberia," Derek said.

Alexander's eyes pinned Carson to his seat—the lone man in existence who could stop him from doing anything. "You will give London space. Forty-eight hours, no contact unless she initiates it."

"Twenty-four," he countered. He knew he wouldn't win a no-separation ruling.

Alexander nodded once, uncharacteristically acquiescing to his demand. "Tribunal?"

"Agreed," Mark and Sarah said in unison.

"Jonathan?"

"Abstain." He rubbed his chin. "If you'd told me to stay away from Christiana for any reason whatsoever, you'd have had to kill me first."

"Derek?" Alexander asked.

Carson threw him a look he hoped conveyed his feelings. *I'll kill you.*

"Sorry, man. One day? I trust Alexander's gut on this one. Agreed."

Untouchable

Carson walked out on rigid legs, his jaw clenched tight. Twenty-four hours? Twenty-four seconds would be too long.

Mark caught up with him in the hallway. "We'll take care of it. If Headler goes to her—"

"I want it filmed, Mark."

"If he shows up, we'll make him a YouTube star."

～

London's key clicked in her lock. The small snick echoed through her empty living room, the sound releasing the tidal wave of tears she'd dammed for hours.

For the next ten minutes, she would allow her body to feel it all—sorrow and loss and a sharp ache in her bones as if she'd been wrenched from the earth's gravitational pull. *From Carson.*

How could he have walked away so easily? *Because your two days of fantasy are over.*

She laid her head on a small pillow on her couch, instantly wetting it with tears. She let her wails rise to the sky. She didn't care if her neighbors called the cops. *Let it go*, he'd told her when she tried to stuff anything down. So, she did.

After many minutes, she turned to her back and laid her arm over her wet eyes.

She sent her mind back to Friday. Forty-eight hours ago, she sat in Whitestone's boardroom, across from Carson Drake, a man she thought she knew. The man she thought about incessantly, the man whose kiss she wondered about. Now she knew how his lips felt, how they tasted.

She took in a stuttered breath and daydreamed about the last two days. Carson pulling her into a private room. His warrior stance against a crackling fireplace. His proposal.

His hands. His *handling*. Overwhelmed with pleasure, flirting with pain, forgetting her life.

How quickly he had lured her into his world. Was she that easy? Did she care if she was easy? He hadn't shown anything but concern for her. No man had ever taken such care of her, paid such *attention* to her, as Carson. He simplified everything in her life. He had done everything he said he would. Shown her what she always wanted. *Shelter.*

Who are you, your mother? Waiting for a guy to come along and right your world? Ha!

She sat up and pushed hair from her face. No more pity party. *Enough already.*

Her responsibilities swooped in from the recesses of her brain and circled her mind like a vulture. Her two days with Carson were over. With that moment of clarity, she rose from the couch.

She stifled a small smile at the thought that Carson may have just showed her the last thing she needed to know to prove she was vice presidential material. VPs knew when to fight and when to regroup. *Time to right a few things.*

She retrieved her employment contract from her fireproof safe. She wasn't good at reading legalese. But she'd figure out how much she could and could not do under her current obligations. Once she understood her options, she'd make the necessary calls and send the requisite e-mails. Who cared if it was Sunday? In mid-September everyone in PR worked long hours, getting ready for fall trade shows and conventions.

First, she'd call the few people who'd tried to hire her in the past.

Her mind spun her messages into a complete story. *I need more flexibility. Less travel, but I can work seven days a week. I'm single. No children.* And—and here was the money line—she'd never leave Washington. Young people in public relations never stayed in D.C. But she would. *Immoveable. Because I have to be.*

After thirty, headache-inducing minutes puzzling out the legal jargon on her contract, she gave up on deciphering what she could and could not do.

What if she just launched her own freelance company? Be the president instead of a vice president? Maybe Carson would help her? Why would he answer if she'd called anyway? He'd deserved so much better than she gave him in the parking lot.

She spent the next hour fingering her cell phone and not calling him.

What was that stupid saying? 'Tis better to have loved and lost than never to have loved at all? *What a load of crap.*

13

Carson wandered through Club Accendos's master library. Less than a dozen people hung around the main space. Two couples engaged in play, and about six other people leaned against equipment and talked. A lazy end to the weekend. Just like every Sunday he'd spent—alone or in the process of divesting himself of Saturday night's "acquisition." *Because that's how you saw them, right? No wonder London fired your ass.*

For the first time in years, he tuned in to the couples surrounding him. An older man laid a diamond rope pattern over a woman's large breasts. His eyes, a portrait of concentration and dedication, never left the Rubenesque redhead's face. Did he look at London like that? Did it matter anymore?

Katie glanced at him from across the room. She pushed off a red spanking horse and walked toward him. He knew her intention. A sudden revulsion washed over him. His disgust wasn't aimed at Katie. It was because of how he'd seen her before. A woman to play with, service and then release.

He turned away. Not in an effort to be rude, but to treat

her honestly and fairly. In the moment Katie's eyes had met his, he'd known. He would never touch another woman again. He couldn't and remain honest. *Not unless her name was London Chantelle.*

For him, temporary was over for good.

On the way home, he placed a call to Mark to see if London's video had been wiped. Mark assured him any evidence of London would be bagged and tagged for his eyes only in less than twenty-four hours.

He jerked his car around a green sedan meandering up Foxhall Drive. When he rounded the corner of his street, he nearly ran into a car idling in front of his gate. London sat in the front seat of the blue Saturn. Panic set in. He jumped from his car before the gate could fully open. Had Headler shown up? No, he would have gotten a call from Mark. Had something happened to Benny?

"What's wrong?"

"Um, I need to ask you something." London looked alarmed. Probably from his wild-man assault on her car door. "Can we talk?"

"Follow me."

As soon as she parked and stepped out of her car, he grasped her arm. He only let go when they were inside. She crossed her arms over her chest—like that first night he'd pulled her into the private room in Accendos.

"Just talking, remember?" he asked.

She smiled in return. "I remember."

"Living room."

After he settled into his large leather chair, she took the seat opposite him. Another reminder of Friday night—a lifetime ago.

"What do you need?" He knew he sounded pissed. Well, he was.

"I need help deciphering my employment contract." She

161

pulled a document from her bag and handed it to him. "I think the clause I marked says they can't stop me from starting my own business if I don't take any of their clients with me. And I'll need a contract, to sign my first client. Jennings Aerospace."

"Busy Sunday night."

"I've run out of time. Jennings tried to hire me before. My contact there said he could use the consulting help."

He almost winced at her words. "Legal assistance. That's what you want."

"Yes."

He flicked the paper back at her and it floated to the floor between them. "The submissive's wishes?"

She picked up her purse and stood. "I made a mistake. I-I'm sorry ... for what I said before. I didn't mean it. And I probably shouldn't have come."

"Make up your mind, London." His voice echoed in the room. "You're not going to keep doing this."

"Doing what, Carson? Asking for your help? You said that's what a Dom does."

"May I remind you, you liberated yourself from me."

"I-I ..."

"Why are you really here, London?" He stood and she backed up a few steps.

"To apologize. And see if you'd be willing to help. But see? We're fighting. This is why ... why—"

"Why, what?"

"Why we shouldn't do any of this!"

"What's *this*?"

"I don't know!" she cried.

"Love." *Damn.* The word had tumbled from his mouth before he could stop it. Her shocked face told him he'd hit a bull's-eye. "You love me," he said softly.

"I can't." She turned as if to run. *Like hell.*

His front connected to her back, and once again, he relished the perfect fit. He glanced down to see she had on the same grey suede boots she'd worn Friday night.

"Damn you, London Chantelle," he said into her hair.

He allowed her to wrest around to face him but kept his arms around her. "You're angry," she said.

"You're damned right I'm pissed. You've ruined me." He clamped his mouth down on hers, and she yielded to his intruding tongue. She sank in his arms as he kissed her hard, stamping out anything she'd dare say to make him—or herself—retreat.

When he finally did release her lips, he stared down into her brown eyes.

"I ruined *you*?" she asked.

"Completely wrecked."

"Define wrecked." She peeked from under her lashes.

"Head over heels, crazy, stupid—"

"Me, too. When I figured out what to do, start my own business, well, you're the first person I wanted to tell." She flushed his favorite shade again.

"Good. If I let you go, are you going to run?"

"I don't think I'm capable of running from you. You're faster than me," she said with a smirk.

He swatted her behind and she hopped further into his hold. "That's not all."

"Yes, you're my Dom. My *Master*." She said the words without a hint of humor.

His cock stirred to life under her words. "I am. But not your owner."

"What am I?"

"My little phoenix." London's list reduced to that one word. *Phoenix*. A beauty rising from the ashes of her life, something he'd make sure she never had to do again.

He finally released his death grip on her body. Yet she

stayed close, and his heart flooded with love. The man who hadn't gotten involved beyond a weekend with any woman in fifteen years was up to his neck in god-damned love.

∼

London tried to fall asleep, but her mind raced. The idea of what she had to face tomorrow had her unable to rest. Carson's constant erection pressed against her ass as they lay in bed, side by side, didn't help her focus, either.

How does he stay perpetually hard? Less than an hour ago she'd hung on to his forearm as he glided into her slowly from behind. His breath was warm on her neck, and for a time she thought of nothing but his chest hairs tickling her back and his cock pitching so deeply and hard into her, they'd scooted closer to the edge of his massive king-sized bed.

She knew if she stirred too much, she'd end right back in that position. *Carson making love to me.*

Instead of pushing her behind back toward him in invitation, she focused on the plan she and Carson had cooked up before attempting sleep.

She'd take the morning off from work and go into the office after lunch. Jason Brennan's public calendar, accessible by anyone at Yost and Brennan, showed he was free at two p.m. Michael's calendar had shown he was busy until at least one. But she couldn't tell if he'd be in or out of the office later. That fact had Carson insisting he go with her. She acquiesced, provided he waited in her office while she went to Jason. *To quit.*

"I'm not going to be able to sleep," she said into the room. She half-hoped Carson stayed asleep. "I'm rethinking about waiting. I should go in first thing and get it over with. Otherwise, Michael has a chance to—"

"Do nothing." Carson's sleep-edged voice stopped her words. "One more time. This is how it's going to go. Michael will arrive early. Try to beat you to the office. When he sees you aren't there, he'll prepare a speech to frazzle you for showing up late. By eleven-thirty, he'll think he's won. He'll see no need to show his hand to Jason if you're already cowed. He'll think he's scared you, which will be enough for him."

"How do you know?"

"I've been in Washington a long time."

"I wish…"

"What, baby?" He pulled her closer against him.

She wished so many things were different. She wished she'd been stronger in standing up to her parents' irresponsibility. She wished for Benny's happiness. She wished she'd never gotten involved with Michael. But even more than all those desires, she wished for more courage.

She wrested around to look directly into Carson's strong and beautiful face. "How do you make everyone listen to you?" she asked. "Sure, you're a lawyer, but that's not why people respect you. You're a Dom, but that's not it, either. What is it?"

"Experience."

"I don't have that kind of time."

He chuckled. "I've heard that from you before. You have to know what kind of experiences to have, London. Tell me, when do you feel the bravest?"

"When I'm with you. The things we've done this weekend. I felt … I don't know, like—"

"Like you could take on the world?"

"Exactly." As usual, Carson's ability to interpret her feelings and fears proved uncanny.

"You can." He tucked a piece of hair behind her ear. "You just have to believe it."

"I mean, when you're *dominating* me, I feel stronger. It should be opposite. It's strange."

Before this weekend, she'd never have believed submitting to a man could make her feel so much. Powerful. Desirable. Chosen.

He pulled her into an embrace. "When you're giving yourself to me, fully, you renounce all other claims over you. Responsibilities. Other people. Even time. You just get to be. And who you are is a strong, remarkable woman. The veneer of who you *should* be is stripped ... Your body certainly enjoys it." The sexy tilt of his lips sent a tingle of new desire through her core.

Carson was so much more than she'd ever dreamed possible. How could she have ever been attracted to Michael?

She chewed her lip. If she were honest, she'd have told him the truth about Michael.

Carson's eyes turned serious. "What crossed your mind? Just then? Something made you angry."

She swallowed. "I'm afraid to tell you."

"There's more to Michael, isn't there?"

"I can't tell you. You'll kill him."

He chuckled. "I already want to kill him."

"But you'll really, really want to."

He sat up against the headboard and beckoned her into his arms. "Now you have to tell me."

"It scares me when you do that. Get so angry on my behalf."

"I'm an attorney. I'm paid for my righteous indignation."

"I'm paid to smooth things over." She placed her small hand against his strong pec. *He really could kill Michael.*

"You need to stop doing that with me. Right now. If we're going to at least live together, you have to open up to me."

She stared up at him, words lodged in her throat. *Live together?* She pushed herself up.

His face broke into a huge grin. "You don't think I'm headed in any other direction, do you? I'm going to do the whole romantic thing, take you to dinner and present you with a key. Hire the movers. Give you more than a drawer. Next weekend."

She held her breath. *This can't be happening. Oh, God, let this be happening.*

"Say something," he said.

Oh my God. Oh my God. Oh my God. "You're telling me in advance?"

"You don't like surprises. I don't either. You're going to say yes, aren't you?"

"Yes." The word tumbled from her mouth with no hesitation.

"I like it when you say yes." He pulled her closer.

She placed her ear against his chest again and listened. His heartbeat remained steady. *Strong.* A surreal wave passed through her body. "I'm not capable of saying anything else with you," she whispered into his pec.

"Good, you're now going to tell me what you thought of. Say yes."

"No fair." She wanted to float on this cloud of happiness for a few more minutes.

"I'm a lawyer. What happened, London?"

She pulled herself from the shelter of his arms. He said to trust him. *Okay, then.* "You asked me why I don't like being watched. Michael might have had something to do with it. And maybe my stepfather, Bert." She twisted the sheets in her hands. "He used to get so angry with me when I wouldn't get ... affectionate with him. And then Michael. Our last time together. H-he was mad." She stopped. Perhaps she shouldn't tell him all the details. Talk about ruining a mood.

"Keep going," he said.

"Are you sure, Carson? I mean, I'm talking about another man. Don't you guys hate that?"

"Tell me."

She sighed. "Okay, remember you asked. We were in his apartment. Fooling around." She felt herself blushing. "Well ... I couldn't come. He was too rough. So, he ..."

"What, London?" His jaw clenched tight.

"I was blindfolded. I didn't see the other two guys come in. They ... touched me." *There. It was done.*

Carson pulled away and rose from the bed. Every muscle in his body was clenched as if he were about to go into battle. *Oh, shit.*

"Keep talking." He stalked the floor, slowly.

"I mean, they didn't have sex with me. One of them refused, and it must have caused the other guy to rethink. Then I kind of freaked out and it was over. It turned out to be nothing, really—"

"Stop. You're right, London. I am going to end him. The other two might be spared."

She should have *never* told him. While some people often threw around words like "murder" and "love" like confetti, she knew Carson didn't say a word he didn't mean.

"Carson. We have a plan. You promised."

He shook his head. "He let other men touch you." He lifted his gaze to her. A fire raged behind his eyes. "That's why you don't like being watched."

∼

Carson stood by the side of the bed and glared down at London. *My London.* A woman who Michael Headler had changed.

London scooted to the other side of the bed and curled into herself. Her whole body quaked with misery. Headler had scared her. Worse, he'd done real damage. *So don't add to the injury.*

As he willed himself to soften his shoulders, he walked to her side and sat down next to her. As soon as his hand descended onto her back, she unwound and launched herself into his chest.

"I-I just want all this t-to end," she cried.

"It will."

"But not like that. P-please, Carson."

His mind fractured into a thousand pieces. Choices and options of what he could do to remedy this situation taunted him. Each piece, each simple, torturous act he could bestow upon the man who harmed his woman, sharpened to a point. If her stepfather were still alive today, he'd feel Carson's wrath, too. What was wrong with these men?

Derek had said, *We're not the mafia.* In that moment his emotions hadn't fully registered the subtle warning. Leave it to the jokester of the Tribunal to know how far he would go for the woman he loved. *What any of us would do.*

He placed a kiss on the crown of her head. She melted a little more into his hold. "Trust me. I'm not going to do anything." *That can be traced.* "I won't let anything happen." *To you.* "I've got you." *Forever.* "No man, except me, will ever touch you again." *The last man who did is about to descend into hell.*

London looked up at him with weepy eyes. "I love you."

"I love you, too." He brushed hair from her damp forehead. "Remember, stick to the plan. Tomorrow, you're going to Jason Brennan—"

"As we talked about."

"In the *afternoon*, London. I'll be in your office at noon to wait with you as long as it takes. Just in case Michael shows up."

She chewed her lip. "Michael won't do anything there."

"I don't trust him. You shouldn't either."

She sighed and nodded.

"I told you the video has been destroyed. You'll quit, start your own business, and be free of any connections with Michael Headler. I won't interfere with any of those plans."

"Thank you." She took in a stuttering breath. "But you're planning something else, aren't you?"

"I'm planning on loving you until the end of time." *And protecting you, even if it means I have to break every law I swore to uphold.*

14

Throughout the night London tossed and turned like a tumbleweed. Carson's arms finally pinned her body next to his, stopping her from tangling the sheets further. Her heart ached with joy at his hold, but her fear kept her on edge, and her thoughts didn't allow her to sink fully into contentment.

Carson won't forgive Michael. He's planning something. He wants to live with me. He'll get us both in trouble. He loves me!

She'd never been good at happiness. Something always came along to remind her of her real purpose, and it wasn't tripping through a field of daisies. She knew what she was good at—taking care of herself and her brother.

Though her ping-pong thoughts kept her awake, Carson lay beside her, deep in sleep. His heavy breathing had both comforted and frightened her. How could have been so calm? At some point in the night she must have drifted to sleep, as she woke with a start.

She rolled over and dipped into the empty imprint of where Carson had lain. She sat bolt upright, panicked. *Where is he?* A soft whooshing sound came from the distance. A rich aroma permeated the air. He was making coffee? She could use a pail of java this morning.

After pulling on her panties and his T-shirt, she padded down the stairs and to the kitchen. Carson stood facing a coffee maker, impatiently drumming his hands on the quartz countertop. He was barefoot and shirtless, wearing a pair of drawstring pants that slung low on his hips. By the outline of his ass, he wore nothing underneath.

Soon she'd get to see him every morning like this. Half nude and gorgeous with ruffled hair. She sighed. *One pull on the drawstring and he'd ...*

He turned and smiled. "Well, good morning. Watching me?"

"Maybe." Curse it, she got caught.

"Come here."

He lifted her up so she sat on the countertop. "You like me up here."

He grasped the back of her knees and pulled her closer to the edge. He leaned in and her thighs parted. "I like any position where I can spread your legs."

"You're going to be late for work."

He laughed. "Unlike the PR reps of the world, clients don't mind the disappearance of attorneys." He held up a buttered piece of toast. "Open."

"Yes, sir." She spread her thighs wider and batted her eyelashes.

"Wicked girl. Eat. You're going to need your strength." He handed her a cup of steaming coffee with a thick swirl of cream.

"Busy day today?"

"Just a few meetings."

"You know, Whitestone really should move forward with that rebranding. I mean, even if I'm not there, it's still a good idea."

One side of Carson's lips lifted in a half smile. "I love you, London. You never give up."

"I'm right about this."

He kissed her on the forehead. "I know you are."

"Then why did you fight me so much?"

"So you'd bring your A game to the table."

"That's manipulative."

"That's smart management."

"You're quite arrogant."

"You love me anyway."

"Yes, I do." She pecked his lips with her own.

His eyes grew serious. "Call me before you leave for the office, okay? I'm meeting you in the lobby."

She knew why he insisted on such a plan. "I might run into Michael anyway, you know."

"That's why you're not going to arrive until noon." Carson glanced up at the clock over the sink. "Michael has a lunch appointment with Sarah."

She stiffened. "When did you do all this?" She appreciated his help. But her suspicions he was planning something arose again.

"I'm starting to like text messaging. Amazingly fast way to get things done." He sipped his latte.

"You'll be addicted now."

He set down his coffee and cradled her face. "You're my only addiction."

She lowered her eyes in shame for her earlier thoughts. She wasn't used to being helped. Looking a gift horse—especially one as beautiful as Carson—in the mouth was foolish. Besides, what he did with that mouth …

"Thank you." Her acknowledgement was swallowed by his kiss. All her worries melted on his tongue.

As his hands began to move up her thighs and under his shirt, she had one fleeting moment of perhaps stopping him.

Solving her fear by losing herself in him? Was that okay? Her now-completely-undisciplined-melt-anytime-near-Carson parts batted away the short-lived question. His hand had cupped her behind and drawn her closer so she connected with his crotch. Oh yes, she was right earlier. He wore nothing underneath those drawstring pants.

She lifted herself up so he could draw down her panties. Before they had a chance to drop to the floor, he'd pulled out his cock and pushed his hardness deep inside her. He thrust inside her, once, twice, three times … and then she came, keening into his shoulder.

If anyone had asked her what she did for a living in that moment, she'd have answered with three words. *Loving this man. Forget public relations. Forget everything.*

So, she did. A few minutes later her body was pressed against the shower wall as he took her again under the pounding hot water. Her sore body didn't protest, but instead opened anew to him. When he finally pulled her from the shower, neither of them spoke.

She sat on the edge of the large tub and watched him dress. Pull his tie knot up to his neck. Secure his cuff links. Shrug his jacket on. Casual, everyday movements that he made the most interesting things she'd ever seen. Was this that afterglow thing she'd heard about? No wonder women got all moon-eyed over men if this is how they woke up every morning.

Now fully dressed, he leaned over her, placing his hands on either side of her legs. "You look better."

"You have a lot to do with that."

"Good." He chuckled and held out his hand. As he led her through the house to the door leading to the garage, her old doubts crept back up her spine. He must have noticed, as he gave her a long reassuring kiss before he stepped out the door. *Like a real couple?*

As soon as she closed the door behind him, any last good feelings vanished like his presence. She trusted Carson, but he had too much confidence in his plan. Michael had been threatened. And if her PR career had taught her anything, all the contingencies in the world couldn't stop the most random component of any plan—the human quotient. Unpredictable and emotional, human beings had one default setting: protect, preserve, and defend one thing—themselves.

God, she wanted this day to be over.

~

Carson nearly crushed his phone in his hand after hearing Mark's news. "Did you get him on camera?"

"Yes, sending now. It was too dark to capture his image well enough. Why does she live there? The outdoor lighting is minimal and it's not safe—"

"She's not going back, Mark."

"Good. Otherwise, I'd think you were slipping, my friend."

He didn't have the time or the patience to share notes on who took care of their women better. "What time did Headler show up at her apartment?"

"Three a.m."

He narrowly missed a Mercedes as he pulled into the coffee shop parking lot. His anger compromised his attention.

"Mark, keep surveillance on her place. In case he refuses the Tribunal, he might go back."

"We'll stay on top of it. And, Carson? Anyone who feels the need to show up at that hour wasn't looking for a friendly chat."

"I know." He killed the call. So, the man didn't take him seriously when he told him what would happen if he showed up at London's apartment. Time to make the Tribunal's power known.

"Good morning," he said, sitting down to join Sarah.

She looked up from her newspaper. "Carson. I see your impatience for justice hasn't wavered. Coffee?"

He waved away her offer to retrieve more caffeine, a substance he needed no more of today. His nerves were already shot. Besides sex, he'd used every attorney trick in the book that morning with London to help keep her composed. Through deep breathing, steady eye contact, and jovial small talk, he'd calmed many juries and clients from leaping into an emotional abyss. Now, after hearing Mark's news on top of London's story last night, no method would calm him down.

"I have more information, facts that you'll need." He glanced around. Even though the coffee shop owner was a trusted friend, he never knew who might be overhearing. Given the later morning hour, only one other person sat in a far corner. A woman sitting next to a stroller. A chubby baby bounced in her seat, cooing in glee as her mother pinched off pieces of muffin and hand-fed it to her.

"You're in love." Sarah took a calm sip of her latte.

He ran his hand through his hair. "Yes."

"That doesn't mean we get to bend the rules."

"Fuck the rules."

She leaned back and appraised him. He knew he looked unyielding. *Savage*. Basically, how he felt.

"You have your lunch set up?"

"As you requested." She ran a manicured finger over her cup.

"Keep him out for a while. London needs time to meet with Brennan without running into Michael."

He held up his phone and played the brief video snippet Mark had sent. They could barely make out a man lurking around the front door. But he recognized the weasel hunch of Headler's shoulders. "He showed up at her apartment last night. Three a.m.," he explained.

"Is she alright?"

"She wasn't home. She was with me."

"So that makes two of you who broke the Tribunal's direction."

"I broke no rule. London came to me."

Sarah's eyes softened as if she finally understood the connection between him and London. Their union was messy, but undeniable.

His attention wandered back to the mother in the corner. The stroller moved in time with the baby's dancing legs. Jesus, he was a goner. "I want you to know that I will adhere to the Tribunal's decision. He's either out or goes with you. If he accepts your training, you will assure he conducts himself in the scene in the proper way. But—"

"There's a condition," Sarah said.

"I'm designing his training."

"No."

His jaw clenched. "You'll think differently when I tell you what I discovered last night."

"Investigating him, are we?"

"I didn't need to. London finally told me everything. Even you will agree he deserves what I'm going to suggest."

She leaned forward. "Go on."

He took a deep breath and steeled himself to recount what London had told him. With Sarah, a dispassionate accounting would resonate with more weight. Her control rivaled his own—or his *past* control. Being in love with London tested his restraint.

As he recounted London's revelations from last night, Sarah's normal cool demeanor melted. Her shoulders stiffened more with each word from his mouth. *Bingo.*

"Now, for my condition. Bring in others—"

"Absolutely not. I will not be party to—"

"I'm not asking them to go through with anything. I just want him to feel everything he put London through. You know a mind fuck is part of this dynamic. If he believes he can get away with certain things, then he has to know what it feels like to be a sub—to undergo certain surprises."

Sarah looked thoughtful. "Sub training. Interesting idea."

"The complete training, Sarah." *Then I'll handle the rest.*

He'd run Headler out of Washington if it was the last thing he did. But he wouldn't inflict the man on another BDSM community. Michael had to go through with Sarah's training—the only other Dominant he knew who could break that haughty countenance of his.

She cocked her head. "Do you know what you're asking?"

"Yes. It's a lot for you to do. But it's the only way he's going to learn." *And buy me time to plaster the world with his smug face so he could never hide again.*

"Agreed. I'll amend the offer letter."

"Today, Sarah. I want him to know his options today."

She appraised him. "Love lights a fire like no other, doesn't it?"

"So does betrayal."

"You'll need to let go of that. We can only do so much, Carson."

"We can do much more." The Tribunal had ways that even most Club members didn't realize. Their reach into intelligence communities, the government and business leaders would have made the CIA blush. Without government oversight, the Tribunal could be more ... direct.

"The planet is a big place. Lots of places to hide." Sarah stared out the window in thought. He caught something in her gaze that told him she wrestled with something, perhaps a past demon their conversation had called forth.

He rose from the table and held out his hand. "Thank you, Sarah. I owe you."

"Yes, you do." She returned his handshake, and her masterful confidence returned to her eyes.

~

London slammed her car door harder than she meant to, probably more from nerves than pure strength. She checked her watch. Eleven thirty. Who cares if she arrived a little early? By now Michael would have headed out to meet Sarah. And she couldn't rattle around Carson's huge house anymore. How does he stand all the echoes? Her envy of a larger living space died within an hour of him leaving that morning.

She had just over two hours before her two p.m. meeting with Jason Brennan. His assistant had booked fifteen minutes for her. She hoped she'd be in his office for less than five. How long does it take to say, "I resign"?

In the meantime, she'd wait out the time in her office with Carson. He'd arrive shortly. Sure, he'd be pissed that she rode an elevator alone without him—did *anything* without him. *Ha!* She smiled inwardly at his protective streak. But *no way* would he accompany her to Jason's office. A girl's got to do some things alone.

The usual office sounds greeted her as she stepped off the elevator. Clacking of keys, muffled voices from conference rooms and people laughing on the phone were all signs Monday had gotten underway with a bang.

As she rounded the corner to her office, she ran into her colleague, Janey. "Where ya been? You missed the staff meeting."

"I, ah, wasn't feeling well, so I took the morning off." She slipped into her office and threw her purse on her chair.

Janey leaned in her doorway. "You okay now?"

"Sure, fine. Um, have you seen Mr. Brennan?" Perhaps she could grab him before lunch. She only needed, like, *one* minute in reality.

"Like I spend time in the executive suites? You overestimate my reach." She flipped her long hair and spun on her heel.

Was London ever that young? She turned to her desk and rifled through some folders. She barely recognized a single sheet of paper on her desk, as if she'd abandoned her life a century ago.

"You missed the staff meeting."

She stepped backward at Michael's voice. "I'm...ah, not well." God, she stammered.

When Michael stepped inside her office, her heart dropped to the floor. "Michael, I don't know what to say."

"Of course you do, sweetheart." He shut the door behind him.

"You had meetings. This morning." Wasn't the Cisco team in today? And what about his lunch with Sarah? He should have been in a cab by now.

"Over."

"I see." She searched her mind for something to direct the conversation. *Damn, he's getting closer.*

"I heard all about your boyfriend's little attempt at arranging my world today. Lunch with that bitch? Pitiful attempt to keep me away from you."

Michael stood a foot away from her, which was twelve inches too close.

"You can make it up to me. You'd like that, wouldn't you?" He ran his hand down her arm and twisted her around. He held her in an arm lock, his breath hot in her hair. "Now that I know how rough you like it—"

"Michael, we're at the office. Please..."

"Begging becomes you." He mercifully released her and walked around to the front of her desk. He folded himself into a chair. "Sit."

She sunk to her chair and nearly crushed her purse. As she pulled it loose, some contents spilled. She picked up her phone from the floor and sat it in her lap. What would she do? Call 911? *Get a hold of yourself, London.* Other people sat less than ten feet away. She wasn't in real danger.

He straightened his cuffs. "I should thank Carson Drake for showing me who you really are. Getting to witness that little flogging scene was a real eye-opener."

"How so?" *Keep him talking. Maybe someone will interrupt.*

"You need a stronger hand. I should have never let you off the hook that last night when we were together. So, this is how it's going to go."

"Nothing's going to go." Good, she sounded strong.

"You're in no position to dictate anything."

Carson was right about his mental state. He believed she'd cave. Revulsion filled her insides. She squeezed her legs together and looked down at her phone. *Think, London.* She tapped the camera icon and quickly swiped her thumb to video mode.

"So, Michael, what do you want from me?" She raised her eyes. "I-I don't want to lose my job."

"Well, since you fucked up my chances with Club Accendos, I'd say you owe me at least a farewell session. Activities of my choosing. Then I'll consider you keeping your job." He crossed his legs and picked a piece of lint off his trousers.

Her eyes darted to his hard-on under his pants. The disgust in her belly changed to rage.

"Michael, you coerced me. And those men ... Why did you do that to me? Bring in other men and threaten me with rape?"

"You needed to have that cunt of yours tamed." His face purpled.

"You disgust me. I doubt Mr. Brennan knows the kind of man you are. He'd have fired you long ago."

"I'm not going anywhere, sweetheart. You'll meet me tonight. My house."

"Like hell."

"Fine. Have it your way. You're fired." He stood up.

"For not sleeping with you?"

"Let's just say you're not well suited for this position, Miss Chantelle. Since you didn't, ah, *assume* the position." His eyes dropped to the floor as if subtly commanding her to her knees.

Of all the choices she had made in her life, ever letting Michael Headler get closer than twelve inches was the worst. Well, her days of poor choices were over.

"You're right about one thing. I'm not well suited to work for a blackmailer." She stood, clutching her iPhone. God, she wanted to scream at him. *Thank you for the recording, asshole!*

The arrogant bastard leaned over her desk, sending coffee breath running over her. Before he launched into a new tirade, her phone rang in her hand. She quickly brought it to her ear.

"Yes, Mr. Brennan." Instinct forced the lie out.

Michael's shoulders dropped at her trick.

"London, it's me." Carson's voice washed her anger in additional courage. "I'm in the lobby. You're on your way?"

"Y-yes. Michael and I were just talking about it. I can get it to you right away."

A curse on the other end told London he understood. "Get out of there."

"Of course, right away. Cisco waits for no one, as you said." She looked in Michael's direction. "Yes, I'll text you right away."

She lowered her phone. Michael's face had cooled. "Don't keep the boss waiting. Then you can pack up."

"I-I have to get this to Jason." Her phone shook in her hand. The five seconds it took to forward the video she'd just made felt like five hours. She managed to hit send before Michael grabbed her phone from her hand.

"You won't be needing this." He slammed the phone against the corner of her desk, a spiderweb of cracks forming on the screen. "Such carelessness, Miss Chantelle. Perhaps a punishment is in order."

15

"Attack on floor six," Carson barked at the security guard behind the desk. He ran to the elevator bank, his only option as the stairwells had to be locked. Every building in Washington had been locked down since the attacks on 9/11—a blessing and a curse.

He burst into an open elevator, earning complaints from two men trying to exit. His phone buzzed, showing London had sent a text. A quick scroll and her distressed voice filled the space. By the time the doors finally reopened on London's floor, he'd dug crescent-shaped indents in his palms, his hands balled into fists. He hadn't hit a man since college. Time to adjust his record.

"Chantelle. London—where?" he yelled at a young, dark-haired girl holding a stack of papers. She startled and pointed down the hallway. A muffled shout came from behind the closed door at the end.

London's office door opened with a loud bang against the doorstop as he threw it open. A black fury flooded every molecule in his body at the sight of London bent over her desk. Michael had his hand on the back of her neck, his other hand cupping her behind.

Michael didn't have time to release London before he threw his entire weight behind a punch. A loud crack filled the room as his fist met his jawbone. Another blow sent Michael further into a large rubber tree plant. Michael threw up his leg, an attempt to stop Carson's advance.

Shouting behind him didn't stop him from raising his fist again. Hands grabbed at his coat, trying to pull him off Michael. But his mission was clear—rid himself of this rage. Feel bone. His fist slid across Michael's chest, blood smearing his shirt. His fists pummeled the air as he felt himself pitching backward. Two guys had pulled him off Headler.

"What the fuck, man?" One of the intruders yelled.

A loud crack of something hard against wood cut through his fury. He shook himself free of the two men who each grasped an arm. He turned to come face-to-face with a security guard holding a baton. He'd brought it down on the desk in warning.

Carson threw up his hands. "Whoa, whoa. This prick attacked Miss Chantelle."

London had crumpled to the floor. But she managed to pull herself up to her knees. He broke free of the other men's holds and rushed to help her stand and bring her close. His hands ran down her face, her arms and over her back. He'd left bloody smudges on her cheeks. "Did he hurt you?"

She shook her head and clutched the front of his jacket. "I'm okay. Michael. I didn't think he would. But he did." She turned her eye to the security guard, who clutched his stick as if violence would erupt any second. "He-he attacked me." An intense tremor ran through her body.

Michael groaned in the corner. His coworkers helped him to his feet. He spat blood on the floor. "Call the cops. Arrest this guy."

"No-no, he was helping me." London's tight voice wavered.

"What the hell is going on here?" Jason Brennan's voice cut into the room's tension.

The security guard stepped forward. "Sir. Altercation between employees."

Michael lifted his bloody chin toward Carson. "This man isn't staff. Jason, this man needs to be arrested."

"Mr. Drake is a client," London said.

"I know." Brennan stepped forward.

Carson shrugged his coat into place and met his advance. "You've got some explaining to do, Brennan. I didn't expect you'd have lunatics on your watch."

"Perhaps we should take this someplace quieter?" Jason Brennan's voice held that same silky quality as Alexander's, but none of its power. Great, he was about to be handed a plate of PR platitudes. Good thing he was immune to such tactics. But London? She stood dazed. Thank God he was here.

Brennan gestured to the doorway. A number of people stood above cubicle walls in the center of the large office, taking in the spectacle. They slowly slunk behind the walls like gophers returning to their holes.

"Curtis, come with us please?" Brennan asked.

The security guard nodded once but urged Carson forward. "Sir. After you."

Jason Brennan told the two men who'd interfered to return to their offices. He then led London, Carson, Michael and Curtis the Watchdog to a conference room down the hallway.

"Gentlemen, please sit." Brennan stood at the head of the large table dominating the center of the room.

"I'll stand." Carson wasn't about to be schooled by a client, especially not one who employed sociopaths. He held

London around the waist. She swayed a little. Behind him, the security guard stood at the doorway, as if someone might try to bolt around him.

Michael walked over to a small bar in the corner. He wet a napkin and held it up to his bloody lip. The smug bastard smiled. Never had Carson wanted to kill a man so much in his life.

"Suit yourself. Michael, do you require medical help? London?"

Michael shook his head and took a seat next to Jason, who'd sat down. He seemed to ignore the fact London didn't answer.

"So, who's going to tell me what's going on?"

"A jealous tirade. One I'm sorry you had to witness." Michael blotted his lip. "Seems London isn't working out here at Yost and Brennan. Her boyfriend, a client mind you, took offense."

"So that's your story? I think I will sit. This should be good." Carson eased London into a chair and took the one next to her. He also pulled out a handkerchief and wrapped his knuckles. "Mr. Brennan. My firm is a client of yours. London is our account executive. And true, we are involved. It's legal." He leaned back in his chair. "Michael Headler has been blackmailing her for some time. I have proof."

"It's all my fault," Seemingly dazed, London shook her head back and forth and stared at her lap. "I should have never agreed to—"

"London, you are under no obligation to say a word here."

Her eyes snapped up to his. Good, she was coming out of her stupor.

"An office romance under my nose?" Brennan asked.

"Hardly," Michael snorts. "Miss Chantelle isn't working out."

"No, I'm not. I resign, effective today." She raised her eyes to Michael.

"You can't resign after I've fired you."

"You can't fire someone for not wanting to date you," Carson said.

Brennan's face held no emotion. "I'm well aware of such things, Mr. Drake. However, let's cut to the part where you assaulted Mr. Headler."

He huffed out a laugh. "As I said, Headler has been blackmailing London. When she refused his advances, he attacked her. I intervened."

"Her word against mine. Jason, you've known me a long time—" He was cut off by the raise of Brennan's hand.

"You mean something like this?" Brennan pulled out his phone and set it on the table in front of him. He touched the screen and London's voice filled the room.

So, London had also sent Michael's threats to Brennan. London's List unfurled another foot. *My smart, brave girl.*

He pulled his phone from his jacket pocket and waved it at the Yost and Brennan CEO. "I've heard it." Brennan's eyes registered his unspoken words. *Don't believe for a second you can erase this evidence.*

Michael leaned forward and tapped his finger on the table. "That's not me."

Brennan's face never left Carson's stare. "Curtis, call downstairs and send up your colleagues. Then will you please see Mr. Headler is secured in my office? Michael and I are going to have a chat after Mr. Drake and I discuss a few things. Oh, and take his cell phone."

Curtis mumbled into his walkie-talkie.

"This is bullshit. A setup." Michael jolted from his seat and headed toward Curtis. "Out of my way." Curtis took hold of Michael's arm. He winced at the hold. Carson hoped the guard had added to Michael's injuries.

London straightened her spine, though she still appeared dazed. "Mr. Brennan, I see you got my text."

Brennan sighed and placed his elbows on the table, though he never took his eyes from Carson's face. "Your terms?"

"Many. Miss Chantelle has undergone blackmail and assault. More than once, Mr. Brennan." He raised his hand to silence London, who moved to speak. Her seething look wouldn't stop him from nailing this company that let a raving lunatic in its midst. *A lunatic who harmed London.*

"What do you want?" Jason asked.

"Headler fired."

"Done."

"London released from her employment contract. A legal agreement saying you will not stop her from launching her own business."

"Without taking any current Yost and Brennan clients with her. Including Whitestone." Brennan placed his hands flat on the table, a signal of non-negotiation. *Fine.*

"Agreed. She won't need it. Letter of recommendation?"

"I'll have one drafted today."

"Your signature."

Brennan smiled. "Of course."

"Letter of dismissal of Headler in my hands by tomorrow morning."

"For?"

"In case he ever goes after London, professionally." He knew the more papers he held in his hands, the safer London would be.

"And in truth?"

"Let's just say Headler won't go near London again." He glanced her way to check her state. She was no longer in shock. Her cheeks flushed bright red.

"Washington has a long memory, Mr. Drake."

"Yes, it does. I expect you to honor our agreement here today. I'll remember every detail."

"As will I."

~

London's ears rushed with blood. The negotiation between Carson and Mr. Brennan continued for some minutes, each word a hammer hit to her head. Every time she tried to speak, Carson's hand squeezed her knee. She grasped his wrist and failed to yank his hold from her leg. Once again, his strength overpowered.

Mr. Brennan looked over at her. "I trust we'll leave as friends?"

"She won't agree to any such thing," Carson answered.

"I wasn't asking for a gag order, Mr. Drake. But I would like some assurances."

"I guess you'll have to take her word." Carson stood up, finally releasing his clutch on her leg. "I want his cell phone before I leave in order to wipe the video. You have our other terms. I expect documents in my office before the end of the day."

Mr. Brennan stood and reached out to shake Carson's hand.

"Miss Chantelle, again, I apologize for what happened." Mr. Brennan held out his hand. She shook it limply. Three days ago she'd have been thrilled to earn such significant acknowledgement from the head of her agency. Today, she wanted never to be touched again—by any man.

As they left the conference room, staff quickly turned back to their papers—props to hide their gossiping. They probably got a real thrill watching a fight. Nothing like that ever happened in civilized Washington.

"Everything's back to normal, folks," Mr. Brennan called

into the room. "Staff meeting at four. Mandatory." Explaining away what happened would naturally be at the top of his to-do list today.

She headed to her office, vaguely aware of Carson following behind her. Her shadow slipped inside with her and shut the door. "London," he said gently.

She held up her hand. "Don't say anything. I can't..."

He reached out to touch her and she jumped backward. "Don't. I mean it." She looked up at his face, stone cold and contained, as if he hadn't nearly pummeled a man to death twenty minutes ago. "I thought you were going to murder him."

"I didn't need to. You accomplished that. The worst thing that can happen to someone here is to lose their job—or their ability to advance. Michael is, in effect, dead."

"No. I didn't want..."

"What, baby?" He ran his hand down the side of her face, capturing a strand of hair between his thumb and forefinger. "London, I thought this was what you wanted."

"What I wanted?" she shouted.

His mask of incredulity only added to her anger.

"What I *wanted* was to quit and—"

"You did."

"On my terms. Not sit there like a deaf, dumb mute while you and Jason Brennan negotiated my future!"

"You needed back up."

"I could have handled it."

"No, you couldn't have. Let me tell you how this would have gone if I hadn't been here. Michael would have probably raped you in this office. Or at least scared the shit out of you and nothing would have—"

"I'd sent Mr. Brennan the video. I could have turned this around—"

"And Brennan would have saved his precious company

first. He would have erased that text, and quite frankly, it's not admissible in court—only arbitration—"

"I could have still gotten—"

"Raked over the coals. Banished from Washington. Who would have hired a girl who's called assault? You know how risk-averse this town is. Now don't be ridiculous. We're going."

A series of long-buried memories burst forward, followed by a sickening sense of déjà vu. *This is how it starts.* First, the promise of protection, then the anger, and then ... She couldn't go back to days and nights worrying when the next explosion would erupt. *I won't.*

"No."

"Why are you fighting me?"

A knock on her door interrupted their argument. She opened it to find Curtis the security guard with two other men behind him. "Miss Chantelle? We heard shouting. Jason wanted me to check on you. Make sure you got out okay."

"I'll bet he did," Carson sneered. "You're being escorted from the premises, London. Curtis, give Mr. Brennan a message for me. Washington never forgets." He took the phone from Curtis' outstretched hand. *Michael's phone?* She didn't care who had it at the moment.

In the parking lot, Carson eased her one box of personal belongings into her trunk. He slammed the lid down and turned to her. "I'll follow you home. Headler's not fully taken care of—"

"I don't give a shit."

~

Carson's instincts kicked in, and he scooped her into his arms. "London, I'm sorry."

"Let me go." She sobbed and struggled in his hold.

He released her. "You can't drive like this. You're still in shock."

"If you care about me at all, Carson, you'll let me go."

Reluctantly, he shut her car door when she slipped inside. She eased the window down. "Don't follow," she said to the windshield. "In fact, don't contact me until I contact you."

He trailed her to her apartment anyway. He watched her struggle with the small carton to get it inside. When the metal apartment building door slammed shut, he felt the full weight of his heart dropping to his stomach.

His eyes wandered over London's choice of address. He couldn't believe he sat idly in his car while she lived in such a place. Every instinct in his gut said to rip her from these premises and lock her away ... He punched his car ceiling with Michael Headler's phone. The sound of the fabric tearing brought him back to reality. *You idiot.* He knew victims of abuse couldn't take violence. *And then you let it fly in her office.* He'd let her calm down, have a little space. He'd return tonight.

A dark sedan sat parked at the end of the street, a shadow barely visible inside. Mark's security contact.

Carson hit his speed dial on his phone.

"Santos," the deep voice said.

"Surveillance arrived. Mark, keep it tight on her apartment building."

"Of course. Headler?"

"Out on his ass."

"Which only makes him more dangerous."

"Don't remind me."

He ended the call, grateful Mark required little chit-chat. He was in no mood to play nice.

After glaring at her building's front door for thirty more minutes, he started his car. But he didn't back out of the parking space. Where would he go? He didn't have anyone waiting for him, anywhere.

∼

"Hi, Mr. Rockingham. It's London." Thank God she had kept a landline.

"Why, London, so nice to hear from you. Is everything alright? Where's Carson?"

Alexander's calm, smooth voice loosened the tension in her chest. No wonder so many people flocked to the man. She prayed he'd understand why she ran to him now.

"Probably still in his car. Outside. In front of my apartment building."

"Is he alright?" Alexander didn't sound concerned, but rather amused.

"That's where I need your help. You see, things are a bit of a mess right now. I have a lot of things—"

"That perhaps Carson could help with?"

"No!" She switched the phone to her other ear. "Sorry. I didn't mean to yell."

"You've been under a lot of strain lately."

"Yes, and that's why I need time to concentrate. You see, it's not just me ..."

"Your brother."

Of course, the Tribunal. They knew everything, right? "I could use your help. Will you please make sure Carson stays away from me? I mean, for now."

"Away." He repeated the word slowly, as if he mulled over the sincerity of her request.

"Yes. I need a break." That was better. Most men understood that word, right?

"A break," he repeated.

Was she speaking in Swahili? "Yes. A break. A separation.

Untouchable

Some time without being stalked, coerced, manipulated or distracted." *Away from anger. Some peace.* "Is that too much to ask? I-I'm sorry, Mr. Rockingham. I don't want to hurt him. I don't want to hurt anybody." Her voice cracked.

"I'll speak with him," he said.

"You'll make sure he's alright, too?"

She heard the creak of Alexander leaning back in his chair. "London, Carson has many friends. More than even he realizes."

"Good." She let her head fall to the back of the couch. "It's the right thing to do. For now."

"Consider your wishes granted."

After they hung up, the expected lightness over her decision never came. She squeezed her palms together and gritted her teeth. *Don't cry.* Just take some time, she told herself. *Regroup.*

She picked up a picture of her and Benny at the beach. In the photograph she looked about twelve. Benny's chubby baby hands held a shovel. She smiled into the camera. *I look happy.* But was she? Did happiness ever matter?

A niggling feeling in the back of her brain kept fighting for attention. *Wrong direction,* the small voice shouted from the bottom of an oubliette in her heart. *Shut up,* she countered. In one weekend, she'd seen more violence and anger than she'd experienced in years. She wasn't going back there. Not *ever*.

∽

Carson pulled into Southland Rehab's parking garage. His conversation with Alexander on the ride over kept beating inside his brain. *London had called him? Asked for his help to keep him away from her?* Alexander related his conversation with London with little passion, simply stating London's "formal request."

Alexander didn't have to threaten him with Tribunal action to ensure her wish for space was granted. The fact that London felt threatened enough to call on Alexander's help filled him with disgrace. To ignore her request would be to turn into Michael Headler, himself—selfish and without moral fiber.

He turned off his ignition and stared at the concrete wall through the windshield. He should go back to work. He could drown himself in endless details of contracts and negotiations, things he could dictate and control. *Yeah, right.*

He opened his car door and headed inside.

As he leaned against the elevator wall, he ran through his conversation with London again. *Our fight.* He couldn't stop retracing his steps. He knew he'd let his temper get out of hand. But London turning to Alexander? A formal restraining order couldn't have shamed him more.

He hung his head and glared at the dirty linoleum of the elevator floor.

Okay, he'd lost before. Court cases hadn't always gone his way. Negotiations sometimes left his clients less than satisfied. But he'd always found a way to get everyone *enough*. Yet now? Nothing from his past—not his career or experience—volunteered an answer as to how to reverse this situation with London.

The elevator doors opened. He waved at a nurse he recognized and headed down the hall. No one stopped him.

He rapped on the doorframe of Benny's room. Benny looked up from the drawing he'd been intently studying.

"London?" Fear colored his eyes, as before.

"I'm afraid it's just me."

Benny shrugged and his face neutralized. "That's okay."

He stepped deeper into the room. "Working on your house?"

"I'm going to build it. Maybe."

"You will." Who was he kidding? He didn't know shit today. "Mind if I sit with you for a while?"

"Sure. You and London have a fight?"

Perceptive guy. "A misunderstanding."

A hint of a smile ghosted Benny's face.

"She's mad at me," he admitted.

"What does she think you did?"

He gave Benny enormous credit in that moment. Benny understood London, and her imaginings. "Probably something I did do."

His almost-smile dropped. "You didn't hurt her, did you?"

"I would never hurt London, Benny. I took care of some things for her."

He picked up his pencil. "No wonder you're in trouble."

"What do you mean?" he asked.

But Benny had returned his full attention to his house, as if he had never entered the room in the first place.

Carson sat with him for a while, quickly growing engrossed in house plans. The man had talent. *More than you do, clearly.* He mentally ran through the last few hours. He wasn't sorry he'd punched the daylights out of London's attacker. He just wished London hadn't been there. He needed to explain to her, reassure her she was safe.

"I'll see you later, Benny." He raised himself up from his chair. He'd go see Alexander. Get this stupid restraining decree off his back.

He stepped off the elevator into the lobby and ran straight into George.

"Hey, man, how you doing?"

"I've had better days."

"You had a fight with Miss Chantelle, didn't you?"

Jesus, did he wear his afternoon on his face?

George gestured him over to a small coffee stand in the corner. "Buy you some coffee? It ain't Starbucks, but it sure beats the stuff upstairs."

After settling onto the lobby's planter retaining wall, he sipped his coffee, avoiding George's stare.

"So, what'd you do?" George asked.

"Why does everyone ask me that?"

"Cuz it's a woman you're involved with, not a giraffe."

He huffed out a laugh. "Giraffes are less complicated. I helped her, that's all. She needed it, too." He took a gulp of the scalding java. "Would have drowned otherwise."

"You sure about that?"

Carson turned to the man. "Not you, too. I just got a little angry. Scared her. I'd never hurt her. Not ever." He wasn't exactly talking to George. He knew he was trying to convince himself.

"Miss Chantelle got a lot of worries." He shook his head. "You know that mother of theirs never came to see Benny once? And the way Benny talks about their daddy. Who does that? Abandon their children? Miss Chantelle, now she's a strong one. But she's got that look on her face, ya know?"

"Like what?"

"Like my Tanya. Her past is like a third person living with us."

Carson stared at the floor. Was he always this self-absorbed, not realizing people all around him had things so much worse than he could imagine? *Like London.* "I need to help her."

"Oh, no, take it from me."

"You think I'd hurt her?" His voice had risen.

"No man. And she probably knows you won't. But their daddies, and whatever they did to them, live in their bones. I figure that's why Miss Chantelle doesn't like the guards, ya know. Sends 'em out. Why I stay back. Women like London, they're always waiting for the next blow. Or our next fuck-up."

Daddies and boyfriends. "She doesn't have to be afraid. Not of me."

"But that's just it. Words don't mean shit. You gotta show her. Man, I thought I was the thick one." George stood up. "Gotta go to work. But, hey, you'll figure it out, smooth lawyer like you." George pitched his paper cup into the corner trash can like a basketball lay-up. "Two points," he called and disappeared around the corner.

Carson sat on the hard wall for several more minutes, mulling over George's coffee shop talk. He mentally ticked through London's List. Wanting help, but then demanding she do everything herself. Wanting to submit, but not. Trusting him, but then acting like he tried to pitch her off a cliff.

Wait. She *wanted* to trust him, but didn't know how.

If he hurt London, he'd throw himself off the top of the Washington Monument. But now that he embraced self-truth, he had to admit he'd taken the wrong tack with her. He had hurt her. He'd opened a wound. Deep inside her sat the anticipation that someday he'd take it too far. It made sense. Every man in her life either left her or mistreated her. *She's nervous about being left. She's worried no one will stay, and when they did? Eventual abuse.* Talk about a rock and a hard place. Ultimately, she wouldn't trust any man—to leave *or* stay. So, she left him.

Ah, this is what it feels like to be on the other side of the preemptive strike. It sucked.

He had misread her entire situation? Hell, he'd misread himself. His pride centered on his self-control, which he'd repeatedly failed at this weekend.

She'd told him what she needed: a protector. But did that

mean someone to fight for her? Or had it meant something entirely else?

He scratched his rough beard. In his haste this morning, he'd done a poor shaving job. That's when it hit him. He'd rushed her and showed her exactly what she *didn't* want. *Rashness.*

London wanted to be protected from a *lack of control.*

He pitched his coffee into the trash can along with his previous plans to march over to Alexander, demanding the Tribunal's release. He had something far greater in mind. London was about to learn that he wasn't like any man she'd ever encountered before. He would evolve into the definition of who he knew himself to be, and who London really needed: a master of self-control. *And loyalty.*

16

Tuesday morning melted into Wednesday, which gave way to Thursday and Friday. Soon London's first week clear of the Bermuda Triangle—as she dubbed Michael Headler, Yost and Brennan and Carson Drake—had passed. Two weeks turned into three weeks. When fall threatened to turn to winter, she stopped counting the days away from those three major stressors of her life. She felt herself propelling farther and farther from her past and toward her future—away from controlling men, violence and threats.

The first threat—Michael—disappeared the quickest. After that day his blackmail crumbled, he'd vanished into thin air. Her colleague, Janey, had simply said he'd been escorted from the building and put into a limo after his meeting with Jason Brennan. London's nightmares about him continued for some time. But imaginary threats were a small cost for surviving assault. She'd live. *If* she stayed focused.

Exiting Yost and Brennan proved easy. Janey had reported that Jason led an all-staff meeting the day Michael attacked her. Few details were given, but Jason had said nice things about London, and his lack of praise for Michael left everyone with the feeling he'd been in the wrong. She should have felt relief. Instead, she couldn't have cared less what anyone at Yost thought of her. She had enough on her plate launching Chantelle Communications.

Two days after she quit her job, a large brown envelope arrived with her amended employee contract, stating she was free to leave and launch her own company. But even more surprising was the letter of recommendation from Jason Brennan. *Stellar employee. Outstanding counselor. Strong competition for Yost and Brennan.* His choice of words almost took the sting out of the final change to her life—Carson's disappearance. *Almost.*

After leaving Carson idling in her parking lot, she'd cried for a whole day. But then she forced herself to grow up. She'd grown dangerously addicted to Carson. Now she started every morning with a new mantra. *I did the mature thing. Dodged a bullet. Unlike Mom, who stayed until bones were broken.*

"I come bearing gifts." Janey's voice from her office doorway shook her from her reverie. Hiring Janey was the smartest thing she'd done to date. They'd never talked about what happened between her and Michael.

Janey lifted up a vase of a dozen roses in salute. Swirls of red graced the sides of the artistic glass vase. "This week's. I can't believe no one can tell you who sent these. I mean, look at this hand-blown vase. You sure it's not—"

"No, it's not." The weekly rose delivery had started arriving the day after she left Yost and Brennan. At first they arrived to her apartment and then to her office. While no card ever accompanied the bouquets, she knew Carson was the sender. Each bouquet—always six red and six white roses—was artfully arranged in a signature glass vase, like the glass collection she had seen in his house.

She tried to get the florist to stop delivering them. But

her not-so-secret admirer ordered them from different floral shops throughout Washington. Carson thought of everything —even how to ensure she couldn't stop his gifts.

She looked at Janey's outstretched arms holding the vase high. Irritation grew in her belly. She was moving on, dammit. He wasn't helping.

Carson now showed up in her dreams. Instead of shrinking with time, like all the dumb women's magazines promised, her ludicrous fantasies grew stronger. Sometimes Carson sliced Michael in half with a sword. Other times, he melted hot wax over her body. Or she'd feel the sting of his flogger.

One night, she came in her sleep during a dream of being bound to the St. Andrew's Cross. She had run to her bathroom mirror, sure she'd find long red stripes across her back. But her skin remained smooth, untouched.

Janey cleared her throat as if trying to get her attention. "Well?" Her eyesight wandered over her office. "By the looks of your office, you don't have room."

At least eight more beautiful vases, each colored and shaped differently, lined every spare surface. Last week's bouquet also still graced her desk.

"Give them to Brenna. Tell her as part of her new AA job she has to deliver flowers to Georgetown Women's Hospital." Their administrative assistant had only been with them for a week, and she already seemed eager for new tasks.

"Benny's halfway house sick of them already, too?"

"You could say that." At first, Benny's new caretakers, the New Horizons House, were thrilled to accept the cheer. But the smell of roses bothered some of the residents.

She would have done anything New Horizons had asked. Benny loved his new home. For the first time in years, he'd made friends and regularly smiled when she visited. That progress alone helped quell her reservations about Carson's help. Even without confirmation, she knew Carson had everything to do with Benny's new address. *So what?* If he'd gotten him admitted to the halfway house that boasted a waiting list a mile long, *fine*.

At least Carson hadn't tried to contact her directly. He'd honored her wishes—sort of. But hadn't he always?

"Well, here's the mail. This just arrived for you when you were on that call. The courier was quite insistent it get to you right way." She handed over a large, stiff white envelope. "Something about a Mr. Rockman or Rockland. Sounds like a scary dude by the way the messenger said his name."

Her heart quickened on sight of her name spilling across the envelope in fancy calligraphy. *Alexander.*

Janey stuck her face in the roses and inhaled. "Man, the person sending these sure has it going on for you. You know, six red and six white roses means unity."

"What?"

Janey turned and called over her shoulder. "It means your love for that person will never die."

"Floral shop nonsense," she called out into the hallway.

"Cynic!" She yelled back.

London swiveled her chair to look out the window. She fingered the thick envelope. *Expensive paper.* Should she open it or just ignore it?

She leaned back in her chair and watched snowflakes drift in the halo of the streetlamps. People scooted along the sidewalk, some appearing giddy, some looking annoyed. The weatherman had said no accumulation was expected. Too bad. Snow made Washington look clean for a change.

Still, she loved the view of Wisconsin Avenue from her little office suite. She could have worked out of her apartment for a while. But the constant presence of that dark sedan, always parked at the end of the street, only reminded her of her past and the dangers that lurked there.

Another one of Carson's gifts. At first, her heart jolted at the sight of a menacing figure behind the steering wheel of the car that never left. One day she got the nerve up to wave, and he waved back. Ever since, she brought him coffee in the mornings. He'd nod and say "Miss Chantelle." She'd hand him his cup of steaming joe. "Sentinel," she'd say.

She was okay with the additional security given Michael's whereabouts being unknown. If Carson wanted to take on her and Benny's safety, well, she'd allow it. She wasn't stupid.

Next month, when her lease was up, she was moving to a new apartment anyway.

She slit open the envelope with a letter opener. The wording was simple, elegant and direct. *A holiday masquerade ball, tonight at nine p.m., hosted by Alexander Rockingham at Club Accendos.* A simple word had been inked in under her name in Carson's handwriting. *Phoenix.*

She dropped it to her desk as if she'd burst into flames if she held on to it any longer.

She picked up her coat. She'd go grab something to eat before the streets grew too slushy. Then she'd figure out what to do. Maybe she'd let Janey and Brenna go home early. Even the threat of snow made travel impossible in D.C. Then she'd go home ... and do what?

Shake it off.

She could hear Janey chatting excitedly on the phone. By the sounds of her speech, she was reeling in a reporter on a story about Jennings Aerospace. Her contact at JA was true to his word, signing Chantelle Communications to an annual public relations program the first week she'd launched.

She took measured steps up Wisconsin, the sidewalk already slick with moisture.

A man and woman headed toward her, the guy chatting away so excitedly he nearly knocked her over. "Whoa," he said and righted her before she fell on her ass. "Sorry about that, ma'am."

The couple continued down the hill toward the water, so lost in one another a pang went through her heart. *They're in love.* She grasped the side of the building and took a steadying breath. She checked her reflection in the window of the shop before her.

Her eyes adjusted and her gaze pierced the glass barrier. A number of feathered and jeweled masks were propped up on satin boxes. Broad silk hats and richly hued corsets adorned fabric-covered mannequins. She'd somehow headed down the side street she'd successfully avoided before today. Since she and Carson broke up, she'd avoided the little masquerade shop and the street it sat on like the plague. Why taunt her heart?

London stepped inside before thinking.

She walked underneath dozens of full-face masks hanging from the ceiling on brightly colored ribbons. When she reached the long glass counter at the back, her attention was drawn to a white mask. Snowy white ostrich plumes cradled the side. An intricate pattern of white and gold crystals were embedded across the plane. Gold crystal drops fell from the bottom to drape across the cheeks of the wearer.

Just what she needed for a masquerade ball. But she wasn't going, was she? No doubt Carson would be there. His face rose up in her mind, and as if he had telepathically hypnotized her, she asked to see the mask. *Just to hold it once.*

The woman behind the counter lifted it from its satin bed and placed it in her hands.

The second she touched it, she had to have the mask. Whether she went tonight or not, it might provide the reminder she required. *Oh, who are you kidding?*

She nodded once to the woman, handed over her American Express and the disguise was hers.

Carson rapped on the doorframe of Alexander's office. An uncharacteristically tense-looking Alexander swiveled in his chair and gestured for him to enter.

Alexander held his phone in a death grip. "No, Ryan, you tell the Dallas Arbiter he can, and he *will*, sit next to a Redskins fan for one evening."

He didn't envy Alexander this time of year. In addition to juggling dozens of holiday parties where his presence would be expected, he had his hands full planning the January Arbiter's Summit. To add more stress, tonight was Club Accendos's Christmas Masquerade Ball, an over-the-top affair that Carson normally loathed. Tonight, he wouldn't miss it.

After pouring himself a healthy dose of Scotch from Alexander's private bar, he sat in a large leather chair. He let the liquor's burn settle on his tongue. It didn't quell his melancholy. He took a deep breath in and held it for a count of three before letting it out in a long puff, like Derek had coached him. *Derek*. Of all the Tribunal members, he'd provided the best help to date. How to still his heartbeat when it threatened to explode from his chest.

"I see the Summit's seating arrangements remain difficult," he said after Alexander hung up.

"That's because everyone has an ego the size of Fort Knox."

"I suspect whatever you tell them to do, they'll do. Everyone attending?"

Alexander fingered his cell phone. "Of course."

The mandatory meeting of the Tribunal Council Arbiters had only one no-show in over twenty years. Alexander's invitations were rarely declined by anyone, ever. He prayed London would be no exception tonight.

Alexander straightened his tuxedo jacket. "You look like hell."

"I'm living in hell."

"She'll show, Carson."

"We'll see." He took a healthy swig of his drink. Tonight could be the last time he saw London. He'd take it. *Just one more time.* He needed to see that long caramel hair swish as she walked. He had to see that haughty chin lift again. Then he'd let her walk out. And he'd live with the knowledge he'd stayed in control.

"You promised your support, Alexander. I promised I wouldn't call or go see her. But I'll need—"

"If she shows up, you'll get to talk with her." Alexander took in a deep breath. "Carson, I realize this is hard—"

"You ever been in love, Alexander?"

"Yes."

"You ever lose it?"

"Repeatedly."

"Then you know wishing doesn't mean crap."

Alexander sighed. "I know."

Alexander had been extraordinarily patient with him over the last eleven weeks. He'd entertained him nearly every night in his office, talking him out of throwing himself off the Memorial Bridge—the place he'd planned to throw Michael Headler from.

Instead, Carson came to Accendos nearly every night. He played chess with Alexander, watched scenes, sipped the one Scotch he allowed himself, and listened to his friends make small talk. After ten days, he finally caught on to their conspiracy. Each one of the Tribunal members had taken turns sitting beside him at Accendos, watching and assessing his state.

Even Katie had gotten into the act, fruitlessly offering

herself time and again—of course, only after he explained why he'd marched away from her without one word.

It was only when Yvette had him and Jonathan over for dinner one night that he knew he must resemble a suicide case. They'd laughed and drank too much wine, and didn't bring up a single thing from the past.

He should have protested such obvious babysitting. But their attention kept him from being buried alive by his own self-loathing for his past behavior. He was in no shape to dispute their care. One day soon he'd have enough of *not* contacting London, and he'd blow his plans to stay away—and losing all hope of reclaiming her.

A shred of hope remained that he could turn things around with London. She hadn't outwardly opposed anything he'd done for her in the last few months. Her security detail reported she caught on to his presence within days, and more importantly, she wasn't angry. She'd seemed relieved, they'd said.

As the weeks unfolded, he realized his epiphanies around London in Southland's lobby were dead on. Perhaps she didn't want him gone, not really. Perhaps she merely tested him. Was she waiting for him to give up? Well, she could wait until the end of time for *that*.

Alexander shook the ice in his glass. "Giving up?"

"Never. I'll take care of her for forever." *Even if she doesn't want me.*

"And her brother?"

"Of course."

"Carson, you may be the most loyal man I've met."

He huffed into his glass. "She can always come to me. But it has to be her choice."

London had admitted she didn't know what a Dominant's role should be. By now, she should have a better clue, because a whole series of Dominants—the entire Washington Tribunal Council—had risen to the occasion to show her.

Jonathan fast-tracked Benny's acceptance into New Horizons. Alexander sent out word of a new public relations firm opening, one that had the best of Yost and Brennan at the helm. Mark's security detail never wavered. Derek provided comic relief for him. *And deep breathing exercises.*

And, Sarah? After one session with the Femme Domme, Michael had sported a hard-on that could have driven tent pegs, according to her. Then Michael ran. The Tribunal found him in a Seattle club, quivering from confusion. He was now back with Sarah, of his own accord, working it out. *If you could call it that.* Sure, Carson remained rattled he'd gotten away with blackmail, but so long as he was off the streets and in good hands, he'd take the victory.

He swirled the ice in his glass. "Alexander, tell me again."

"You're doing the right thing." Alexander leaned back. "Even though hitting the pause button never was your strong suit."

"No. I suppose not."

"But I give you credit, Carson."

He laughed into his glass. "Yeah, I'm on the verge of winning the Nobel Peace Prize."

Alexander smiled. "The Nobel might be stretching it. But something tells me you'll be rewarded for all you've done—and not done."

"From your lips to London's ears." He finished his drink in one gulp. The burn down his throat did nothing to ease the parasitic grief that lived in his chest. A constant thrumming, like a homing beacon, refused to be silenced. He had reached the end of his endurance.

Tonight would mark eighty-one days since he'd seen London. He hadn't moved farther than the ten miles between his office, his home and Club Accendos. He refused to vary

Untouchable

his route, afraid he'd find himself in front of London's apartment by accident. Demand she acquiesce. *And push her further away.*

Alexander refilled his glass—with water.

"Carson, do you know why I chose you to be on the Tribunal Council all those years ago?"

"I'm the best attorney you'll ever know."

"You have unshakeable integrity."

He puffed air and rubbed his neck.

"She'll show," Alexander said. "And when she does, you know what to do. Just remember who you are."

He knew Alexander was right. He needed to stop running through his mistakes in his head. *Easier said than done.* He'd fucked up that first night they were together. He shouldn't have made love to her when she'd declared no sex. He should not have let her change terms midway through their weekend half a dozen times. Most of all, he shouldn't have let her get scared because he ceded control. He needed to show her he was reliable, calm, and not at all like the men she'd encountered before. So, he would. He would be everything she needed. *Loyal.*

~

London watched her reflection grow in her darkening window. She picked up the embossed invitation sent by Alexander. Holding the heavy weighted card made her feel special. She hadn't felt like that since... *Carson.*

Janey rapped on her door "Hey, you headed out?"

"Soon."

"Well, don't wait too long. And you sure you don't want to come? It's Friday night in D.C. and holiday season. Who cares about snow? A bunch of us are going to go to Club Dirty. We'll dance the week off."

She smiled at her younger counterpart. "You go. Have fun."

Janey frowned but left her to stare out the window and get lost in debate again. Though only a few years apart, she felt their age difference was sometimes akin to the Grand Canyon and a ditch. As of midnight, London would turn thirty years old. *Too old for clubs and illusions.*

She fingered Alexander's invitation again and stared at the mask's box on her desk. She'd clutched it all the way back to her office as if she'd carried a heart for transplant. What on earth had she been thinking? She hadn't been thinking. That was the problem. And it had felt so good. To not tumble in the maelstrom of choices? *Just act.*

Should she go to Accendos? Her logical brain told her one look at Carson and she'd cave ... *Would that be terrible?*

Yes, she would go. Truth was, she wanted to talk to him. Sort out a few unresolved issues. *Like how I still love you.*

17

"Miss Chantelle. I'm Tony. I'm to escort you inside."

London took the man's outstretched hand and let him help her exit the cab. She lifted her dress's train, careful not to let the hem touch the growing dusting of snow. Another man, who she vaguely recalled from her last visit, held an umbrella over her head.

Once inside, she stopped at a mirror in the vestibule and slipped on her mask with shaky fingers. Her stomach churned like an awakened hornet's nest. Eleven weeks had passed since she'd seen Carson. Perhaps this time the mask would cloak her true self. She barely recognized the woman staring back at her in the mirror.

"London." Alexander's voice pulled her attention to the far end of the entryway. *So much for the disguise.*

Two strides and the elegant man had crossed the round room. "You look ravishing." He lifted her hand to his lips.

"You look ravishing, too," she said. Alexander stood tall and regal as ever in a clearly expensive tuxedo. He may have been the only man on the planet who would look strange *out* of formal wear.

"Thank you for the invitation. I, ah, wasn't expecting it."

"I'm delighted you could join us. We have special delicacies planned tonight." He entwined her arm around his.

"You say that to all the girls."

He laughed. "Only the beautiful ones."

Her smile dropped as they entered the ballroom. While the room looked smaller than she remembered, the large crowd presented an intimidating scene. A mass of richly hued gowns and tuxedos spun around the floor in time with chamber music. Ornate feathered and bejeweled masks covered many of the guests' faces. A puff of air whispered by her legs as a gown hem swished by.

Garlands of holly, ivy and pine dripped from the walls. A Christmas tree, tall enough to nearly touch the two-story ceiling, rose high in one corner. Its large gold balls glinted amongst tiny white lights wrapped around the tree boughs. She'd stepped into a Christmas greeting card.

Alexander must have sensed her trepidation as his hand gave her a gentle, but clearly intended, push until she had to step forward.

"Someone is waiting for you." His eyes sparkled with amusement.

"I'm not sure I can," she said.

"Remember when we first met?"

"Of course. You were so kind to me."

"Nothing you didn't deserve. Do you remember when I said you're either the most reluctant submissive I'd met to date or the strongest?"

"I haven't thought about those … things in a while." *Liar. It's all you think about.*

"You were both. Now it's time to choose." He winked and left her standing, alone.

What the hell did that mean? She shook her head and headed to something she did recognize—the bar. She had spent an hour curling her hair into an updo. That effort alone deserved a drink.

She smoothed down the front of her gown as she waited behind a gentleman in a dark blue velvet jacket at the small bar. The few minutes' wait gave her an opportunity to scan the room. Large green wreaths hung every few feet from the edge of the balcony. A couple standing in the center of a balcony parted to reveal a man in a tuxedo, holding a crystal tumbler in one hand. A swath of dark hair casually fell across his brow. His gaze found her and pierced her heart.

Carson.

If she hurried, she could get to the vestibule before he descended the stairs. If no cabs were outside, she'd simply have to hoof it down the drive to the gate. Because, wow, she'd made a mistake. What made her believe she could talk to him? *And fall out of love.*

She set her champagne on a small table by the gabled arch leading to the entryway. She felt his eyes on her bare back, her skin exposed down to her waist. Warmth filled her insides—an automatic reaction to the possibility of his gaze on her. Before she could think, she turned. She wanted just one more look.

Carson hadn't moved. His dark eyes glistened in the light. He lifted his drink to his lips. *What the hell? He was going to just stand there? Sipping his drink? What a cocky son of a bitch.*

She squared her shoulders and lifted her chin. *Screw you.*

∼

Oh, how he'd missed that chin.

Carson gripped the edge of the railing and sucked in his breath. The crystal pattern on the glass ate into his other hand from his clasp. London's large topaz eyes peered up at him from behind a white mask. The swell of her breast, exposed by the deep V of her white gown, rose and fell. He held her gaze. He held his breath. He held every hope he'd amassed over eighty-one days in his gut.

He ran his finger along the edge of his glass and absorbed every detail his eyes could observe. Her torso had twisted, allowing the long, single ruffle cascading down the side of her gown to part. He glimpsed the skin of her leg, and his cock pressed against his pants in response.

He took another casual sip of his water and watched her anger grow. London Chantelle, his little phoenix, stood in the gabled arch, not moving, but clearly debating. Seeing her standing there, defiant, fiery and gorgeous as ever, Alexander's earlier wisdom rang in his mind. Let her come to you, he'd said. *Then show her.* He threw her a smile. He hoped she caught his secret message intended just for her. *Your move, sweetness.*

He steeled himself and then turned away, giving her a full view of his back.

∼

Oh, no, you don't. What kind of game was he playing? Ignoring her but not—the flowers and the sentinel and the halfway house for Benny and the ... *Argh.*

She tore her eyes from the balcony and glanced over at the spiral staircase in the corner. *Where he intercepted you three months ago.* She stepped around a man in a dark blue tuxedo. He'd stopped in front of her, an expectant look on his face. He held out a white rose to her. "Madame?" His accent, thick with sin and promise, only added to the ridiculousness of the situation. She didn't have time for such frivolity.

"Pardon," she said quickly and swished around the man. She made slow progress on the stairs, as she angrily tugged on her gown hem, which kept getting caught. When she finally stepped onto the balcony, Carson stood stock still in the middle of the long gallery. He stared at her as if he couldn't place her face. *Well, let me remind you, Mister Cocksure.*

~

Carson held his breath. He knew how capricious the moment was. If he moved, she might change her mind. He didn't want to spook her.

Her hips swayed a delicious beat as she grew closer. Her scent had changed, no longer smelling of cinnamon Christmas cookies, but something deeper, earthier.

"You changed your perfume." That wasn't what he expected to say first. What was he planning on doing? He knew what he *wanted* to do—fist her hair, pull her head back until she exposed her long neck. He'd press his lips to her pulse, testing to see she was real. Then he'd growl in her ear, *never again*. Because she came to him. She wasn't through with him at all. And he wouldn't be without her another day.

He set his glass down on a table and reached out his hand. Miraculously, she placed her palm in his.

"Just talking," he said. *Then we'll move into what you really need.*

~

His large hand clasped her possessively. Warmth and wetness pooled between her legs. *You silly woman.* One word from his mouth and London had melted. She still followed him despite her inner critic.

He led her to the end of the balcony and pushed on a panel. She had to duck as he pulled her through a small hidden door. *They were in a library?* Books lined shelves on every wall. A large oil painting of a hunting scene hung over a lit fireplace, flames crackling over two large logs.

"What is this secret place?" she asked.

"The Master's private library." A muscle in his cheek flexed.

The angles in Carson's face were more pronounced, as if he'd dropped weight. His body still maintained that weightlifter's physique she'd admired in the past. *Past?* Her body's reaction hadn't changed. Her panties had dampened at the first sight of him.

"You came," he said.

"Yes. Well … Alexander invited me."

He laughed in a rich, throaty way that made her stomach clench.

"I knew you'd wear white." His dark eyes travelled over her body—liberally and without apology. She felt a welcome relief at his appreciation.

"Untouchable?"

"Pure." He gestured for her to sit in one of the antique leather club chairs before the fireplace. "Sit."

~

By the time London had lowered herself into the cushion, all the blood in his brain had travelled south. His cock swelled at her following his command.

Carson eased himself into a chair and laid his arms casually on the chair's armrests. "Take off your mask." When she did, his erection grew impossibly harder.

"Uh, thank you for the sentinel."

"His name is Brad. He appreciates the coffee."

A flash of irritation crossed her eyes. "Getting daily reports, are we?"

"Yes. That makes you angry."

Untouchable

She sighed. "Michael is—"

"Not going to be a problem."

"Of course not. You've taken care of everything, right?" Her voice dripped with sarcasm. But London kneaded her palm with her thumb like she had that first night in a room just like this one—containing a fireplace, twin chairs, and a very reluctant submissive, back as rigid as a steel beam.

"I see we've come full circle."

She slowly shook her head. "I'd like to think we've moved past all that. I'm not going to argue with you, Carson."

"Good. Because I'm through fighting."

Her eyes widened. So, he'd taken her by surprise.

∼

Carson stood and walked to the fireplace. When he turned around, the memory of watching him lit by firelight that first night they'd met at Club Accendos threatened to overtake any shred of sense she clung to.

"Fighting you doesn't interest me." He stated his words with such conviction she almost believed him—almost. "All I want is for you to be happy, and for you to be yourself."

"I am." *Liar.*

"Perhaps."

"Always doubting me, aren't you Carson?"

"I have never doubted you, London. But I know you're scared to let anyone inside. You think your safety depends on staying in control, every second of every day, and never allowing yourself to need anyone."

She lifted her chin. "You don't—"

"Yes, I do." He stepped toward her. "I'm familiar with the practice. We chose blue, by the way."

"What?" She felt her forehead wrinkle at his abrupt change of topic.

"The new logo colors. We went with your suggestion. Whitestone debuts a new brand in January."

She looked down at her hands. "Thank you. It means a lot to me that you took my suggestion." *More than a lot.* His admission clamped down on the speech she'd spent all afternoon preparing—the one where she told him he was off the hook. *Where he could just walk away now.*

She rose. "Listen, Carson. I came here to talk with you. To tell you, you can stop now."

"Stop what, London?" His jaw clenched.

"The gifts. The roses. The security—"

He moved closer. "And Benny?"

"Thank you. For Benny." Her eyes pricked with tears. "I've never seen him so happy. I-I can repay you. My business is doing pretty well, and … well, just stop—"

He was close enough to pull her chin down. "No. I will never stop. I will always love you. And you will always be safe with me. I will never hurt you. When you decide to stop torturing the both of us, I'll be here. You've asked me to stay away. I have. But I'm not leaving you. When you need me, call. Or text." One side of his mouth quirked up. "In the meantime, the gifts, the security, it will all remain."

He drew his face closer, as if he might kiss her. But he pulled back quickly and released her jaw. He wrinkled his brow as if deep in thought. But then he abruptly moved toward the door.

∼

Carson had only gone two steps when he heard her gown rustling behind him. Her hand clasped his forearm. "No, please. This isn't what I intended. I just …"

"Just what, London?" He focused on the door and held his breath—again.

"Please, Carson. Will you look at me?"

He slowly turned and nearly came undone. Her eyes glistened with unshed tears. But he couldn't do what he craved—capture her trembling lips with his own until she dropped her mistrust and yielded. He had to let her cross that final line and ask him to return to her.

London drew closer. "I did love you."

"Did?"

"Okay, *do*. I just can't. I'm sorry." Firelight glinted in the pool of tears rimming her eyelids.

"You're scared. Admit it." He crossed his arms. "I won't kiss you until you do."

"What?"

That chin was going to be the death of him.

"You arrogant ... if you think—" She stopped her words when he stepped backward. "Where are you going?"

The first night, they'd had a similar conversation. She'd lured him in with her witty banter—call and response, like thunder and lightning. She *dared* him. Well, he was calling her bluff.

"You've made a preemptive strike for nothing. I'm familiar with the pattern. We're the same, you and me. You're afraid of being left. Well, I'm not going anywhere. I'm your Master. But you have to admit you want me for me to ever touch you again."

Her lips parted and she stared at him. Good, he'd surprised her again.

"I'll help you. Tell me, London. Are you happier with me or without me?" he asked.

"Oh, Carson, please. Don't."

"Your Master asked you a question, London. No delay."

"With. But I have trouble with men. I didn't want to hurt you. I don't know what I wanted ... or want."

"I do. You want to do good work. You want Benny to be

healthy. You want to be respected, loved and free. You have all those things. Right now. So, why do you look so sad, London?"

"I-I don't know."

"Come here," he said.

She blinked. "Why?"

"Afraid I'll hurt you?"

"I know you won't ever hurt me, Carson."

His insides warmed. *One hurdle over.* He beckoned her closer.

"No. I can't—" She took one step forward anyway.

"Yes, you can. Now just say it. I'll respect whatever answer you give. What do you want?"

She took in a shuddering breath. "You. I've always wanted you. I just don't know how." She leaned into him and placed her cheek against his lapel. "I think..."

He placed his hand on her silky hair and breathed in her scent.

She relaxed against him. "I've never had the luxury of being happy. I'm not sure what to do with it."

The truth of her last statement couldn't have rung any louder. He was surprised the walls hadn't shook. He allowed one second of gratitude to fill the space before he engulfed her in a tighter hug. When he felt her whole body melt under his embrace, he turned her gently to face the antique club chair. He pulled on her hair until it released from its tight coil. Her long locks unfurled down either side of her face.

"It's okay if you're afraid. But don't be afraid of me." He grabbed handfuls of her dress. His hand climbed the fabric until he felt the slip of lace covering her backside. As he traced a fingertip along the edge of her panties, she groaned. "Do you know what I fear the most? Being without you."

She released a choked sob and tried to wrest around.

"No. You'll have to call sugar. You remember your safeword, don't you?"

"Yes. I remember." He lowered her over the chair until her glorious ass presented.

"Good." He smacked her butt and she yelped. "I'm not going anywhere. Ever. Now spread your legs."

She widened her stance and clutched the sides of the chair harder. She took a shaky breath when he slipped his fingers inside the lace of her thong, meeting damp, soft folds.

"Beautiful." His acknowledgement earned a release in her shoulders.

He let her dress hem fall back down to her ankles. He unzipped the back. As it fell open, her bare, creamy, tanned skin taunted him. He pulled the thin straps over her shoulders. The heavy material dragged the dress down to her ankles. His mouth watered as he thought of tasting every inch of her skin tonight.

"Step out of it."

She complied and resumed her widened stance. His throat tightened with emotion—and the fact he'd been right —more than right. He'd reached the dead center of her maze. London craved unerring control … and loyalty. So long as he offered both, she responded. *She feels safer.*

London swayed on her high heels, left only in the small thong. His mouth watered anew at the sight of her breasts hanging heavy over the chair. So many parts of London taunted him, he almost didn't know where to begin. He started by shedding her of her panties.

He swatted her behind and she startled. "That's for making us wait. In fact, I should spank you for every day we've been apart."

Now bent over the chair, her pussy glistening with her desire for him, she must be brought to understand he meant every word he'd spoken.

"Would you agree, London?"

She peered over her shoulder and slowly nodded.

His hand came down on her bare flesh. He nearly came in his pants from her grunt. A flash of her quivering lips peeked from under her curtain of hair. He started a rhythm of smacks, her flesh singing under his slaps. By the time he reached ten, her bottom was bright red and she writhed her ass backward toward him, panting and squirming. He couldn't wait any longer.

He was about to owe Alexander one antique chair.

He freed himself from his pants and pushed inside her in one long glide. He began fucking her brutally, as if he tried to drive out the last eighty-one days of hell. She keened an impending orgasm with a long cry. *Not yet.*

He smacked her ass and she gasped.

"Yes, sir." She understood.

After wrenching himself out of his tuxedo jacket and abandoning it to the floor, he pulled his cock back in a leisurely slide. She wiggled her behind backward, trying to capture more of him, earning her another slap.

He returned to undressing. It look far longer to undo his cufflinks, but they finally dropped to the carpet. After ripping off his shirt, buttons skittering across the floor to land God knows where, he fisted her hair.

She tensed her inner muscles as if egging him on. He inhaled noisily to steady himself. *Make her wait.*

~

When Carson thrust deep inside her, reaching her farthest point, the spike of pain made London cry out. His clever fingers rimmed her clit. As he pitched deep inside her again, pain and pleasure began their dance. Her whole body relaxed over the chair as he used her mercilessly.

"Carson. I ..."

"What, baby?" His voice was gentle, not at all like the cock spearing her to the core. He stopped moving and held her against his hot body.

"I'm so sorry," she whispered.

He pulled out, the loss of connection excruciating. "Oh, no, please, I meant—"

"Yes, London. I know."

He grasped her forearms and helped her straighten. When she turned, his eyes had reddened, as if he held tears at bay. "You did nothing wrong. *I'm* sorry." Then, with no warning or hesitation, he fisted her hair and pulled her head back. "But never again will we play this game," he growled. His ferocious turn should have scared her. Instead, an overwhelming sense of being safe and whole replaced any anger she harbored. Instead, she felt ... centered.

She'd tried so hard not to be stupid about men. But she had been. She'd been a fool. Carson gave her everything she'd ever dreamed. *An anchor.*

"No, Master," she whispered. "Never again."

He lifted her up. "Put your legs around me." He wrapped her in a chenille blanket hanging off the back of the other chair. She clung to him as he lowered them both to the floor. Within seconds he seated himself inside her again. With his gaze intent and needy, he drove inside her body.

"Mine." He suckled and nipped her ear lobe while rocking into her slowly and deeply. He claimed her mouth and another slow slide inside until his pelvis ground against her clit. Back and forth until her pleas filled his mouth.

He freed her mouth. "I'm not leaving you. Say it, London."

Twin tears escaped her eyes and trailed down the side of her face. "You're not leaving me." Her voice was small, tentative, as if she tested the veracity of her words.

"Now come with me." He kept up a slow rocking until she arched her back into him and released.

~

Carson played with her hair as she sat on his lap, wrapped in the blanket. She nuzzled her face against his neck. His heady aroma, masculine musk and tobacco filled her nostrils, her heartbeat slowing. She didn't remember being lifted from the floor. Her orgasm had spiraled her from the earth. She could only recall her final words before she came completely unglued. *You're not leaving me.*

"Forever?" she asked.

"Yes, London." He traced the outline of her face with a gentle finger swipe. "I told you you've ruined me. I love you."

"You were right," she said, lifting her head off his neck. "The only time I'm happy is when I'm with you. Even in my dreams."

"You've dreamt about me?" He grasped her chin.

His voice was so devoid of ego, she risked answering truthfully. "Repeatedly."

"And what were we doing?"

She clasped her bottom lip between her teeth. She couldn't possibly voice the visions that danced in her head at night. She shook her head and dropped her gaze again.

"Your Master asked you a question, London."

Her sore pussy tightened at his words. *My Master.* At that moment she couldn't believe she had let so much time become between them.

She lifted her chin—on purpose. "We did many things. You see, I've been ... bad."

"Tell me what you've done." His voice, edged in steel, only made her insides grow wet again.

"I took off your collar by myself." That last night she had

seen him, she'd thrown his belt across the room and left it in the corner. She'd been afraid if she'd picked it up again, she'd have burst into flames.

Emotion filled his eyes as if he finally believed she loved him. He fisted her hair and pulled her head back. "Never again," he said.

"No," she whispered. "Kiss me?"

His mouth captured her lips in a rough, possessive kiss. She yielded, a small purr rumbling in her throat.

A loud cheer echoed from some faraway place. She broke the kiss, eyes darting to the door. "What was that? Did they hear us?"

"It must be midnight. Alexander always plans a special toast."

"Like New Year's Eve."

"Only better, which reminds me." He reached down and retrieved his jacket from the puddle of clothes. He pulled out a long black box. "I have something for you. Your birthday present."

"How did you find out? No, wait, don't tell me. *The Tribunal is powerful.*"

"But we only use our power for good."

She sat up and pulled the blanket around her middle, suddenly shy. "I'm not sure I deserve it."

"You deserve everything."

Nestled inside the box, on a bed of satin, lay a choker. Pearls interspersed with diamond-encrusted filigrees that would wrap around the wearer's neck. But it was the centerpiece that commanded attention. A delicate bird with outstretched wings clung to each filigreed end, as if in flight.

She touched the belly of the bird with her fingertip. "It's a collar, isn't it?" The phoenix's tail would dip into the hollow of a woman's throat, a gentle reminder of what she wore.

"Yes. A phoenix." He lifted it from the box. "I had it made

for you." He held it up, but didn't make any move to put it on her.

"You assumed …"

"Hoped. It's always your choice to submit. I have no right to demand," he said.

"You might." Her face flushed. "I still have it. Your belt, I mean."

He nodded. "Keep it. Consider it a training collar."

She laughed but swallowed it back at his serious expression.

"If I put this on you, London, it means you're mine. Forever. Not until our next fight. Not until the next job. And only I can take it off you."

"You may want to sometimes, you know."

"No, I won't. I went through hell being separated from you."

"You said you wanted me to be happy."

"Always."

"I'll only be happy if I'm yours." She eased herself off his lap and knelt before him. She lifted her hair in invitation as she dipped her chin. After he secured the collar around her neck, she touched the phoenix that nestled against the hollow of her throat. *My collar.*

She looked up at him, and an infinite and all-knowing comfort settled in her middle when their eyes met.

"You'll be mine, too?" she asked.

"I've always been yours."

He leaned down and kissed her mouth again, and the world silenced. There were no words left to say. So, she let go and let in the happiness.

EPILOGUE

"It's done." Mark relayed the words with his characteristic certitude. "His plane landed in Caracas an hour ago."

Carson scrubbed his face and loosened his grip on the phone. "I owe you. Banishing Headler couldn't have been easy."

London's face shot up from her dinner. He reached across the table to stop her from wearing a hole in her palm with her thumb.

"Michael agreed quickly to Alexander's suggestion. Practically begged to go. I don't trust him," Mark said.

"Neither do I. But I trust Seraphina." *And Alexander's judgment.*

"She must owe Alexander big time."

He huffed. "Who doesn't? Let's hope Seraphina's Domme reputation proves true."

After twelve unsuccessful sessions, Sarah had declared Michael unsalvageable. The fact that she had uncovered his own submissive desires just made him angrier. Carson couldn't believe Alexander would spend another second on Headler and call in the queen of all Dommes. He couldn't believe Headler had *agreed*. But what choice did they have? They couldn't cut him loose in his current state, bewildered and mad as hell at who he had discovered himself to be.

"Yeah, so you might not see me for a bit," Mark said. "Taking some time off."

"You finally going to get off your ass about Isabella?"

"Something like that. London throw you out yet?"

"Not yet."

"But she didn't say yes?"

"She's about to." *God willing.*

Mark laughed into the phone. "Gotta go."

"Mark? Don't let Isabella get away."

"Not planning on it."

"Well, good luck."

"At the rate you're stalling with this phone call, sounds like you're the one who needs luck." The phone went silent.

Mark had stood in the wings pining for Isabella for, what, ten years? And he accused Carson of stalling? Okay, so maybe he had been moving slower than usual. He'd wanted to know Michael was handled. *Yeah, right. Truth, remember? You're nervous about what you're about to do.*

London peered at him from across their dining room table. "Michael?"

"He won't be back for a very long time. Hey, none of that." He leaned over and caught a tear before it could fall from her eye.

"I can't believe it's over."

"It's over. Now wait here." He rose and left London sipping her wine, surely deep in thought over the final loose end of her life being tied and bound. *Literally and figuratively.* Time to change her focus. He might not get another chance to be alone with her for a while. Benny moved in with them tomorrow. London's mind would be on nothing else but making him comfortable in their home. *Theirs*. He liked that word—now.

After retrieving two boxes from his office, he returned to London, who sat fiddling with the phoenix pendant resting in the beautiful hollow of her throat. Her eyes grew wide when he pushed the small red leather box toward her.

"Consider Michael's 'deporting' an engagement present," he said.

"Engagement?" She stared at the box like it might bite her. "Cartier."

He chuckled. "Only the best for my future wife. The woman who always says yes, remember?"

"Yes."

"I haven't asked yet." He walked around to her side of the table.

She giggled and peered up at him. "Are you going to get on your knees?"

"Not in your lifetime. Stand." London stood on her feet in a flash, an automatic reaction to his command. She'd gotten quite good at immediately responding.

He lifted her up to sit on the kitchen counter.

"You really do like me up here."

"It puts us at eye level. Hold out your hand."

She offered her left hand, and he slipped a diamond the size of a gumball on her ring finger. Sure, three carats was a bit much. But in case another man's eyesight wasn't good, he wanted to ensure no one missed his mark of commitment.

"Now I'm asking. Marry me?"

"Yes. Always yes." Her face cracked into a blinding smile, and his nerves she might say no finally retreated. *Damn*. His eyes had misted. Before he'd be forced to turn in his man card, he grasped her behind and sharply pulled her toward him until his hard-on filled the last molecule of space between their bodies. "That word has quite an effect on me, Mrs. Drake."

He placed his lips on hers, and his tongue did impolite things inside her mouth. She responded by writhing against his cock, captive in his pants.

Her face flushed when he pulled away. "I might not be the best wife. I mean—"

"Stop. Time for one more present." He eased her off the counter, but kept her banded close to his side. After reaching into the second box he'd retrieved, he pulled out a long wooden paddle. "For domestic discipline needs. In case you burn the toast. Or forget who you are." He showed her the flat end.

"A phoenix." She fingered the bird etched deep into the wood.

"If I ever hear you deny yourself, I'll brand your ass until you wear it." He released his hold and twirled the paddle between both hands.

"Who am I?" She asked him that question daily.

He'd never change his answer. "My phoenix. A woman of incomparable spirit ... and mine."

"You might have to prove that."

His lips twitched into a grin. "Remember your second lesson."

"Don't force discipline with a smart mouth."

He chuckled when she leaned over the table and widened her stance without him having to ask. "I think you need to remind me."

"Perhaps." He stepped backward. He wouldn't waver in his authority again, not since he promised her he wouldn't that night in Alexander's master library. He was her Master. He loved her, and he would never, ever cede control to her again. Just the way she needed it.

"Please, Master. Paddle me. But, of course, only if you

wish it." Her lashes fell to her cheeks in a sign of obeisance. Okay, a little dramatic. But he'd take it. On cue, her panties darkened with moisture, a sign of her willingness.

After he lifted her short skirt, he palmed her flesh only half covered by her tiny lace panties. She wiggled her behind in invitation. He fingered the phoenix's wings. Its edges weren't rough enough to cut her but would still imprint its design on her glorious ass. He drew back and landed a blow on her flesh. The etchings left a faint pink mark of a bird.

He smacked her once more, and her breath shot from her lungs from the impact. "Hmm, I wonder how many I should give you?" he asked.

She peeked back at him from the curtain of her hair. "You're never going to stop, are you?"

He straightened. "No. Now say it."

"You're never leaving me."

"Never."

~ The End ~

Thank you for reading **UNTOUCHABLE**.

If you enjoyed this hot story, you'll love **PERFECT**, where Marcos Santos finally makes his move on the woman he's loved from afar for ten years. Of course, Isabella *was* married to his brother. Not any more...

For a sneak peek at **PERFECT**, turn the page!

PERFECT

Chapter One

Isabella stood on the front porch of her abandoned Arlington, Virginia home and willed herself not to cry. She hadn't stepped inside in eleven months, twenty-eight days and sixteen hours. She slipped the key in the lock, and her body began to shake like a skeleton in a windstorm. She stepped backward.

Returning was a mistake. She should have obeyed her mother and father and stayed in Miami.

No. Dios mío! Just open the stupid door.

The loud crack of protesting wood followed a screech of hinges left unused for too long. She hitched the mailbag higher on her shoulder and stepped inside before she chickened out.

Bed sheets draping the furniture resembled deflated, mismatched ghosts. The silence in the house rivaled her husband's gravesite.

She needed to do something fast before she turned and

Perfect

fled. Coming here alone? *Stupid.* She whipped the sheet off the couch. Another mistake. Dust clogged the air.

When her coughing subsided, she wiped the tears from her eyes and scanned the abandoned room. More cautiously, she pulled the sheet off Jorge's beat-up leather chair. She ran her hand over a small tear on the armrest. *He sat here.*

Stop it. She reminded herself why she'd returned without telling anyone she was in town. *You're going to get in and get out, remember? No maudlin reminiscence.*

Wandering through the hushed rooms, she quickly identified what she'd set aside to take with her. Her grandmother's antique saltcellars and a small painting by Albrecht Dürer made the "save" list. As for the rest? 1-800-JUNK could haul the rest of the household items away. Who needed the reminders of all she'd lost here? Tomorrow she'd hire a realtor and never, ever come back to this place.

She remained undecided about visiting Jorge's gravesite.

After dropping to her knees in front of the coffee table, she dumped the bag of mail she'd picked up from the post office. Her eyes rested on her late husband's *Guns & Ammo* magazine. She winced at the reminder of one of the many pastimes that had supplanted her, and eyed the mound spilling across the surface and onto the floor. There were bound to be others. She should leave sorting mail to another day when she didn't feel so fragile.

Little squares of fading daylight on the floor led toward the back porch, as if beckoning her to follow. Rising, she padded through the kitchen, averting her eyes from anything that might spark more memories of her life here. She focused on the simple deadbolt on the back door that led to her garden—what had once been her pride and joy.

Pausing on the back stoop, she scanned the scruffy-looking backyard. She barely recognized the yard she'd designed, planted and cared for all by herself. Years ago, the

Perfect

National Wildlife Federation had certified the small quarter-acre lot as a backyard wildlife habitat. Her father had his own certificate made up from his company, Sandoval Landscaping, and shipped it to her pre-framed.

Isabella Sandoval Santos, *Ángel de la Tierra*. The Earth's Angel.

Not anymore, Papi.

Rogue grass blades invaded her herb garden. Only a lone rosemary bush remained to fight the interlopers. A neglected hummingbird feeder hung sideways from the Japanese maple.

It looked like she'd felt that last year with Jorge. Forgotten.

When she stepped off the flagstone patio into the thick grass, her kitten heels sank into the moist ground. She kicked off her shoes, scrunched her toes in the cool green, and took in a lungful of the earthy air. Sounds of not-too-distant cars mixed with the peter-peter-peter of a titmouse in the oak trees.

She took slow steps around the perimeter of the small, fenced-in yard and took inventory. A pool, the length of a refrigerator, fed a too-small trickle of water into the larger pool below choked with leaves. Large hydrangea bushes lined the back wall, tiny buds forming on the ends of their rounded mopheads. Had they always bloomed blue?

As she circled around the yard to the side of the house, more signs of neglect showed. Cigarette butts lay in the side yard, likely thrown by the guy who cut her grass.

She turned and a dewy, sticky mass of white strings hit her face. She swatted at the gluey fibers. *Gah!* She backed up and sticky strings pulled across her skin.

"*Mierda!*" She brushed at the gummy strands. Her fingers touched a squishy little mass, and a crawl across her forearm crushed her in fear.

Perfect

"*Ay, Dios! Quítamela!*"

Something moved on her neck. *There's more than one.* She could feel their hairy legs. *Get off! Get off!*

More stickiness tangled in her fingers. She had to get away before she was covered in long-legged, furry spiders. They might bite. Get into her hair, her eyes, her mouth... She kicked and the earth pitched sideways as she lost her footing in the wet grass.

"Isabella!" A male voice boomed in her ear.

Marcos? What was he doing here?

His shirt pressed into her face as he pinned her to his hard, male body with incredible strength. With her arms and hands immobilized against his solid abdomen, his hands swept over her back.

"*Pare, pare*, stop," she cried into his chest.

He released his grip. She pushed him off and ran to the middle of the yard. She couldn't catch her breath. The ground crashed into her knees. A sharp pain radiated up her arm as she landed on her wrist.

"Calm down." His body covered hers from behind, his hold gentle as if she was made of glass. His heartbeat drummed against her shoulder blades.

"Jesus, I thought someone was attacking you."

"Something was."

She turned her face to look up into a pair of familiar, steel-grey eyes. Her heart climbed into her throat. "Marcos."

Dios. She wasn't strong enough to see him yet. The temptation he presented was too much. It wasn't fair, damn it! She hadn't seen Mark since Jorge's funeral—on purpose.

A lazy smile stretched across her brother-in-law's face. "*Ella.*" His chuckle rumbled against her back.

Her breath hitched at hearing his nickname for her.

He lifted her to standing and twisted her to face him. "For

Perfect

someone who likes to play in the dirt, you've always had quite the overreaction to spiders."

She backed up a little to make space between their bodies. "Why are you here?"

"Are you okay?" His gentle hand descended on her shoulder. She peered up at him, not quite sure what to say.

"Let's get you inside and cleaned up." Mark's muscles glided under his T-shirt as he led her toward her back stoop. She tried hard not to stare.

She stopped at the steps. "You have a gun tucked into the back of your jeans."

"Thought someone was hurting you."

"Well, spiders can bite, you know."

His warm chuckle shook some of her tension away and the tightness in her stomach released.

"How did you know I was here?"

"The security firm called and told me someone had entered the house." He gestured her inside.

Oh, wow, her mind resembled a sieve these days. She'd forgotten about the security cameras. Mark had arranged for them while the house sat empty. At the funeral, he'd offered to watch over the place while she was gone. Of course, since his work frequently took him out of the country, it made sense he would hire a security company.

She paused and eyed the back screen door. It hung on one hinge as if a wild lion had crashed through.

"Your screams... well, the door was in my way." He grimaced, yanked the door off its final hinge and leaned it against the siding. "I'll fix it."

"Don't bother. I'm calling a realtor in the morning. They'll likely have a long list of things to fix."

As soon as she entered the kitchen, he pointed to a stool. "Here, sit for a minute. Let me look at that wrist."

She gratefully sat her butt down.

Perfect

Mark's muscles strained the capacity of his T-shirt as he wet a cloth with cold water. His well-defined forearms flexed as he wrung it out. Mother Mary, he had glorious muscles. She ripped her gaze away. She shouldn't notice Mark in *that* way.

As he wrapped the cloth around her wrist, she tried not to think about his strong fingers.

"There. So when did you get into town?" He sat down on the stool next to her.

"I, uh, arrived yesterday. I was going to call. But, well… I wasn't sure you'd be in town." It was a lie, and lame. Mark deserved better. "Thanks for this." She lifted her wrist a little.

"Does it hurt?"

"Not really."

He studied her face as if he almost didn't recognize her.

"The house is dusty," she said. What a moronic thing to say. As usual, around Marcos her intelligence deserted her. Her hormones took over.

"I'm sure. I haven't stopped by much. And, well, I wasn't sure if you'd want to see me."

Shame colored her insides, and heat crossed her face. "I'm sorry about not returning your calls after his…" She couldn't bring herself to say Jorge's funeral. She didn't know what to say to Mark at all. How could she talk about what happened after the burial services? Even if she'd never stopped thinking about how his lips felt when he suddenly kissed her. Nice. Too nice.

"I was calling to apologize. My behavior was… well, I wasn't me that evening. I should never have kissed you… and I shouldn't have brought this up now. Timing never was my strong suit." He scrubbed his chin. "It's good to see you, Isabella."

"You, too."

Her heart hitched a little when his lips pulled back,

Perfect

showing perfect white teeth in his perfect face. Okay, so what if he turned her insides to mush? No woman could be unaffected by a smile in such a package. Was Mark still single? Perhaps he had a girlfriend now.

"How are... things?" She hoped she sounded casual and not prying.

"Good. Not travelling as much. Went to work for Congressman Brond. He's off the taxpayer's payroll now, and he's getting married."

"I'd read about that. So, you're not doing that... other job?"

She hoped not. She knew his former career had involved danger, given the number of times he'd disappear only to reappear with bruises and stitches. Yet over the years he'd dodged all questions about his secret work and ignored Jorge's ribbing about his silence, calling him James Bond and Rambo.

"No. I stopped altogether. Was too distracted. Put others at risk."

"I'm sorry, Mark. You lost Jorge, too. It must have been hard." She touched his forearm. Her fingers met human concrete.

Before she could withdraw her touch, his hand covered hers. "Death I can handle. It's worrying about the living that's hard."

A slight chill travelled up the back of her neck. In a way, she understood his words.

Jorge's death had brought emptiness but also a strange peace. At some point, she'd given up fearing for Jorge. His drug addiction was pointless, and later, his extreme sports addiction seemed such a waste of his sobriety. She never stopped fearing for Mark. His risks, although unknown to her, seemed commendable.

"You back working for your father?" he asked.

Perfect

"Yes. Lots of new construction in Miami. He needed landscaping help."

Mark unwrapped her wrist, as if to check for bruising. "Did your father tell you I came to see you in Miami?"

"No." A sliver of anger flared at the thought she'd been cloistered by her family. "But that sounds like Papi. Overprotective." She'd have to confront her father later. Not telling her Marcos had visited? She couldn't let that slip. It was rude. *Like not calling him back wasn't?*

"You also changed your cell phone number." His shrewd grey eyes cut into her heart. God, he had beautiful eyes. She couldn't lie to those eyes. *So, tell him the truth.*

"That cell phone's at the bottom of Biscayne Bay, the victim of a rough day on Papi's boat. Since I was living in Florida, it seemed better to change to a local number." Plus, no amount of blocking had stopped the disturbing calls she got for weeks after Jorge's funeral. Changing her number was easier, and she had needed easy.

His eyes didn't seem to buy the story. Okay, so it wasn't the whole truth. He gave her a look she'd seen before—a look sported by her husband when he wasn't pleased. It made her insides go soft.

Marcos and Jorge... so alike, yet not at all.

She'd met the brothers at the same time. She'd been pulled more strongly to Mark, but his mysterious disappearances scared her. Jorge had seemed safer, and almost as attractive, and he'd understood her—sort of. He'd turned out to be not safe at all.

Dios! She reached out to grasp the edge of the counter. She'd grown dizzy. She always did whenever she thought about how opposite life had turned out from what she'd expected when she married Jorge.

"Ella, do you want to rest upstairs?" Mark's hand moved to her arm to steady her.

Perfect

Warmth spread across her whole body at his obvious concern. *Right.* She loved the feel of his hand on her.

"You should—"

"I'm not staying here," she blurted. Besides, no way in hell was she entering her old bedroom. "Today's just been... "

"Overwhelming. Just take a minute."

Seeing Marcos, as strong and indomitable as ever, she realized how much she'd missed him.

"Thanks for being here, and I'm sorry, Mark."

"Nothing to apologize for."

"Yes, there is. My father shouldn't have dismissed you. But, more importantly, I should have returned your calls. I should have done a lot of things before now."

Sold the house. Handled her estate. Could her to-do list grow any longer?

"If you need help sorting through anything, I'm here. Not planning on going anywhere."

Her to-do list suddenly seemed petty. Because of Mark's secret occupation, her heart lightened whenever he reappeared—alive.

"Where are you staying?" he asked.

"Marriott."

"A hotel?" His brow furrowed.

A long groan from the basement captured their attention. Mark pushed off the sink with a start.

"The furnace," she said quickly. "It's always done that."

"I'll go check on it. Will you be alright?"

She nodded.

As Mark pounded down the basement steps, memories pounded on her brain.

She hated that basement. Hairy-legged spiders lived down there, their webs guarding climbing harnesses, grappling ropes, motorcycle helmets—all remnants of Jorge's life that didn't include her.

As if his disappearance into cocaine wasn't enough, once clean, he'd escaped into base jumping, rock climbing, motocross—anything that offered a new kind of high. She'd lost herself in the stillness his absence left behind. With no role to play in his life, her world diminished to nothing. *She* diminished to nothing.

Another loud moan sounded from downstairs, and that familiar ache she'd harbored for too long welled up hard and fast. She clutched the edge of the island and held on. She'd badly miscalculated the impact visiting her old house would have. Yes, returning was an *epic* mistake.

~~~~

Perfect can be found at most online retailers or visit Elizabeth's web site at www.ElizabethSaFleur.com

ALSO BY ELIZABETH SAFLEUR

Elite

Holiday Ties

Untouchable

Perfect

Riptide

Lucky

Fearless

Invincible

The White House Gets A Spanking

Spanking the Senator

Tough Road

Tough Luck

Tough Break

Tough Love

ABOUT THE AUTHOR

Elizabeth SaFleur writes romance that dares to "go there" from 28 wildlife-filled acres, dances in her spare time and is a certifiable tea snob.

Find out more about Elizabeth on her web site at www.ElizabethSaFleur or join her private Facebook group, Elizabeth's Playroom.

Follow her on Instagram (@ElizabethLoveStory) and TikTok (@ElizabethSaFleurAuthor), too!

Made in the USA
Middletown, DE
12 April 2025